The Twitter Diaries

A TALE OF 2 CITIES, 1 FRIENDSHIP,
140 CHARACTERS

Also by Imogen Lloyd Webber

The Single Girl's Guide

The Twitter Diaries

A TALE OF 2 CITIES, 1 FRIENDSHIP, 140 CHARACTERS

GEORGIE THOMPSON
AND
IMOGEN LLOYD WEBBER

BLOOMSBURY READER

LONDON · NEW DELHI · NEW YORK · SYDNEY

First published in Great Britain 2012

Copyright © 2012 by Georgie Thompson and Imogen Lloyd Webber
Cover Design by Melanie Lloyd

The moral rights of the authors have been asserted

Bloomsbury Publishing Plc
50 Bedford Square
London WC1B 3DP

www.bloomsbury.com

Bloomsbury Publishing, London, New York, New Delhi and Sydney

A CIP catalogue record for this book is available from the British Library

ISBN 9781448209866

10 9 8 7 6 5 4 3 2 1

Typeset by Hewer Text UK Ltd, Edinburgh
Printed in Great Britain by Clays Ltd, St Ives plc

To girlfriends the world over and @Mums everywhere.

#CONTENTS

#AUTHORS' NOTE

This is a work of fiction and we have taken some liberties.

According to Twitter rules, tweets must be 140 characters or less. We have obeyed this and when our heroines exceed the tweet limit they go onto a new one, indicated by the symbol '>>'.

"Twitter handles" have been created by the authors and they have no connection with any real individual or corporate entity. For anyone who shares a Twitter handle with any of our characters – the coincidence was inadvertent.

If you subscribe to Twitter you can follow the exploits of @TuesdayFields and @StellaCavill on Twitter and join in the conversation at www.TheTwitterDiaries.com.

Georgie **www.twitter.com/officiallygt**

Imogen **www.twitter.com/illoydwebber**

Every reasonable effort has been made to trace holders of any proprietary interest in this publication but if any have been inadvertently overlooked the publishers would be glad to hear from them. The list of acknowledgements constitutes an extension of the copyright page.

Twitter is a trademark of Twitter, Inc.

#CHARACTERS

OUR HEROINES

@TuesdayFields

Tuesday Fields, 33, is, professionally, coming into her own. Having grafted for years in local newspapers and national titles, where she met her one time boss and now infamous trans-Atlantic TV host, Peter Mignon, @PM_TV, she has found what she's really good at – TV. Tuesday is working morning, noon and night to make her mark as a sports reporter for Wake Up Britain, @WUBTV. Things are going well, Tuesday's boss, @TheBossWUB, can see her potential, but the station's main anchors, @AnchorManTV and @KateKingTV, are not making things easy for her – they are threatened because they can see her potential too.

Personally, Tuesday has the unfortunate ability to choose all the wrong men. This is much to the despair of her mother, @Mum, who has already satisfactorily married off Tuesday's two older sisters in a timescale her favourite read @TheDailyGB would approve of, but is failing to get Tuesday down the aisle. Tuesday's retired, browbeaten Dad, when he is not playing golf, finds he enjoys a much quieter life if he just agrees with his wife, @Mum. Tuesday's most recent dating disaster was @HugoPr1nce, a self-made millionaire who, along with social mountaineering his way through London, was cheating on her with his bit of fluff, @RedS0ledShoes.

Suddenly, at a loss about what to do for New Year, @PM_TV comes to Tuesday's rescue and invites her to New York for a party he's throwing. It is a long way from her Kensal Rise postage stamp-sized flat but she thinks what the hell and jumps on a plane bound for the Big Apple. What has she got to lose?

Nothing, it turns out, to lose but everything to gain. Tuesday finds a welcome salvation in a girl she meets at @PM_TV's party, Stella Cavill.

@StellaCavill

Stella Cavill, 33, gives off the impression that she is the most together girl in the world. The only child of a thrice-divorced, flighty mother, @Supermodel_1971, Stella has moved to NYC with her boyfriend Will Moss, @MerchBanker. Having hit upon the concept that men have no taste whatsoever when it comes to shoes, she has ambitions to be the Tamara Mellon of male footwear. Stella has built her company, Stellar Shoes, from nothing and although may come across as 'posh' she is a grafter and a worker. There is no silver spoon in her mouth unless she earns the right to put it there herself. Stella is supported in her work endeavours by Iris, @SINternUK, 25, who started out as an intern at Stellars and now runs things from London for her manic mistress.

Stella's mother, @Supermodel_1971, made her career out of divorce and cannot understand why Stella wants to 'play about' with work. Stella does her best to ignore the on-going suggestions that she should simply get on with it and marry @MerchBanker. Stella has never had a father figure in her life, he exited the picture some time ago, but in a number of respects that role is filled by her main backer, the mysterious @AllThatGlittersIsGold.

However, all that glitters is not gold, and Stella's company is seriously struggling in the recession. Added to which, since @MerchBanker and Stella moved from Islington to their Soho loft a year previously, their relationship has hit the rocks. The starry-eyed man that Stella once knew has been inundated with attention from NYC's multitude of predatory women. Not ideal when he's taking an ego battering from the economic downturn and his girlfriend is working night and day trying to save her baby – her business.

THE SUPPORTING CAST

@AllThatGlittersIsGold

Stella's main investor and an impossibly rich hedge fund manager with contacts from London to Langley. A fifty-something, he normally plays with women half his age. Despite that, Stella is determined he never meets her mother, @Supermodel_1971. She has the habit of changing men's habits – and breaking their bank balances in the process. Stella can't afford a fall out of that magnitude and what it might mean for Stellar Shoes.

@AnchorManTV

The co-host of Wake Up Britain, @WUBTV, and a tangerine-coloured national treasure. Happily married to Audrey for decades despite his protestations of eternal youth. He is the first to judge others, but you know what they say about people who live in glass houses . . .

@BugsBunnyMovie

A mystery admirer turned follower of our heroine, Stella. Is there more to him than his cartoon Twitter name suggests?

@HugoPr1nce

One of the most successful British thirty-something men of his generation – or so he keeps telling everyone. A self-made million-aire, he specialises in social mountaineering with his eye on the prize of being elevated to the House of Lords. However, his genius for self-promotion takes a turn for the worst when he cheats on Tuesday with @RedS0ledShoes.

@JakeJacksonLive

Jake, a baby-faced 24-year-old, hard working junior correspondent at Wake Up Britain. An only child to a single mother who dotes on him, he is desperate to be seen as a man and a serious journalist, not just the boy next door – both personally and professionally.

Jerry Reuben

Triple Oscar, four-time Emmy, seven-time Tony award winning director, @MichaelAngeloMovie is his go-to film star of choice. Reuben is not on Twitter. Or so he claims . . .

@KateKingTV

The demonstrative Kate King, co-host of Wake Up Britain, TV age 49, Real age 55. She has had to become a first class diva in her fight against the world's glass ceilings and has been ensconced on the @WUBTV sofa for what seems like forever. However, all good things must come to an end. With her strops-a-second, how much longer can she stay on top?

@LordTw1tter

A self-made billionaire thanks to his mobile phone business and an avid Spurs fan, he has a friendly but public rivalry with @PM_TV. The main beneficiary of this is his charitable foundation, which regularly reaps the rewards from big money bets between the two on anything from follower counts to football results. Childish? You bet!

@MerchBanker

Will Moss, 33, and Stella Cavill's boyfriend. A geek when Stella met him in London, she turned him into something of a sophisticate and many (women mainly) are happy to buy into the Black Amex and British accent. However, times are tough and as the market swings wildly, so do Will's moods and fortunes.

@MichaelAngeloMovie

Michaelangelo, 38, is the biggest film star in the world and, despite his mother's inability to look up the correct spelling of the great Italian artist and sculptor he was named after, he's made the world his stage, with multiple Oscar nominations to his name. Although he has yet to see a win, his favourite director, Jerry Reuben, assures him it is only a matter of time. Addicted to

Twitter, he uses it to expound his ideas of how to save the planet – usually from the comfort of his private jet.

@Mum
Tuesday's mum, 64 (admits to 59), flits between pride and panic over her career-driven, but still childless daughter. She can't help but offer up advice about Tuesday's 'predicament' and thus tweets her, daily, with, @TheDailyGB inspired thoughts.

@No1Sportsman
Forget David Beckham, the five-time Formula 1 world champion, 34, is the most famous sports personality in the world. Ruthless, incredibly bright, he dominates both on and off the track. Rumour has it he selects his girlfriends out of the Victoria's Secret catalogue. Winning is everything but he enjoys a good chase/race too.

@PM_TV
Peter Mignon, fifty-something, is a mutual friend of Tuesday and Stella's and a famous transatlantic TV host. He had at one point in his career edited @TheDailyGB, which is where he met Tuesday. Arsenal-loving with a dubious dress sense, he is obsessed with global notoriety and has an on-going battle with twitter rival @LordTw1tter over their follower counts. Underneath it all, he has a heart of gold and the girls adore him in his role of benevolent uncle.

@RedS0ledShoes
Hugo Prince's most recent squeeze post Tuesday. What she does day to day remains a mystery but whatever it is, it is always with his money, perfectly coiffed hair, unsoiled Louboutins and, without exception, documented in @TheDailyGB.

@RubyRainerUS

Fifty-something, single, American, and the biggest daytime talk show host in the world since @Oprah hung up her microphone. Hers is a suitably tough story to global domination and her army of fans applaud and admire her in equal measure. Ruby Rainer has the power to change lives for the better, and she does.

@SINternUK

Iris is Stella's 25-year-old fabulous flame-haired former intern, who now runs Stellar Shoes from London. Whoever crosses her path tends to fall for her charms – male and female alike. Iris, however, has only ever had eyes for another redhead . . . a redhead with blue blood.

@Supermodel_1971

Stella's mother is a model from the 1970s, the pinnacle of her career being a Vogue cover in 1971. She still has style in spades but is of the opinion that the only career a woman should really have is marriage (read divorce) and looking good. She has had three husbands, three extraordinarily large divorce settlements, and one child, Stella. She's also a devotee of Botox, fillers and any other form of facial or body enhancing surgery.

@TheBossWUB

Tuesday's boss at Wake Up Britain and a workaholic prone to shouting. He is frustrated by the powers that be slashing his shoe-string budget for the show and distraught by the subsequent downward spiral in viewing figures. He finds Tuesday frustrating and fabulous in equal measure.

@WUBTV

Wake Up Britain. The one time top breakfast TV show in the UK but currently ailing in content and viewers. Hosted by the ever-present @AnchorManTV and @KateKingTV with Tuesday doing the jobs they don't want to do – sports reporting in the field. Literally.

@TheDailyGB
Newspaper revered by middle England and @Mum's bible. According to @TheDailyGB the biggest danger to society are single, childless women. Women just like Tuesday Fields and Stella Cavill . . .

#PROLOGUE

TUESDAY

I am late.

All things considered I suspect my host, Peter Mignon, will be uncharacteristically sympathetic. After all, I've travelled the Atlantic to be here, making a short detour to the London townhouse I shared up until about ten hours ago with my boyfriend, Hugo Prince. Make that ex-boyfriend, Hugo Prince, who I just caught on top of a brunette, on top of a pool table, in Home House. Which is why I am now 3,000 miles from London and a world away from the latest man to break my heart.

It was all Mignon's idea, me being here.

Something to do with the endless run of espressos I supplied him with as his intern at The Daily, has since seen him return the favour in the only way he knows how; with a string of outlandish but occasionally brilliant suggestions, of which me being here is just one.

The only thing is, I'm not where I need to be right now, which is at Mignon's New Year's Eve bash at The Waverly Inn in downtown Manhattan. Instead I am stuck on the Tarmac at JFK, watching the snowstorm that has brought the city that never sleeps to a complete standstill and wondering when, if ever, my luck will change.

Apparently that isn't going to happen anytime soon. Well, not tonight anyway. Immigration ... check. Customs ... check. Luggage on the other hand ... MIA. Sod it, my Virgin Atlantic sleepsuit will just have to do. When I told Mignon I may be fashionably late, this wasn't what I had in mind. Into yellow cab minus bags, Blahniks and LBD I go.

Of course it doesn't help that my head is mush. It's almost as messed up as my makeshift outfit. Almost. And so I do what I always do at times of distress and regress, going over and over in my mind the events that have taken me to bolt from Big Ben into the arms of Lady Liberty.

I'm not a frequent flyer to The Big Apple, but even I know this journey into Manhattan is taking an age and, tonight, I am the worst kind of passenger, the ultimate backseat driver. Thirty minutes late and counting.

The thing is, it felt like it was all going so well. With Hugo Prince, that is. Was. Until I caught him shagging a younger model senseless in the games room of the members club where we'd actually met each other, two years ago.

I should have known better than to trust a man who sleeps fortnightly with a teeth-whitening gum shield. But seriously, did I really read the signs that badly? Because after only minor resistance from the aforementioned s**t, I moved from my one bedroom in Kensal Rise into his 35 Ovington Gardens in the autumn, armed with all that I have, own, am, crammed into several battered old suitcases. He had money, buckets of the stuff, but no real class to mention of and, like all successful people in this world, what Hugo Prince didn't have he simply craved more and more – a place at the top table. To be specific, he wanted in, into the establishment and into the House of Lords. If I'm being brutally honest with myself I always suspected I wouldn't be the woman he had on his arm when he arrived at his final destination, but I sure as hell didn't think he'd trade me in for some brash brunette either.

So my love life is once again in the gutter and I'm back to my postage stamp sized flat in NW10. Any day now my mother will start to send me her The Daily inspired thoughts of freezing eggs, suggesting I settle for Mr. Average and start finding fault with women like me – women who work rather than marry for a living.

Well there's something, I suppose – I may be a personal disaster but at least I'm not a professional one. Not yet anyway.

We pull up outside The Waverly Inn. Oh hell. Having got here I'm not sure I want to go in. How am I ever going to go from tramp to vamp in a five-minute trip to the ladies with only a blunt black eye pencil and lip-gloop for company?

Where is Gok Wan when you need him? Please let him be at Mignon's party. That would be just perfect.

On first glance I can't see Gok Wan. Lots of women who look like the one I caught Hugo Prince with are here, though. Excellent. But I can't miss Mignon. He is in the place I expect him to be, slap bang in the middle of the bar, in the middle of an assortment of blondes, brunettes and redheads who are squirrelling around him like scavengers. He is wearing a ludicrously lurid suit and relishing every minute. The only thing that can top this moment as far as Mignon is concerned is if he were to turn around and see me, his old intern, at the entrance of this fabulous place, wearing my Virgin Atlantic sleepsuit.

And then he does.

STELLA

I am late. In London I was never late. But six short months in New York and Stella Cavill, Little Miss Control Freak, is late for New Year's Eve. It's not as if the timing has changed at the last minute.

Although the location has. Thank God Peter Mignon stepped in with this invite, even if it is at the Waverly Inn with a whole load of 'meeja' underlings of his. Will still gets impressed by Mignon and the tales of guests on his transatlantic ABC chat show. Will still gets impressed by The Waverly Inn. You can take the geek out of the style but not out of the boy, especially one but months off the boat.

I find it hard to muster up the enthusiasm anymore. It's all work to me. They're just people and it's just a restaurant and really there are more important things going on in the world. Or maybe they're all merely keeping up appearances too and, like me, behind the façade they are all dancing on the recession's knife-edge.

In I walk to the crowded West Village cubbyhole that defines pretentious. I am so late that coat checking will have to wait. Still wrapped up against the bitter snowstorm I totter into the bar area with my array of bags – there was no way I was leaving my alternative outfit option – my one precious Leger and pair of Blahniks – in Stellar Shoes' Seventh Avenue s**thole offices. I'd thought it essential to be in the middle of Fashion Avenue, the trade-off being that to stick to my backer's budget I'd ended up with a studio where security amounted to an easily prised padlock.

I force a smile on my face – you never know when you may meet a client who needs some shoes on his feet. That's how I met Mignon after all, when his producers took away the desk from his set and realised his footwear was as tasteless as his tweets.

Stop it, Stella. Beneath Mignon's bluster there is a warm-hearted human being. And he's a Brit. It's odd how being away from home makes you gravitate towards the familiar, even if it's just the accent, a better immigration lawyer, and the shared experience of Grange Hill with beans on toast for tea. Is that why Will and I stay together, familiarity? In our last row he dared to intimate it was because I didn't have the bank balance to move out and on. How could he even think like that let alone say it?

I spy Will. Very much the Goldstein Smythe banker. He certainly looks the part, now. According to my mother, his transformation is my greatest achievement. No mention of her only child building a business up from scratch without taking a pound from her mother's divorce settlements. This particular mother-daughter chat had taken place over the summer on a boat Will had chartered. When she'd declared that 'now it's time to close the deal darling, I always managed it within six months', I'd almost thrown her still-perfect body into the Med.

My mother's screams of displeasure were still ringing in my ears from Christmas. Hell hath no fury like a former supermodel (if one Vogue cover in 1971 made you, officially, 'super') – without a wedding to organise.

The news we'd cancelled St Bart's had sent her over the edge. 'What do you mean, you're both working? That's not part of the plan,' she screamed down the phone. 'I'd had you and three husbands by the time I'd hit your advanced age of 33. The ring was the plan, the RING!'

Of course, I denied I had a plan. But it was a truth universally acknowledged that I, Stella Cavill, always had a plan. A plan to break free from my family (well, my mother). A plan for world domination (or at least to become the Tamara Mellon of male footwear). And yes, of course I'd had a plan for Will.

But life's rich tapestry keeps getting in the way with ever increasing intensity.

Will kisses me hello. Breathe, Stella. It's fine. Everything's still fine.

We'd moved to New York together. Will Moss and Stella Cavill had an American dream of conquering the Big Apple from their trendy Soho loft. And we had come so far. I knew the minute I met Will in those heady, pre credit crunch days. The suit was dreadful, the shoes unspeakable and he had looked like a waiter in Annabel's rather than a member with that haircut. But there was something about him. A kindness. And he could banter. Men who can't answer back don't last three minutes in my company let alone several years. We were blissfully happy for all that time in Islington. And then came our attempt to take our bite out of the Big Apple.

I survey the scene. Mignon has assembled the usual array of minions but there's someone I don't recognise. She is teasing him relentlessly about his Twitter follower count, despite the fact she is attired in a Virgin Atlantic sleepsuit.

I like her already.

TUESDAY

Mignon and I are having a heated debate. It was always going to happen at some point this evening, it nearly always does, but I didn't bargain on it happening already, and certainly not with me arguing my case dressed in a big red baby-gro. He's obsessing over Twitter. I'm doing my best to wind him up over his follow-ers. It's not difficult. I just tell him @LordTw1tter is trending. 3-2-1 and I've lost him to his iPhone.

I stifle a giggle. It feels good. The law of probability suggests I'm within a whisker of being cut a break sometime soon and then, just as in all the finest Richard Curtis films, I get my break.

Standing at the doorway a matter of moments after I've made my own embarrassing entrance is another of Mignon's blonde dinner guests – a slim and glamorous thirty-something swamped with bags and visibly harangued by her own appalling time keeping.

I like her instantly.

STELLA

Three minutes later and Tuesday Fields is filling my spare Leger rather better than I. But after hearing her story I certainly don't begrudge the poor girl this.

Hugo Prince. I'd heard of him of course – you'd have to be hiding under a rock not to know of his business success. But since when did such ambi-tion translate to personal happiness, for either the egocentric Prince or the invariably neglected Princess in his life?

It hadn't for my mother.

I can see Tuesday trying to keep it together. Time to face the music. Or at least Mignon's placement. Somewhat predictably for New York – and our host – there are too many women for the table. Which creatures will be attaching themselves to Will this time?

Thanks to our outfit changing expedition we are last to the table and I draw Tuesday Fields. I quickly surmise I get the luck of the draw. I think this girl could be a soul sister and it's not just because of the uncanny physical similarity between us. The 22-year-old PR, whose hand is glued to the small of Will's back, has squealed in confirmation 'you could be twins'.

TUESDAY

Thank God for this girl Stella. Gok who? Out of sleepsuit and into slinky Hervé number I go. Of course looking the part doesn't mean you belong and I still don't. Not really. Not even a little bit. But then neither, it seems, does the shoe designer sitting to the left of me. Quicker than Harry Potter can say expelliarmus Stella had spotted my predicament, whisked me off to the restrooms and waved her wand (and a generous dousing of Jo Malone Pomegranate Noir) all over me.

Over dress fittings and a pocket sized can of Elnett I spill about Hugo Prince and she spills about her boyfriend, Will. Now there's a boy who looks right at home in this crowd, from the luscious locks to the beautifully cut Saville Row suit (no tie), to the great watch and even better shoes. Some would say he's practically perfect in every way. Except for the fact he isn't.

STELLA

Tuesday is now abusing Mignon about Arsenal's lack of success, her encyclopaedic sporting knowledge crushing his. I find myself laughing. Loudly. It's been a while. Somehow, in her presence, the problems of a never ending supply of women ten years younger than me falling over my sharp-suited boyfriend, along with the issues in my shoes' supply chain, start to dissipate.

As my giggles ring forth I find Will catching my eye with a glint that I haven't seen in months.

TUESDAY

There aren't many things in this world I'm certain of but here are some things I do know; a glass of fizz solves everything and Mignon knows how to throw a party. A combination of the two is a guaranteed good time and that is precisely, against all the odds, what I am having.

Oh hell. He's on his feet. Speech incoming . . .

STELLA

Our host has declared we need to announce our New Year's Resolutions.
We have all drunk enough to be bordering on honest.

Tuesday's is to get the coveted sofa spot on Wake Up Britain.

Mine is to dress the feet of men Mignon could only dream of kissing the feet of on his much hyped new TV show – while shifting serious stock.

Mignon's, @PM_TV, is to hit a million Twitter followers by the end of the year, crucially exceeding that of his rival, British businessman, '@LordTw1tter'.

Tuesday and I roll our eyes, get out our phones and pretend to unfollow @PM_TV immediately.

Of course, while we're on there, well it would be rude not to, @TuesdayFields and @StellaCavill are each other's newest followers on Twitter.

#JANUARY

TUESDAY FIELDS

@TuesdayFields: London
Intrepid newshound with a nose for a good sports story.

Monthly Must:
Get over @HugoPr1nce.

Monthly Must Not:
Sleep with @JakeJacksonLive.

Followers:
Not enough to declare publicly.

STELLA CAVILL

@StellaCavill: New York, New York
Saviour of men's feet.

Monthly Must:
Do anything and everything to get
@MichaelAngeloMovie wearing Stellars for the Oscars.

Monthly Must Not:
Put overdraft even deeper in the red even if there's
frost inside the windows at Stellar Shoes' offices.

Followers:
Embarrassingly low.

@StellaCavill
New York calling London. Did you get back to Blighty OK?

@TuesdayFields
Are you really 100% sure only we can read these direct messages, Stella Cavill?!

@StellaCavill
Positive, Tuesday Fields. So . . . did you get home alright?

@TuesdayFields
Seriously . . . no one else can see these tweets?

@StellaCavill
Seriously.

@TuesdayFields
Direct from me to you, and you to me?

@StellaCavill
Correct.

@TuesdayFields
So just to be clear . . .

@StellaCavill
Tuesday! Why do you think they're called 'direct' messages?

@TuesdayFields
Well I hope you're right, for both our sakes . . .

@StellaCavill
How revealing do you think our Twitter conversations are going to end up being?

@TuesdayFields

Well, you never know, we may end up dishing the dirt on all sorts.
Our innermost thoughts on love, life, the universe . . .

@StellaCavill

We may . . . but not this morning, I'm preoccupied with a
hangover.
>> Was just checking you're back in London, out of sleepsuit and
in something more constrictive, that's all?

@TuesdayFields

Sleepsuit bagged and binned. Sad really. We went through a lot
in that short time we had together.
>> If it's any consolation I feel terrible too . . . still.

@StellaCavill

At least our heads are bound to be better than @PM_TV's. I
thought he was never going to stop drinking . . . or talking.

@TuesdayFields

If you hadn't accidentally on purpose spilt the Cabernet all over
that TV exec he might still be banging on about his follower count.

@StellaCavill

Boring @PM_TV.

@TuesdayFields

How to stop him reaching a million . . .

@StellaCavill

I sense an @GossipGirl style plot coming on. Speaking of plots . . .
How's the saga of the loathsome @KateKingTV?

@TuesdayFields

Still rooted to the sofa, naturally. She's also doing her level best to
get me sacked and it's only January.

11

@StellaCavill

You're younger, prettier and brighter. Of course she's trying to get you sacked. Just keep doing what you're doing.

@TuesdayFields

And what's that exactly?

@StellaCavill

A damn fine job!

@TuesdayFields

Hardly.

>> My last live hit saw me face-planting over the handlebars of a bike whilst delivering a piece to camera in the company of @MayorOfLondon.

@StellaCavill

Think glass half full. A YouTube moment?

@TuesdayFields

'This is Tuesday Fields, reporting from The Gherkin with a bruised chin and ego . . .'

>> On a much more positive and attractive note, how's project @MichaelAngeloMovie going?

@StellaCavill

Launched my Twitter campaign but not so much as an inkling of a reply, let alone a follow . . . yet.

>> He's going to be on @PM_TV's show next week . . .

@TuesdayFields

Can't you casually insert yourself into their inevitable public slanging match then?

@StellaCavill

I plan to.

>> I'll wax lyrical about the environment, something @MichaelAngeloMovie is passionate about and something @PM_TV couldn't give two hoots about.

@TuesdayFields
If neither bite abuse Arsenal's latest performance, that always gets @PM_TV going.

@StellaCavill
His love for them knows no bounds or boundaries. Ahh, love . . . dare I ask how the heart is?

@TuesdayFields
Well supers**t @HugoPr1nce is back from St Bart's. He's on page 20 of @TheDailyGB and so is the brunette I caught under him at Christmas.

@StellaCavill
Googling now . . . wow, trout pout! It'll never last. But seriously, how are you, T?

@TuesdayFields
Somewhere between lucky escape and heartbroken. Small crumb of comfort is, I can't see her being the eventual Lady Prince, can you?

@StellaCavill
Not. How to derail his career with one easy slag/shag . . . You know what you need, Tuesday Fields? A distraction.

@TuesdayFields
Well there is an interest of sorts, but that's all it is unless I can get past the elephant in the room.

@StellaCavill
Which is?

@TuesdayFields
He's cute but he bloody should be, having been born in the 1980's . . .

@StellaCavill
Well if it's good enough for Madonna . . . Gainfully employed?

@TuesdayFields
Ish. He's the new kid on the block at Wake Up Britain, making a play for the Afghanistan assignment.

@StellaCavill
And for you?

@TuesdayFields
Look, if @JustDemi had issues holding onto Ashton, what hope do I have?

@StellaCavill
Madonna.

@TuesdayFields
Enough about the boy crush @JakeJacksonLive. Cougar connotations making me cringe. Changing the subject, how's Will?

@StellaCavill
@MerchBanker is away in the Far East. I'm now sleeping, badly, at the office.

@TuesdayFields
All work and no play . . .

@StellaCavill
Makes me a very dull girl . . . I know!
>> Head is banging . . . while I'm compos mentis enough to remember could you do me a favour and follow @SINternUK?

@TuesdayFields
@SINternUK?

@StellaCavill
She LOVES Wake Up Britain. Watches you most mornings apparently.

@TuesdayFields
Great, but who is this masochistic creature?

@StellaCavill
@SINternUK is Iris. Ex-intern. Multi-tasking redhead who runs things for me from London. She could be useful to you too.

@TuesdayFields
OK you've got my attention, although I warn you it won't be for long in my current condition.

@StellaCavill
@SINternUK's quite something.
>> Stays out all hours trying to tie down minor royalty at The Box while simultaneously cluttering up my inbox.

@TuesdayFields
Already love her. What I'd give to be 25 again.
>> Breaking up with yet another boyfriend has led to an inevitable string of helpful conversations with @Mum. Today's gem . . .

RT: @Mum 'page 24 of @TheDailyGB darling – interesting piece on why successful women are so unlucky in love'.

@StellaCavill
Question for @Mum: why is doormat preferable to dynamic?

@TuesdayFields
Love @Mum but onslaught of advice unwelcome. Do Mums always know best? Don't answer that Stella. Unless it's a big fat 'no'.

@StellaCavill
I quote mine:
>> @Supermodel_1971, 'to lose one boyfriend without a ring, may be regarded as a misfortune; to make a career out of it looks like carelessness'.

@TuesdayFields
Wilde.

@StellaCavill
I retorted with a real rather than butchered quote: 'in married life three are company and two none.'

@TuesdayFields
Touché . . .

@StellaCavill
Well it always has been in her case anyway. Turns out my expensive boarding school education wasn't such a waste after all.

@TuesdayFields
Oh hell. @TheBossWUB screaming blue murder at @WeatherWoman for predicting drought not downpour again. Must jump, who knows how high today . . .

* * *

@StellaCavill
I did it! @MichaelAngeloMovie replied. Probably all thanks to @PM_TV. Should I thank him, do you think?

16

@TuesdayFields
I advise not on health and safety grounds. His head would explode. There is something you should definitely do though . . .

@StellaCavill
And what's that?

@TuesdayFields
Get @MichaelAngeloMovie to follow you, on and off Twitter . . .

@StellaCavill
The problem is . . .

@TuesdayFields
His mother can't spell Michelangelo properly?

@StellaCavill
That pesky 'a'! But there's something else too . . .

@TuesdayFields
What?

@StellaCavill
He's just so very . . .

@TuesdayFields
Hot?

@StellaCavill
Green! I've had to follow every @SaveThePlanet organisation going and it's completely cluttered up my news feed.

@TuesdayFields
Bet he drives a Prius he flew in privately from Japan like all those other bloody faux-green types. Hypocrite.

@StellaCavill

I'm just grateful I don't have to make him shoes the size of his carbon foot print. Then my business would be even more up the spout.

@TuesdayFields

How is the Tamara Mellon of male footwear's empire?

@StellaCavill

On edge. Need a good awards season, get some shoes on some celebs' feet. Golden Globes next week.

\>> My backer @AllThatGlittersIsGold is putting the pressure on. Let's hope he doesn't pull the plug too.

@TuesdayFields

What does @MerchBanker say? He's got a head for figures.

@StellaCavill

@MerchBanker has enough on his plate at the moment.

\>> There's a limited amount even he can do when the world seems to be in a perpetual state of financial Armageddon.

@TuesdayFields

A problem shared is a problem halved, S . . .

@StellaCavill

To tell the truth, I'm too embarrassed to ask him for help. I've always been Little-Miss-In-Control for the both of us.

@TuesdayFields

Despite appearances, you are not Wonder Woman, Stella Cavill.

@StellaCavill

I know that. I'm just not willing to give up that outfit just yet – it's why he fell for me in the first place.

@TuesdayFields

Hang on; I'm trying to picture the scene.

>> Your eyes met across a crowded room at a fancy dress party, you were Wonder Woman, @MerchBanker had come as He-Man . . .

@StellaCavill

I was being metaphorical you muppet.

@TuesdayFields

I haven't finished . . .

@StellaCavill

I don't think I like where this is going . . .

@TuesdayFields

Trust me, you will. Wonder Woman and He-Man live happily ever after in NYC and are fabulously successful in shoes and banking. The End.

@StellaCavill

She-Ra would be so pissed off.

@TuesdayFields

She-Ra is too busy using her extreme powers of strength to save Planet Etheria to worry about He-Man's living arrangements.

@StellaCavill

But they're an item aren't they? She-Ra and He-Man?

@TuesdayFields

They're brother and sister, Stella!

@StellaCavill

No way. Are you sure?

@TuesdayFields
Yes! Although to be fair they didn't realise that until it was almost too late. Very @JeremyKyle.

@StellaCavill
By the power of Grayskull! Well whatever She-Ra was on back then, I need some of it pronto if I'm going to sort out Stellar Shoes. >> Damn the recession.

@TuesdayFields
Sadly, I'm no She-Ra, but can I help? I can't stand @AnchorManTV but his feet do get three hours of live airtime every morning.

@StellaCavill
There's an idea! I'll tell @SINternUK to touch base on shoeing him immediately.

@TuesdayFields
You know what they say about a man with big feet?

@StellaCavill
Big . . .

@TuesdayFields
. . . hold that thought for another because @AnchorManTV has the smallest feet on a man I've ever seen!

@StellaCavill
Too much information, Miss Fields. Tell me, is @TheBossWUB cutting you some slack on Wake Up Britain?

@TuesdayFields
Still making me jump through hoops. He's not being a total bastard, it's his twisted logic.

>> He thinks me working fourteen hour days, seven days a week will help somehow.

@StellaCavill
And is it? Helping?

@TuesdayFields
Sort of, I suppose in that I have no time to even think about @HugoPr1nce, but nothing for @KateKingTV to worry about just yet.

@StellaCavill
Hang on in there, give her enough rope and all that . . . old bags get binned for new ones as soon as budgets allow, unless they're much loved . . .

@TuesdayFields
And @KateKingTV certainly isn't that. Thanks, S.

* * *

@StellaCavill
Question: Who has the biggest . . . feet . . . in Hollywood?

@TuesdayFields
Answer: Is it @SteveJones? Word is his are more than generously sized . . . haha!

@StellaCavill
Ubiquitous he may be, but I'm talking A-list here, Tuesday.

@TuesdayFields
A-list? In which case my next question is . . . are his shoes actually made of recycled cardboard?

@StellaCavill
Answer: . . .

@TuesdayFields
!!!

@StellaCavill
These Golden Globe gifting suites are incredible, T.
>> So far I've given @AllThatGlittersIsGold's profit margin away in shoes but the things I've taken . . .

@TuesdayFields
Not @JustinBieber's virginity? Please God, not that.

@StellaCavill
Seducing young men? You're one to talk, mentioning no names @JakeJacksonLive.
>> Anyway, didn't @SelenaGomez get there first? Why and how do I know that?

@TuesdayFields
@PM_TV's news feed probably. You know he's obsessed with knowing everything and subsequently retweeting it to everyone.

@StellaCavill
You're right. That's exactly where I heard it. Me, and it would appear an ever increasing number of his followers . . .

@TuesdayFields
Let's not get bogged down in @PM_TV. Back to Bieber. If not his virginity, what have you taken?

@StellaCavill
A free Botox voucher, an infrared sauna and a state of the art home gym.

@TuesdayFields
You've got to be kidding me?

@StellaCavill
I kid you not.

@TuesdayFields
Is there still space for @MerchBanker in that Soho loft of yours with all those new acquisitions?

@StellaCavill
That's another story. Put it this way, it's a long way from the life Will and I had together in Islington.

@TuesdayFields
And from my humble abode in Kensal Rise! Your work is evidently going a lot better than mine, S.

@StellaCavill
Why? How did @TheBossWUB humiliate you this time?

@TuesdayFields
Had me reporting live from a third division football club threatened with closure.

@StellaCavill
That doesn't sound so bad?

@TuesdayFields
Wouldn't have been bad at all had a rainstorm not washed away my notes and mascara.
>> @TheBossWUB banned the use of umbrellas last month citing they look messy on air.

@StellaCavill
Suspect he didn't know what messy on air looked like until he saw you without one this morning!
>> Where were you anyway? @PM_TV's beloved Emirates?

@TuesdayFields
Not. They, my football-loathing friend, are in a different league in more ways than one.

@StellaCavill
How could I forget? I'm constantly reminded by @PM_TV and his incessant tweeting about them. I do know they are called the 'Gooners'.

@TuesdayFields
'Gunners'.
>> Anyway you're forgiven for doing them down, on grounds that @PM_TV's team's form of late has been almost as bad as his addiction to tweeting.

@StellaCavill
Haven't seen him since New Year in the non-virtual world. Does he still exist? I mean in real life?

@TuesdayFields
Thought he might be in La La Land with you . . .
>> . . . trying to lull a poor unassuming starlet onto his show for the inevitable display of public shaming and tears.

@StellaCavill
Only A-Listers allowed in town this week so @PM_TV not here.

@TuesdayFields
Not yet in any case but rest assured he'll be working on it.

@StellaCavill
Well, if he is here, I've not seen him.
>> Probably trying to talk his way into the gifting suites as we tweet – or trying to blag a Botox voucher.
>> How's tricks your end?

@TuesdayFields
@KateKingTV and @AnchorManTV at each other's throats.
>> Microphone issue this morning broadcast row over who gets
to open and close show. P45 for sound guy Derek.

@StellaCavill
Poor Derek. What a pair of prima donnas. Anyway, they ought to
watch out, I hear there's a new TV marriage on the cards . . .
>> How is your baby-faced foreign correspondent?

@TuesdayFields
OK. He's . . . OK.

@StellaCavill
Come on Tuesday, you can do better than that.

@TuesdayFields
Well, he's making a real effort. But I'm not. I can't get my head
around this cougar thing.
>> My one time acceptable rear is these days a dimpled disaster
area.

@StellaCavill
How bad is it?

@TuesdayFields
What? My bum? Not good.

@StellaCavill
Not your bum! His age?

@TuesdayFields
He thinks the 'landline' belongs in a museum.

@StellaCavill
Ah.

@TuesdayFields
He is sweet Stella, but sweet makes me want to throw up.
Yesterday, coffee and croissants. Today, lunch . . .

@StellaCavill
Tomorrow, breakfast in bed! Might be just what you need.

@TuesdayFields
Reminds me of a bad joke. 'How do you like your eggs?'

@StellaCavill
I don't know. How do I like my eggs?

@TuesdayFields
'Fertilised!'

@StellaCavill
@Mum would love that.

@TuesdayFields
Yes she would!

@StellaCavill
I don't think @Supermodel_1971 is ready to be a grandmother.
Plan a wedding, yes? Granny? No.

@TuesdayFields
Why do mothers make it their life's work to get their girls hitched?
>> @Mum would consider her 'career' a failure is she doesn't get
me away soon.

@StellaCavill
You'd think with mine's track record she'd be more liberal and
less bothered.

@TuesdayFields
You'd think . . .

@StellaCavill
Mind you, I wouldn't be surprised if she slipped me the number
of a good divorce lawyer at the wedding breakfast!

@TuesdayFields
At least you're moving in the right direction. I'm going backwards,
in life and possibly into the bedroom.
>> Imagine what @Mum would make of @JakeJacksonLive?!

@StellaCavill
Well the first thing she'd do is trawl through her @TheDailyGB
archive cuttings . . .
>> . . . to find a very good reason why it's a very bad idea for
older girls to date younger men.

@TuesdayFields
'The truth behind men who pursue older women'

@StellaCavill
'10 reasons not to date a younger man'

@TuesdayFields
'Heartbreak and humiliation, the real life story of a 30 something
woman who dated a 20 something boy' etc. etc.

@StellaCavill
Don't you just love @TheDailyGB? Informative, advisory and
total and utter bollocks. No wonder @PM_TV once edited it.

@TuesdayFields
I still think the time I was interning there was when I made
@Mum most proud – she believes every sodding word!

>> Oh well, bring on the damning headlines. Right now I fancy making a bit of mischief for myself . . .

@StellaCavill
That's my girl.

@StellaCavill
On second thoughts can you still be considered a girl post 30 do you think?

@TuesdayFields
Don't you start, for God's sake!

@StellaCavill
Just asking. Onwards and upwards and into the arms of a naughty but nice boy you go . . .

* * *

@StellaCavill
Oscar nominations are out. Guess who I'm heeling?

@TuesdayFields
Not Mr. Environmentally Friendly?

@StellaCavill
Correct! @MichaelAngeloMovie has clearly fallen for my faux green credentials and is now following me!

@TuesdayFields
You might have to do a line in 'green Crocs' . . .

@StellaCavill
Unfortunately @AllThatGlittersIsGold is unconvinced star power is enough to shift sales in environmentally friendly footwear.

@TuesdayFields

Sod that. Great exposure, S. And if his shoe size is anything to go by . . .

@StellaCavill

I know where you're going but don't! @MerchBanker is feeling very neglected.

@TuesdayFields

Nothing like an A-list movie star being interested in his girlfriend to remind @MerchBanker of what he's got at home.

@StellaCavill

@MerchBanker's not at home. Neither of us is. That's the problem, Tuesday. We're both travelling with work constantly. >> Not even ships in the night – more like oceans apart.

@TuesdayFields

@MerchBanker adores you, Stella. Without you, where would he be? >> More importantly what on earth would he be wearing – especially on his feet?

@StellaCavill

I don't know, Tuesday. @Supermodel_1971 asked me last night if he was a 'wheel's-up bachelor' >> (i.e. plays away from home the minute he jets off anywhere).

@TuesdayFields

Will, really? Not a chance.

@StellaCavill

I told @Supermodel_1971, no. Not yet in any case.

@TuesdayFields

At least you have something decent to 'declare'.

>> My inappropriate flirtation with @JakeJacksonLive is not for any sort of public consumption, least of all in polite company.

@StellaCavill
So he's not about to get introduced to @Mum anytime soon I take it?

@TuesdayFields
Not. Even if I do cave to his boyish charms – which I haven't by the way . . .
>> . . . I'd have had to have a lobotomy to think an introduction to @Mum was a good idea.

@StellaCavill
Modern women, modern times, Tuesday Fields. Don't discount it. Think about it.

@TuesdayFields
On the subject of @Mum. Today's nugget:

RT @Mum: 'Not having a go, just a gentle warning darling, @TheDailyGB reporting fertility rates plummeting in plus 30's.
>> Thought you should know, that's all!'

@StellaCavill
Wish that paper's readership would plummet.
>> To them public enemy number one isn't crime or corruption – it's the single woman, scourge of society.

@TuesdayFields
Sadly it speaks @Mum's language so perfectly.
>> What she means is, at 33, I'm to consider my fertility, well, plummeted.

@StellaCavill
You and me both, Tuesday Fields. You and me both.

* * *

@TuesdayFields
Am office angel all thanks to visit from @SINternUK. Consider
@AnchorManTV well and truly reeled and heeled!

@StellaCavill
Yes! @SINternUK has that effect on most men. Especially those
twice her age.

@TuesdayFields
Well @AnchorManTV is now completely in love with your
flame-haired assistant and as a result being so much nicer to me.
>> I owe you one, S.

@StellaCavill
I owe you! Maybe it'll work out after all. You get a break from the
nasty bastard and I get a better looking balance sheet.

@TuesdayFields
@KateKingTV isn't best impressed! If looks could kill,
@SINternUK and I would be pushing up daisies by now.

@StellaCavill
I bet. Let's just hope that @SINternUK's dalliances with the
house of Windsor don't break the red tops.
>> And @AnchorManTV realises she isn't interested in an
ageing breakfast show host with hair plugs.

@TuesdayFields
By which you mean I should make the most of him being a naïve
and horny old fool . . .
>> . . . before he figures out @SINternUK has no intention of
seeing anything other than his feet bare?

@StellaCavill
Precisely.

@TuesdayFields
Urgghh. I need to banish all thoughts of @AnchorManTV with the horn.
>> Let's talk about something or someone more attractive, like @MichaelAngeloMovie . . .

@StellaCavill
Swoon . . . I'm allowed at least to do that, the rest of womankind do.

@TuesdayFields
Except the rest of womankind don't have @MichaelAngeloMovie following them on Twitter.

@StellaCavill
Or getting flirty direct messages from him . . .

@TuesdayFields
OMG. Really?
>> I know you're mere moments away from happily ever after with @MerchBanker, but be honest, S, if you could, would you?

@StellaCavill
In my mind I think already have! But like @SINternUK with @AnchorManTV, the only part of @MichaelAngeloMovie I plan on seeing naked is his feet.

@TuesdayFields
Ha. So you have thought about it?

@StellaCavill
Could you not? @People's sexiest man alive is asking me how I am, almost daily.

>> Apart from you, I'm not sure who else asks how I am at the moment. But I couldn't do that to Will.

@TuesdayFields
But he looks like a real life version of the original Michelangelo's David with a far bigger package in his pants!
>> In fairness marble David wasn't wearing pants, but you get my drift.

@StellaCavill
What can I say? I love @MerchBanker. @MichaelAngeloMovie is strictly business.

@TuesdayFields
I know how much you love that absent banker boyfriend of yours, but if it was me he was DM'ing I'd be there in a vodka shot!

@StellaCavill
I know you would! I'm convinced that's why @MichaelAngeloMovie likes me though, T.
>> I'm a challenge. Let's face it; he'd drop me as soon as he had me. I'm determined to make it work. With Will and I that is.

@TuesdayFields
@Mum was right about one thing. No such thing as the perfect man is there?

@StellaCavill
Not. Speaking of which, how is @JakeJacksonLive whose only flaw is his age? Poor boy.

@TuesdayFields
Wants dinner, then who knows what else. Christ.
>> After the disaster that was @HugoPr1nce I'm not so sure taking my ageing body to bed with a younger model is the answer.

@StellaCavill
From what you've told me, @JakeJacksonLive is nothing like @HugoPr1nce.
>> What I mean is, he doesn't sound like a total scumbag. If anything he's behaving like a lovelorn pup!

@TuesdayFields
I am undecided. My own judgment too clouded by @Mum and @TheDailyGB projections.

@StellaCavill
The right response is to ignore both, you do know that. Right?

@TuesdayFields
We'll see. In other news I heard from @PM_TV today. He's coming back to London for the Arsenal cup final.

@StellaCavill
You'll find him in a rage. He's been telling anyone who will listen – i.e. his dwindling Twitter followers – how most of the first team need selling.
>> I don't need to know. Yet I continue to follow and be updated. Why?

@TuesdayFields
Well it's not for the inner workings of the footballing world.

@StellaCavill
And certainly not for his charm and good looks!

@TuesdayFields
How that man loves to ruffle football feathers! I suspect most who follow him have a perverse attraction to controversy.

@StellaCavill
Or live in hope of a retweet and a few more followers if they insult him enough.

@TuesdayFields
I have to admit his tweets do make me laugh.

@StellaCavill
I have to admit I find his obsession with @No1Sportsman highly amusing.

@TuesdayFields
Only sportsman I can think of who could give @PM_TV a run for his money.
>> There's a reason why he's worth big bucks and front of the grid most of the season.

@StellaCavill
Well he can spell for starters, which removes much ammunition for @PM_TV.
>> And God @No1Sportsman looks the part. Did you see his @VanityFair shoot?

@TuesdayFields
Just yesterday I made it my screen saver. Sorry, Chuck Bass. You were divine, but I've moved on.

@StellaCavill
@AnnieLebovitz did a great service to womankind – and gay men everywhere – when she put @No1Sportsman in a string vest. Inspired.

@TuesdayFields
Possibly the only man on the planet who can make one of those look good.
>> Why don't you add @No1Sportsman to your growing list of fiendishly fit celebrity clientele who you won't sleep with?!

@StellaCavill
Why don't you interview – and then sleep with him?

@TuesdayFields
That would really piss off @HugoPr1nce . . .

@StellaCavill
I'm not sure @HugoPr1nce should be your primary motivation, Tuesday Fields.

@TuesdayFields
I'll do some research, try and be a good journalist, find an angle etc.
>> Ooo! Am suddenly living up to my Twitter title billing and am intrepid news hound!

@StellaCavill
Do what @PM_TV does, wear @No1Sportsman down to the point where it's just easier and less hassle for him to say yes. Get sniffing . . .

@TuesdayFields
Speaking of @PM_TV, I've arranged to see him at that pub of his when he's over in London for the game.

@StellaCavill
The one with the silly name? The Ferret and Trouserleg? How very apt!

@TuesdayFields
Isn't it? Quick question before I'm summoned by @TheBossWUB for yet another meaningless meeting.
>> If you could ask @No1Sportsman any question what would it be?

@StellaCavill
That's easy. What's his shoe size, of course . . .

TUESDAY FIELDS

@TuesdayFields: London
Working hard, playing harder.

Monthly Must:
Make a professional impact.

Monthly Must Not:
Get sucked into Valentine's Day hysteria.

Followers:
Little growth unlike waistline.

STELLA CAVILL

@StellaCavill: New York, New York
And the award for best men's footwear goes to . . .

Monthly Must:
Boost sales. End of.

Monthly Must Not:
Get carried away with stories of Valentine's Day proposals . . .

Followers:
Can they go down as well as up?

***

@StellaCavill
I'm seeing red.

@TuesdayFields
Red? Why?

@StellaCavill
Valentine's Day. I'm seeing red. Literally. Everywhere.

@TuesdayFields
You're the attached one. I'm supposed to have jurisdiction over this particular grievance.

@StellaCavill
The pressure. Who needs the pressure? It's just a day. Spoke to Will in Shanghai last night.
>> He was talking about flying back for one night only.

@TuesdayFields
But that's romantic?

@StellaCavill
It was. But then we had a slanging match.

@TuesdayFields
About what?

@StellaCavill
I said he sounded reluctant. He said I sounded reluctant. Which of course, I am.
>> I'm right in the middle of Awards Season and I'm sinking. Don't have the money for the staff to swim.

@TuesdayFields

Surely he understands, S?

@StellaCavill

Stuck on the other side of the world? What he needed was a devoted girlfriend saying, 'it would be lovely to see you'.

>> Instead I was a complete cow.

@TuesdayFields

Valentine's Day, AKA VD, can be about as welcome as an STI – and as impossible to ignore.

@StellaCavill

Quite. Anyway, I BBM'd him and apologised. He's read it but not responded.

@TuesdayFields

He will. What will you do instead?

@StellaCavill

Need you ask? Work! It's the BAFTA's, the Brits and the Grammy's that week.

>> I'm going to be prostituting myself to the @RZRachelZoes of this world.

@TuesdayFields

You going?

@StellaCavill

@SINternUK is going to cover the Brits and BAFTA's.

>> I'll be stuck in LA, first loitering in the gifting suites at the Grammys, followed by the Oscar brownnosing.

@TuesdayFields

Sounds like a slog but just think of how good this month should be for business!

@StellaCavill
Speculate to accumulate and all that, just what I was saying to @AllThatGlittersIsGold while explaining my hotel bill. Again. How are you?

@TuesdayFields
See below . . .

RT @Mum: 'Darling I've been thinking. Important just to crack on with life. Unmarried girl of your age, life's too short.
>> Happy Valentine's! Love Mum x'

@StellaCavill
February 15th has always been one of my favourite days of the year. Bring it on.

***

@TuesdayFields
This February 15th is one of the most disastrous days of my life. @Mum and Madonna to blame.

@StellaCavill
What for?

@TuesdayFields
Last night.

@StellaCavill
Why, what did you do? Got to be more exciting than my evening. Spent it stuffing gift bags and my face with @GreenandBlacks chocolate bars.

@TuesdayFields
Not what Stella, who . . .

@StellaCavill
@AllThatGlittersIsGold was right then. Hard work, persistence and perseverance do pay off . . . ?

@TuesdayFields
@Mum's message, endless pictures of Madge with various toyboys and prospect of spending Valentine's Day alone with bowl of cereal . . .
>> . . . made me have sex with @JakeJacksonLive.

@StellaCavill
Because sex becomes compulsory after a few pics'n'tweets?!

@TuesdayFields
Now it does! Christ, I am a fully-fledged cougar.
>> Last night I behaved like a total tart with a man far too young to see me naked in anything other than a blackout.

@StellaCavill
If you can't laugh about bedding @JakeJacksonLive then at least humour me. God knows I could do with a laugh and a bit of romance.

@TuesdayFields
Heavy on laughs, a little light on romance . . .

@StellaCavill
If you discount the fact he's been following you around like a puppy dog for ages.

@TuesdayFields
Discounted. Cook in the kitchen I am not, but whore in the bedroom I most certainly am/was.

@StellaCavill
Well, spill. I'll take what I can get which wasn't even so much as a VD card let alone a red rose. So, full details please. Leave nothing out.

@TuesdayFields
You want to know the worst part?

@StellaCavill
Every part.

@TuesdayFields
He woke up first.

@StellaCavill
Don't suppose you remembered to set the alarm in the middle of the night in order to wake up cleansed, toned and moisturised?

@TuesdayFields
I set it but hit snooze. Missed critical minutes to sort morning breath and apply full but natural looking war paint.

@StellaCavill
So he went to bed with TV's Tuesday Fields and woke up with . . .

@TuesdayFields
. . . her gin-fuelled and distinctly less attractive evil twin. Yes.

@StellaCavill
Was it bad enough that you woke up wondering 'where am I?'

@TuesdayFields
Check.

@StellaCavill
'What did I . . . ?'

@TuesdayFields
Check.

@StellaCavill
'Why did I?'

@TuesdayFields
Check! I spent half an hour pretending to be asleep whilst figuring how to get from bedroom to bathroom naked . . .
>> . . . without @JakeJacksonLive seeing me, well, naked.

@StellaCavill
Slightly late in the day for that don't you think, darling?!

@TuesdayFields
But for a random shoe obstructing my sodding path the plan to back into the bathroom shrouded in sheet would have gone well.

@StellaCavill
?!

@TuesdayFields
Let's just say if last night wasn't enough to put him off, seeing me landing legs akimbo on the bathroom floor will have done it.

@StellaCavill
Small flaw in your theory there Tuesday . . .

@TuesdayFields
. . . and what might that be, brain box?

@StellaCavill
Well once you've stopped beating yourself up about sleeping with @JakeJacksonLive, you might want to remember that he actually likes you.

@TuesdayFields
Morning after the night before will have put paid to that. It doesn't matter how much he likes me or I like him, it's the last thing I need.
>> That and to see Gordon again.

@StellaCavill
Who the hell is Gordon and how was he involved?

@TuesdayFields
Gordon, as in the gin, not the person. I don't know anyone called Gordon.

@StellaCavill
Well that's a relief. I thought for one horrible moment there . . .

@TuesdayFields
Anyway it doesn't matter. I am never ever locking lips with Gordon again.

@StellaCavill
Not until at least Saturday, when that tonic will be itching to have a splash of him in it.

@TuesdayFields
What's happening Saturday?

@StellaCavill
I think you'll find you've got an ego to entertain in @PM_TV down the Ferret and Trouserleg?

@TuesdayFields
Bollocks! You're right. Forgot he was flying in. Thought I was the one who got to break bad news around here?

@StellaCavill

Suspect you'll need Gordon for medicinal purposes on Saturday.
>> You can't have missed @PM_TV's buzzing after
@BarackObama agreed to a one-on-one.

@TuesdayFields

Are you saying @PM_TV needs swatting?

@StellaCavill

Exactly that. If he gets really objectionable just . . .
>> . . . remind him that if he had real clout he wouldn't have had to
leave Hollywood because he couldn't get into the Vanity Fair party.

@TuesdayFields

When @BarackObama airs he'll never look back. I will need
Gordon. Claiming duvet day. Going under.

@StellaCavill

Sweet dreams, Tuesday Fields. I've got a pair of shoes for
@MichaelAngeloMovie to think about.

@TuesdayFields

Then you'll be the one having the sweet dream. I'm the one living
a nightmare.

* * *

@TuesdayFields

I am in love with Peter Jones.

@StellaCavill

Which one? Maker of duvets or dragon in den?

@TuesdayFields

Maker of duvets of course. While I've been entertaining ideas of a relationship with a department store, how've you been?

@StellaCavill

La La Land even more otherworldly than usual. Oscar obsessed. It's rubbing off on me.

>> Perfecting @MichaelAngeloMovie's pair of patents taking its toll.

@TuesdayFields

Why?

@StellaCavill

I might as well be working on a foot double. I've not been allowed to meet him yet.

@TuesdayFields

No way! Feet dwarfed by ego?

@StellaCavill

His size double-zero stylist won't allow me past her billowing maxi skirts 'at this time'.

>> Wants to do the whole thing, fitting included, by email.

@TuesdayFields

How is that supposed to work?

@StellaCavill

I've gone over her head. DM'd him and set up our first proper meeting face to face.

>> The power of Twitter – the ability to get round sulky starved and thus bitch from hell.

@TuesdayFields

What does @MerchBanker think about you having a one on one with @MichaelAngeloMovie?

>> I'm surprised he's not there with you offering to hold the shoehorn.

@StellaCavill

On a scale of 1-10 his level of interest in this particular project is about a 2.

>> @Supermodel_1971's is an 11. Me heeling a Hollywood actor is giving her scope to reminisce . . .

@TuesdayFields

Confessions of a cover star or a mother is bad enough, but both combined? Christ.

@StellaCavill

It was one Vogue cover. I'm sorry, but that does not a super-model make.

@TuesdayFields

At least she got a cover! I've been slogging away at this TV thing for ages now without so much as a mention in the back pages.

>> Positive or otherwise.

@StellaCavill

It doesn't necessarily translate into success, Tuesday.

>> I may have made it into the fashion mags but a mention on the party page in Twatler or Hello! is no substitute to shifting stock.

@TuesdayFields

What's that expression? Something about it being better to be noticed than not noticed at all?

@StellaCavill

But then what about the fall? If that happens I'll be remembering anonymity with nothing but fondness.

@TuesdayFields

If it's alright with you, I'd like to try being noticed sooner rather than later. I'm running out of resolve. @TheBossWUB is being unbearable.

@StellaCavill

When he goes on his next rant, picture him on the loo. It helps if you can bear to conjure the image.

@TuesdayFields

Yesterday's outburst was so severe I swear he came within a whisker of losing his stomach through his arsehole.

@StellaCavill

'Restroom' analogy spot on then?!

@TuesdayFields

@KateKingTV doing her best to give him a coronary.
>> Rest of us caught in the crossfire and, if particularly unlucky, in direct trajectory of spit too.

@StellaCavill

In which case, keep your head down!

@TuesdayFields

I am doing so in more ways than one. Been ducking and diving @TheBossWUB and @JakeJacksonLive.
>> I don't know which corridor encounter fills me with more dread.

@StellaCavill

I'd sooner be in your shoes than mine.
>> @AllThatGlittersIsGold is in NYC as I type, taking a look at

the books in between meetings on businesses that actually make him money.

@TuesdayFields
Nothing you can do to paper over the cracks?

@StellaCavill
Nothing.
>> What with me in LA and @SINternUK in London there's no way to even attempt to manage the fallout with soothing tones and eyelash fluttering.

@TuesdayFields
Can't you send in @Supermodel_1971?

@StellaCavill
Tempting but . . . no.

@TuesdayFields
What harm could it do?

@StellaCavill
With her track record? Plenty.

***

@StellaCavill
I have just met the embodiment of male perfection.

@TuesdayFields
I take it the @MichaelAngeloMovie rollercoaster of flirtation just got a whole lot more fun to ride?

@StellaCavill
Considerably. Window shopping only. No trying let alone buying. How's tricks your end?

@TuesdayFields

@DaveTV playing out a repeat of Dragons Den last night. One where they decided not to go with those suitcases for kids. Doh.

@StellaCavill

Are you actually obsessed with anyone/anything called Peter Jones? >> If you can be bothered to lift yourself off the sofa and onto a plane I could just snag you an interview with @MichaelAngelo Movie?

@TuesdayFields

Really? Access all areas?

@StellaCavill

Well maybe not all areas . . .

@TuesdayFields

Bet he'd like to access all your areas!

@StellaCavill

Tuesday! I'm looking forward to getting on a plane back East. NY may be full of Americans but at least they're real. >> Here the smiles are as fake as the breasts. For all I know @MichaelAngeloMovie won't even be wearing Stellars.

@TuesdayFields

Downtown LA at the Kodak with @MichaelAngeloMovie or down the Ferret and Trouserleg with @PM_TV? >> I think we both know who drew the shorter straw this weekend, thank you very much.

@StellaCavill

Are you really sure you can't get on a plane? >> I'm not going to the ceremony but we could watch from my minis- cule hotel room and then go gatecrash some parties afterwards?

@TuesdayFields

@KateKingTV refusing to cover the cup final. Says it's not in her contract to do weekends or football related stories. Hag.

@StellaCavill

@TheBossWUB will be shutting the doors to the studio and her career if she keeps that up.

@TuesdayFields

@AnchorManTV would be loving every minute of it if he was here, but he's gone to see a show or something in Amsterdam.

@StellaCavill

Show – or something? Amsterdam? Did he go with that wife of his he parades around in @TheDailyGB?

@TuesdayFields

Audrey? No. Flying solo apparently.

@StellaCavill

Allegedly. My imagination is running wild.

@TuesdayFields

My stomach is turning. 11AM meeting today saw @KateKingTV call her agent in front of newsroom to confirm . . .

>> . . . she doesn't do weekends or football and me told I do and I will.

@StellaCavill

@KateKingTV is gifting you that sofa spot quicker than you can possibly imagine.

@TuesdayFields

Hold your horses, S. Let me get through @PM_TV and the cup final unscathed first.

>> But yes, things are looking better, although nowhere near as good as @MichaelAngeloMovie!

@StellaCavill
He is something else. I mean, the man has beautiful feet.

@TuesdayFields
@MerchBanker must be out of his mind letting you spend all this time with the likes of @MichaelAngeloMovie.

@StellaCavill
@MerchBanker is convinced everyone in my world is a friend of Dorothy's, no exceptions.

@TuesdayFields
Not even @MerchBanker can be that naïve when it comes to @MichaelAngeloMovie. His little black book reads like FHM's sexiest 100.

@StellaCavill
Yes it does, but Will maintains it's all a front. Which it usually is, but I'd hazard a guess not in this case.

@TuesdayFields
On what basis?

@StellaCavill
Think of the logistics of putting shoes on a man's feet and where that leaves my face . . .

@TuesdayFields
Moving forward you may well need a chastity belt. Hope you picked one up at JFK?

@StellaCavill
I looked but there weren't any. Must all be in Amsterdam . . .

@TuesdayFields
With @AnchorManTV. Replacing thoughts of him this minute with @MichaelAngeloMovie.

@StellaCavill
I would.

@TuesdayFields
So would I!

@StellaCavill
That's not what I meant!

@TuesdayFields
It's precisely what I meant.

* * *

@TuesdayFields
Save me!

@StellaCavill
From yourself? Only you can do that Tuesday.

@TuesdayFields
From @PM_TV!

@StellaCavill
How is The Ferret and Trouserleg and its charming proprietor?

@TuesdayFields
Well, when he suggested a drink I didn't think it would be with a cast of thousands.

@StellaCavill

You know as well as I do @PM_TV can't stand one-on-one combat, much prefers crowds and audiences, preferably television ones.

@TuesdayFields

Am standing at the bar next to Ross Kemp and Sarah Brown.

@StellaCavill

What are they talking about?!

@TuesdayFields

Afghanistan, gangs, the Amazon . . .

@StellaCavill

Predictable.

@TuesdayFields

Uh-o. Sarah just said she and Gordon loved the part on the Amazon shows where Ross gets involved with tribe life.

@StellaCavill

Isn't it Bruce Parry who does that?

@TuesdayFields

Yup! Ross is looking pissed off. Sarah doesn't seem to know why. I'm going in.

@StellaCavill

Keep me posted.

***

@TuesdayFields

Found @PM_TV. He was dodging various bullets freezing with the smokers in the beer garden. He's insisting I send you this:

RT @PM_TV: 'Darling Stella. Tuesday tells me you're getting up close and personal with a rather racy film star although she won't tell me who . . .
>> . . . once you've heeled him, whoever it is, perhaps you'll put in a good word for me to grill him, so to speak.
>> Off to watch Arsenal storm to victory in cup final tomorrow. Chow x'

@TuesdayFields
Sorry. Spanish inquisition etc. Managed to keep identity of said star secret. Just.

@StellaCavill
Is he, as I suspected, telling everyone and anyone who'll listen about the Obama exclusive?

@TuesdayFields
How did you guess? Am going to need a bigger fly swatter and a much bigger glass of Gordon's!

@StellaCavill
Told you that you would have to get reacquainted with your old friend, Gordon.
>> So the pub is open then, despite complaints from the neighbourhood's @TheDailyGB reading Chelsea tractor brigade?

@TuesdayFields
For now . . .

***

@TuesdayFields
This is Tuesday Fields reporting from Wembley on a historic day for the underdog, and I don't just mean Millwall!

@StellaCavill
It went well then?!

@TuesdayFields
I am broadcasting success after special weekend coverage of cup final went without so much as a stutter!
>> Shame the same can't be said of @PM_TV's beloved Arsenal . . .

@StellaCavill
What's the betting that after a good old rant about players not playing and managers not managing he stays off this topic for a while?

@TuesdayFields
Highly likely. Saw him briefly afterwards and he was fuming. He wants everyone sacked and an inquiry.

@StellaCavill
Suspect legal will get involved and persuade him to at least publicly pipe down.
>> I've lost track of the amount of lawsuits pending in his direction.

@TuesdayFields
Not sure police closing pub early last night or @LordTw1tter's follower count overtaking @PM_TV's will have helped . . .

@StellaCavill
Rubbing salt into the proverbial wound.

@TuesdayFields
Speaking of which, @Mum could not resist her own form of prodding this morning:

RT @Mum: 'Darling, what have you done with your hair? I don't like that. Dad says he prefers it down too. Off to play golf with your father.
>> Good luck! Mum x'

@StellaCavill
Suggest reply to @Mum: 'I'm 33 not 3 and am perfectly entitled to wear my hair however I choose.'

@TuesdayFields
Well at least it wasn't lashing down with rain this time so my make-up stayed in place and on my face.
>> That's got to count for something, right?

@StellaCavill
Any word from @TheBossWUB? Please don't tell me he filed a complaint against your hair too?

@TuesdayFields
No news, which I'm assuming is good news.
>> Hoping lack of major blunders will have gone some way to restoring my slightly battered reputation after previous OB.

@StellaCavill
@KateKingTV will be seething from under her Egyptian cotton bed spread.

@TuesdayFields
You don't think she shops at Peter Jones for bed linen?

@StellaCavill
Well if she doesn't she should. I hear it's the best . . .

@TuesdayFields
Oh shut up! I know it's supposed to be the case but how hard can it be to get this waterproof mascara off?

@StellaCavill
Baby oil. Can be used on most surfaces, including your face and my clients' shoes.

@TuesdayFields
Seriously

@StellaCavill
Just putting a bottle of it in @MichaelAngeloMovie's shoe bag for later.

@TuesdayFields
Don't give it to him till the last possible minute or he may want to rub it all over you!
\>> If you believe @TheDailyGB, @MichaelAngeloMovie epitomises the toxic bachelor . . .

@StellaCavill
Since when did you start believing anything printed in @TheDailyGB?

@TuesdayFields
Since @MichaelAngeloMovie was quoted in it this morning saying someone special had caught his eye but he wouldn't say who . . .
\>> . . . just that she wasn't in the business of show . . .

@StellaCavill
No?!

@TuesdayFields
Yes.

* * *

@StellaCavill
I feel sick. In hotel watching E!'s 'Live From The Red Carpet'. You up?

@TuesdayFields
We all are. Oscars equal compulsory insomnia for those of us on

breakfast telly. What's @MichaelAngeloMovie done to make you
so green?

@StellaCavill
He's just DM'd me to say he's about to get out of the limo and
that he's wearing my shoes!
>> Well technically speaking his shoes, but you know what I mean.

@TuesdayFields
Just switched to E! I see him and more importantly I see his feet!
You really wouldn't know they were cardboard.

@StellaCavill
Stop being facetious. He looks good though, doesn't he?

@TuesdayFields
He looks like a movie star. Oh that's right, he is a movie star and
he's mad about you!

@StellaCavill
You don't know that. He could have been talking about anyone.
And it's @TheDailyGB – when have they ever been accurate
about anything?

@TuesdayFields
Slandering @Mum's bible. How dare you.

@StellaCavill
Well he didn't say a word about any of it this afternoon. Actually
he was the consummate professional.

@TuesdayFields
Because he had an entourage of payroll people around, not to
mention his mother!

@StellaCavill
Maybe.

@TuesdayFields
Hang about! You're disappointed aren't you?

@StellaCavill
No!

@TuesdayFields
Not even just a teeny weeny bit? You are!

@StellaCavill
It's just nice to feel a frisson that's all. You know, a little something that I haven't been feeling with Will away. Again.

@TuesdayFields
What girl wouldn't be at the very least flattered? Would you just look at him!

@StellaCavill
Stay tuned . . . @MichaelAngeloMovie being ushered into the 360 degree camera by @RyanSeacrest.

@TuesdayFields
That is one well-fitting suit and I don't mean the one @RyanSeacrest is wearing.
>> Although the GAY crowd will love that muscle shirt he's got on.

@StellaCavill
Shoes, Tuesday! Look at the shoes!

@TuesdayFields
Oh yes, the shoes. They look good, great even.

@StellaCavill
OMG. Did he just say that to @GulianaRancic?

@TuesdayFields

Apparently he did! The biggest movie star in the world has name checked you in 'who are you wearing'.

@StellaCavill

And said they were the favourite part of his ensemble! That, Tuesday Fields, is my stay of execution. Emailing @AllThatGlittersIsGold.

***

@StellaCavill

Save me!

@TuesdayFields

From yourself? Only you can do that, Stella!

@StellaCavill

No, you muppet. From @MichaelAngeloMovie!

@TuesdayFields

Told you you'd need the chastity belt! What's happened? I saw he lost, but his short hirsute-in-all-the-wrong-places director won.

@StellaCavill

I ended up seeing him after, T. @MichaelAngeloMovie said he wasn't in the mood to mingle.

@TuesdayFields

Just in the mood for you?

@StellaCavill

Judgment impaired. I'd hit the mini bar in celebration when he said I was the favourite part of who he was wearing.

@TuesdayFields

So where are you now? It's 4AM in LA right? Is he wearing anything now and, more importantly, are you?

@StellaCavill

I am and he better be. I'm hiding in his downstairs bathroom. Embossed black loo paper.

@TuesdayFields

Gold taps? Marble floors? Stupidly folded hand towels?

@StellaCavill

Yes, yes and yes. What does that mean other than he's got bad taste in bathrooms?

@TuesdayFields

It means, Stella Cavill, he can afford to buy anything and right now he thinks he can buy you too.

@StellaCavill

I need a plan. I can't go back in there without one. He's mixing me a martini. I need to leave. Tuesday, help! Tell me what to do.

@TuesdayFields

Suggest he shows you around, he'll like that, will appeal to his gargantuan ego.
>> Alternate sipping with tipping and you won't lose your head, or the deal to heel him.

@StellaCavill

OK. DM me in 20. That way I can blame you for me having to leave, friend in crisis etc.

@TuesdayFields

Will do. Roger that.

@StellaCavill

I won't, if it's OK by you!

TUESDAY FIELDS

@TuesdayFields: London
Growing old (well older) disgracefully.

Monthly Must:
Secure exclusive interview with @No1Sportsman.

Monthly Must Not:
Do not sleep with @No1Sportsman.

Followers:
On the up. Ish.

STELLA CAVILL

@StellaCavill: New York, New York
Making mankind leap.

Monthly Must:
Enjoy the fact @MichaelAngeloMovie wore Stellars to the Oscars.

Monthly Must Not:
Stop worrying about the fact it had little impact on sales.

Followers:
Slide has stopped and tide is turning . . .

***

@TuesdayFields

I did it! I got the interview with @No1Sportsman! Probably @PM_TV's doing, although naturally I'd never admit that to him.

@StellaCavill

Naturally.

@TuesdayFields

So you'll never guess where we're doing it . . .

@StellaCavill

Doing it?!

@TuesdayFields

The interview!

@StellaCavill

Monaco? The only Grand Prix I've ever heard of/would consider attending.

@TuesdayFields

Wrong! Am off to the land of the kangaroo and Kylie, Oz, for Melbourne GP!

@StellaCavill

Congratulations! @KateKingTV must be throwing every toy out of her pram. And surely @TheBossWUB has managed to raise a smile?

@TuesdayFields

Could have knocked me over with a feather in this morning's meeting about a meeting. @TheBossWUB held me up as example to all.

>> @KateKingTV's polyfilled face was fuming. I think.

@StellaCavill
You deserve the break, Tuesday. Just don't sleep with him before the interview is in the can, promise?

@TuesdayFields
Since you managed not to sleep with @MichaelAngeloMovie at all, I promise! At least until after the piece airs.

@StellaCavill
That's my girl.

@TuesdayFields
And how are you, S, what's new? Any fall out from @AllThatGlittersIsGold poking his nose where it's not wanted, i.e. in the books?

@StellaCavill
I'm worried, I have to admit, that he's about to cut his losses and pull the rug out from underneath me.

@TuesdayFields
He can't! Not when everyone's starting to take notice. @AnchorManTV showed me the love letter in @GQMagazine about Stellars.
>> And @RollingStone were banging on and on too.

@StellaCavill
Unfortunately a few good articles and some positively written pieces in black, doesn't change the fact that I'm seriously in the red.

@TuesdayFields
Well you're with the right bloke for all that stuff. What's @MerchBanker's take on it all?

@StellaCavill
@MerchBanker doesn't have a take. Have lost him to China. Which is where we should probably have expanded in the first place.
\>> East not West, emerging markets and all that.

@TuesdayFields
He doesn't know?

@StellaCavill
I don't think he's registered the seriousness of it.
\>> He's blinkered on his work – it's not exactly the easiest market in the world for him to deal with at the moment, either.

@TuesdayFields
You don't do failure and you won't here. Chin up. Sending you a big hug from across the pond.

@StellaCavill
Appreciate it. Just what @MichaelAngeloMovie said, too.

@TuesdayFields
What? He's sending you a big hug from across the pond as well? You mean he's in London?
\>> If you don't want him point him in the direction of Kensal Rise, would you?!

@StellaCavill
No, you muppet. He's in LA and you're missing the point – he was still sending a hug!

@TuesdayFields
Uh-o . . .

@StellaCavill
@MerchBanker hasn't even read my latest BBM yet. @MichaelAngeloMovie however, has been DM'ing on Twitter. What does that say?

@TuesdayFields
That @MerchBanker needs to step up his game?

@StellaCavill
He does. I'm scared, Tuesday. Maybe @Supermodel_1971 is right and @MerchBanker has become a wheels-up bachelor after all.

@TuesdayFields
Don't go into a meltdown just yet. He's probably just run out of juice on his Crackberry.

@StellaCavill
Maybe. I'm dreading my birthday later this month. Staring down the gun barrels at 34 with a disastrous company – and relationship.

@TuesdayFields
You sound like you've read @Mum's latest tweet and worse still, listened to it:

RT @Mum: 'you can't have it all, darling. Something has to give. You better hurry up before you're past your sell by date. Clock's ticking.
>> Tick tock, tick tock!'

@StellaCavill
Boom! She's talking bollocks. You don't have to choose.

@TuesdayFields
Neither do you. You're just going through a bad patch.

@StellaCavill
Just the thought of losing Will and my company is too much. What am I without him and my work?

@TuesdayFields
Look, before @MerchBanker and Stellar Shoes there was Stella
Cavill and if it comes to it . . .
>> . . . (which it won't) after @MerchBanker and Stellar Shoes
there'll still be Stella Cavill.

@StellaCavill
I guess so.

@TuesdayFields
And for what it's worth, I think @MerchBanker will come good.
He usually always does, albeit belatedly.

@StellaCavill
I hope you're right, Tuesday. I really do.

@TuesdayFields
When am I not? I'm always on the money about other people's
love lives, just mine that I can't figure out!

@StellaCavill
Speaking of other people's love lives, have you seen
@HugoPr1nce's bit on the side's latest tweet?

@TuesdayFields
Not. Avoiding where possible.

@StellaCavill
Only drawing your attention to it so you'll see what a lucky escape
you had . . .

RT @RedS0ledShoes: '@HugoPr1nce has brought me the best
present ever! A Vertu phone with pink diamonds and everything.
So lush.'

@TuesdayFields
Dodged a bullet. Now before you throw yourself off the Empire State over your own relationship, do you want some good news from my end?

@StellaCavill
You've gone back for seconds with @JakeJacksonLive?

@TuesdayFields
No! Guess again.

@StellaCavill
You tampered with @KateKingTV's autocue scripts and she's unknowingly just announced her retirement on air?

@TuesdayFields
Food for thought but um, no! I've found out @No1Sportsman's shoe size . . .

@StellaCavill
And how big is he?!

@TuesdayFields
Big. So I'm thinking if you've got two of the biggest stars in the world wearing your wares, @MichaelAngeloMovie and @No1Sportsman . . .
>> . . . you're going to be just fine, S.

* * *

@StellaCavill
Are you there yet?

@TuesdayFields
This is Tuesday Fields reporting for duty from the country that gave us Vegemite and Jason Donovan! In other words, yes I have arrived.

@StellaCavill
When's the big interview?

@TuesdayFields
This afternoon. It's only 8am and already 40 degrees! Fearing my make-up will slide off my exhausted-looking face.

@StellaCavill
I know the feeling. Sleep eludes me at the moment too. How was the flight?

@TuesdayFields
@TheBossWUB sent me out economy, the bastard, was sat between a screaming baby and a verbose seven year old.
>> By the time we arrived my tubes had tied themselves.

@StellaCavill
Have you told @Mum yet? She'll be writing a letter of complaint to @BritishAirways and cc'ing in @TheDailyGB.

@TuesdayFields
I wouldn't put it past her. Anyway, thankfully, there is an upside.
>> Snooze-free flight means there is now nothing I don't know about motor racing or @No1Sportsman.

@StellaCavill
@PM_TV had better watch his step. This goes well and you'll be swapping sport for his spot soon.

@TuesdayFields
Lucky for him he has a day job. His career as a pub landlord has, shall we say, hit a roadblock.

@StellaCavill
Why? What's happened? Thought the Ferret and Trouserleg was doing a roaring trade bar the odd grumble from the locals.

>> Or so @PM_TV keeps telling us on Twitter.

@TuesdayFields
'Was' being the operative word. Guesswork suggests that's why it got closed down. Local residents complaining about the noise.

@StellaCavill
Bet @TheDailyGB has had a field day.

@TuesdayFields
Well, bearing in mind he left @TheDailyGB under a cloud, they are making the most of dragging @PM_TV's name through the mud on this one.

RT @TheDailyGB: '@PM_TV told turn the volume down and get out of town'; '@PM_TV's pub shutdown for being like him; too loud!';
>> 'Will @PM_TV turn to drink after local residents shun his?'

@StellaCavill
Nothing like an @TheDailyGB hate campaign. That just over the last few days?

@TuesdayFields
Yup. I'm guessing Twitter silence for the next few and then he'll do what he does best and hit back with both barrels.

@StellaCavill
Suspect you're right. Hope they know what they've started.

@TuesdayFields
I'll put my house on it, they don't!

@StellaCavill
So who are you wearing for your close up with @No1Sportsman?

@TuesdayFields
@DVF. Let's hope we're not up too close and personal. Just reapplied foundation for a second time.
>> Am going to look like a cake-face by the time this interview comes round.

@StellaCavill
Whatever is @Mum going to say?

@TuesdayFields
Luckily @Mum is several thousand miles away and will have to go some to figure out time zone differences. I'm hoping she won't manage to.

@StellaCavill
I'll put my house on it she will! Well, Will's apartment.

@TuesdayFields
To be honest, Susan the make-up artist in London is so bad that @Mum probably won't notice the difference.

@StellaCavill
You don't need me to tell you that your mother notices everything.

@TuesdayFields
@Mum is as far from my mind as @HugoPr1nce and @JakeJacksonLive are right now. For the next few hours my only focus is @No1Sportsman.

@StellaCavill
I bet! Have fun and good luck. Remember no sex before marriage. I mean interview.

@TuesdayFields
Roger that.

@StellaCavill

I was worried you were going to say that.

* * *

@StellaCavill

Full report on the main feature and the post-match please. I saw he won. Impressively.

@TuesdayFields

Hello from LHR. Have landed to emails from @TheBossWUB singing my praises – fantastic ratings apparently!

@StellaCavill

I'm presuming then, that you got what you went for?

@TuesdayFields

@No1Sportsman really opened up, S. Got much more than I thought I would.

@StellaCavill

On or off camera?

@TuesdayFields

. . .

@StellaCavill

TUESDAY!

@TuesdayFields

Pipe down. Nothing happened. Not really anyway. We went to dinner after he won, but that was it, honest.

@StellaCavill

@No1Sportsman doesn't do just dinner!

@TuesdayFields
Actually he does! Well he did with me anyway.

@StellaCavill
Good looking, successful, your age, can spell – what's stopping you?

@TuesdayFields
We're talking about a guy who has supermodels for breakfast, lunch and dinner. I'm not up to that, Stella.
>> It's a whole other level of legs and loveliness.

@StellaCavill
You're gorgeous, Tuesday, stop doing yourself down.

@TuesdayFields
I'm just being realistic. Supermodel I'm not.

@StellaCavill
I still think he'd be lucky to have you. Only room for one super-model in my family and it's not me with my long old torso and dimply thighs.

@TuesdayFields
Will you listen to us both! Don't worry. We'll get wrinkly and crinkly together. Sod supermodels and sod the modelisers who go with them.

@StellaCavill
Any word from @JakeJacksonLive?

@TuesdayFields
Not lately. Seen him on air. Read his Twitter. He got the Afghanistan gig. Leaves town next month for Kabul.

@StellaCavill
And how do you feel about that?

@TuesdayFields
Honestly? I'm sort of hoping it'll be a case of out of sight, out of mind. Struggling to get him out of mine at the moment.
>> Been so bloody awkward since Valentine's. Been dodging proverbial bullets round the office.

@StellaCavill
Have you considered @JakeJacksonLive is days away from dodging actual bullets?!
>> If you'd shown more interest he probably wouldn't be going at all.

@TuesdayFields
That, S, would be career suicide. @TheBossWUB is taking a flyer sending him at all.
>> @JakeJacksonLive wore him down to the point where he couldn't say no.

@StellaCavill
That sounds familiar . . .

@TuesdayFields
I'll ignore that! This could be huge for him though. Great opportunity.

@StellaCavill
To get shot at!

@TuesdayFields
You're so dramatic! It won't come to that. @JakeJacksonLive can talk his way out of most things.

@StellaCavill
And into some too . . .

@TuesdayFields
Let's not go there. How's work?

@StellaCavill
Let's not go there.

@TuesdayFields
Like that, is it?

@StellaCavill
In the middle of warzone of my own right now with @AllThatGlittersIsGold. Every chance I'll get taken out by friendly fire sometime soon.

@TuesdayFields
Well here's something to cheer you up. Page 19 of @TheDailyGB. Check out who's wearing your shoes in our favourite Fleet Street rag . . .

@StellaCavill
Hold on, Googling . . . OMG, you've got to be kidding me?!

@TuesdayFields
Got @SINternUK to send some over before I left for Oz. @No1Sportsman and I may not have swapped bodily fluids but we did swap something.
>> I gave him a pair of your shoes.

@StellaCavill
You should break good news more often. It suits you. Thanks, Tuesday!
>> That should keep the firing squad and @AllThatGlittersIsGold at bay for the time being.

@TuesdayFields
Stella Cavill, you live to fight another day!

@StellaCavill
Thanks to you I do.

@TuesdayFields
Got to go. @Mum's birthday dinner at @Quaglinos. Tried telling her it went out of fashion in 1996 but she wouldn't hear of it.
>> She's convinced she can get a table because she's a repeat customer.

@StellaCavill
She can be excused this time on the grounds of it being her birthday.
>> By the way, you never told me – you gave @No1Sportsman a pair of my shoes, what did he give you in return?

@TuesdayFields
His mobile number . . .

@StellaCavill
TUESDAY!

* * *

@TuesdayFields
Happy Birthday, Stella! Let's not age, let's just marinate in gin and tonic.

@StellaCavill
Now that sounds like a plan. Thanks, T.

@TuesdayFields
How are you going to celebrate your first 25 years?!

@StellaCavill
25! I wish.

@TuesdayFields
You could be you know, in TV world.

@StellaCavill
You mean while my passport says 34 my TV CV says 25?

@TuesdayFields
Precisely. Alas for me it's too late. Blabbed my real age to the Wake Up Britain website a while ago before realising no woman in TV does that.
>> Well no women who still want a job post 35 anyway.

@StellaCavill
You're only as old as the man that you feel . . . @JakeJacksonLive – and I – will help of course, with all the enthusiasm my 25-year-old self can muster.

@TuesdayFields
He's going to war, remember?! And you're not 25.

@StellaCavill
I am in my dreams . . .

@TuesdayFields
Well back in the real world I am considering Botox.

@StellaCavill
What? Why?

@TuesdayFields
Fallout from not having a TV age. If I at least look good for my years then hopefully I'll buy a few more on air.

@StellaCavill
Before you go filling your face with Botox, try vodka. Cheaper and paralyses more muscles!

@TuesdayFields

Do you know, I'm not sure I could do that to Gordon. We go too far back.

@StellaCavill

Such loyalty. If Gordon wasn't gin and was a person and could talk – what on earth would he say?

@TuesdayFields

He'd tell me I'm much more fun when he's around.
>> Oh, and that I'm a terrible judge of character with a penchant for bad men and @GreenandBlack's butterscotch chocolate.

@StellaCavill

I could tell you that!

@TuesdayFields

You already do! Anyway what's @MerchBanker doing for the big day?

@StellaCavill

Will's still away. He managed to bunch me a dozen half-dead roses but he hasn't called.
>> And my BBM didn't make it through to his 'berry, so he's switched off from it and me.

@TuesdayFields

He'll be in touch. He's probably, as we tweet, picking you up something sparkly in Shanghai.

@StellaCavill

Maybe – as long as it's not someone. Have to admit, someone else did bother to call me . . .

@TuesdayFields

Who?

@StellaCavill
You really have to ask? @MichaelAngeloMovie.

@TuesdayFields
What? @MichaelAngeloMovie not only remembered your birthday but called you on it too? Blimey Stella.

@StellaCavill
I know.

@TuesdayFields
What've you stored him as under in your phone? Surely not Michaelangelo?!

@StellaCavill
'M'. I feel so guilty, yet I've got absolutely nothing to hide. I've not done anything!

@TuesdayFields
Yet. Good on the phone? If he's good on the phone you can bet he's even better in bed!

@StellaCavill
His voice did bring a smile to my face – you know how husky it is. Felt for a moment like the female lead in one of his rom-coms.

@TuesdayFields
Yes, except this time you're the love interest and there is no film!

@StellaCavill
He sent me something too . . .

@TuesdayFields
Don't tell me, an @NetJet to heaven and back? I mean LA.

@StellaCavill

Not. But he did send flowers. Lots of them. Five dozen pink roses.

@TuesdayFields

Money doesn't always buy class or imagination, but it can buy you great flowers.

@StellaCavill

Yes it can! Problem is, Tuesday, it looks like a florist in my office and it's mostly @MichaelAngeloMovie's doing, not Will's.

@TuesdayFields

Well with @MerchBanker away, at least you won't have any explaining to do.

@StellaCavill

As long as I bribe my interns here to keep schtum.

@TuesdayFields

What are you doing tonight? Turning 25 needs celebrating!

@StellaCavill

I did celebrate it, Tuesday, 9 years ago!
>> The girls here have been making suspicious noises about the Boom Boom room, egged on by @SINternUK in London no doubt.

@TuesdayFields

And the problem is . . .

@StellaCavill

I hate that place. It's full of men my age trying it on with girls ten years younger, with legs ten times longer than mine.

@TuesdayFields

Ever seen Ferris Bueller's Day Off?

@StellaCavill
Of course. Why?

@TuesdayFields
Because someone needs to wake up and smell the coffee! Hollywood's hottest heartthrob is sending you birthday bouquets. >> Get your LBD and Blahniks on and get your backside down there.

@StellaCavill
But what about the supermodels?

@TuesdayFields
What about them? The only 'M' they've got in their phones are their mothers or their management.

@StellaCavill
Love you. Night!

@TuesdayFields
Night!

* * *

@StellaCavill
Tuesday, you there?

@TuesdayFields
Yes, I am waking up Britain. Why are you not in bed or still out celebrating?

@StellaCavill
Celebrating? Right now I have absolutely nothing to celebrate. Birthday Armageddon.

@TuesdayFields

Why, for God's sake? I thought we'd established that despite turning 34 you have plenty going for you?

@StellaCavill

You'd almost convinced me that was the case. That was until about midnight.

@TuesdayFields

What happened, Cinderella? Did your carriage turn into a pumpkin or your @DVF dress into a hessian sack?

@StellaCavill

Tuesday, this isn't funny. My interns were banging on about The Boom Boom room because that's what Will had booked as a birthday surprise.

@TuesdayFields

So far, Stella this doesn't sound like a disaster. Your boyfriend flew back from Shanghai to surprise you. Am I missing something here?

@StellaCavill

Well I was missing there. After tweeting you I got to thinking about how I was going to turn this business of mine around and I lost track of time.
>> I was a 'no-show' at my own bloody birthday!

@TuesdayFields

What about @MerchBanker? Presumably when you didn't turn up, he came looking?

@StellaCavill

And guess where he found me?

@TuesdayFields

Holy crap! At your office surrounded by flora and fauna provided by none other than @MichaelAngeloMovie!

@StellaCavill

Exactly. Cue the row, the tears, the tantrum and the accusations . . .

@TuesdayFields

He thinks you're having an affair?

@StellaCavill

He does now!

@TuesdayFields

He actually thinks you're having an affair with @MichaelAngeloMovie. OMG. What did you tell him?

@StellaCavill

That I'm not! So he demanded to see my phone and I refused to hand it over.

@TuesdayFields

Principle?

@StellaCavill

My phone is full of DM's from @MichaelAngeloMovie and you. I thought with that can of worms opened . . .

@TuesdayFields

Got you. Annoyingly it doesn't look anywhere near as innocent as it all is.

@StellaCavill

No, it doesn't. S**t.

@TuesdayFields
OK, Going into crisis management mode. Where is @MerchBanker now?

@StellaCavill
Will stormed back to Boom Boom at The Standard.
>> He's probably going to take some 22-year-old tartlet back to the suite he said he booked for us.

@TuesdayFields
Stella, count to ten. You weren't to know.

@StellaCavill
What have I done? What should have been a wonderful romantic reunion has degenerated into him probably cheating on me.
>> Right now. Oh God . . .

@TuesdayFields
OK, call him, leave a voicemail if he doesn't pick up.

@StellaCavill
What in the world am I going to say that I haven't already?

@TuesdayFields
Just apologise again for being such a doughnut and not making your own party.
>> Then tell him in no uncertain terms that he's got it wrong and you are 100% not having a fling with a movie star.

@StellaCavill
But I'm not!

@TuesdayFields
I know that. You know that. But he is probably yet to be convinced.

@StellaCavill

Oh God. What a mess. I should never have led @MichaelAngeloMovie on.

>> I gave him completely the wrong idea and as a result have stuffed up everything.

@TuesdayFields

You've stuffed up nothing. If you're guilty of anything, it's being a gullible girl flattered by some attention.

>> When the dust settles @MerchBanker will see this for what it is.

@StellaCavill

That's if Will hasn't given up on me already.

@TuesdayFields

He won't have done. Bet you he's at Boom Boom nursing his battered ego with a hideously overpriced whisky sour and nothing more.

@StellaCavill

I hope you're right, T, or I'm in for a rougher ride than I thought in the coming months, at home and at work.

@TuesdayFields

Go home and get some sleep. This will all look a lot better in the morning. I promise.

>> Just make sure you square this off with him before you go into the office.

@StellaCavill

That's the last place I want to be right now. Carting all of @MichaelAngeloMovie's flowers to the nearest dumpster right now.

@TuesdayFields
What a waste.
>> Next time @MichaelAngeloMovie wants to send you the entire contents of a florist tell him you've moved back to London and give him my address will you?

@StellaCavill
Willingly. Night, T.

@TuesdayFields
Night, S.

TUESDAY FIELDS

@TuesdayFields: London
Have a spring in my step. Crediting Fitflops and not time of the year.

Monthly Must:
Be perfect daughter to demanding mother.

Monthly Must Not:
Encourage @No1Sportsman.

Followers:
Increasing, slowly but surely.

STELLA CAVILL

@StellaCavill: New York, New York
"Keep your eyes on the stars, and your feet on the ground" – Theodore Roosevelt.

Monthly Must:
Repair relationship with @MerchBanker.

Monthly Must Not:
Spend entirety of Easter on Crackberry to the office.

Followers:
Plateaued.

@TuesdayFields
Mother's Day. Remembered. Am perfect daughter. You?

@StellaCavill
I am world's worst. Forgot. How the hell did that happen?

@TuesdayFields
You've got me. You're in America for God's sake.
>> Forgive me but don't they have the copyright on commercial exploitation of days such as these?

@StellaCavill
You're forgiven. I, on the other hand, won't be.

@TuesdayFields
Prepare to say goodbye to unconditional love forever . . .

@StellaCavill
Maybe it's just because I was distracted patching things up with Will.

@TuesdayFields
You're both OK, now though, post the birthday drama?

@StellaCavill
We've agreed to go away over Easter. It's proving hard to sort things out when you're on different sides of the world.

@TuesdayFields
He's back in China?

@StellaCavill
Yes. But aha! On a cheerier note, your bragging rights are short-lived on Mother's Day, Miss Fields.

@TuesdayFields
How so?

@StellaCavill
Those helpful people at Google have reliably informed me Mother's Day US is not the same as Mother's Day UK.

@TuesdayFields
Really? What about Father's Day?

@StellaCavill
Father's Day we get to be commercially exploited in UK or US on the same day.
>> So if I actually spoke to my errant Dad, he wouldn't have his nose put out of joint by me forgetting it.

@TuesdayFields
You never talk about your Dad, Stella.

@StellaCavill
He stopped talking to Mum before she gave birth and never saw much reason to speak to me, so we're not all that close.

@TuesdayFields
I'm sorry.

@StellaCavill
Don't be. @Supermodel_1971 is parent enough. So I'm feeling guilty about today. We're both British so British rules should apply.
>> I'm present-less.

@TuesdayFields
And no doubt she'll be expecting something thoughtful and expensive.

StellaCavill
But I've not got the time or the money. Suggestions?

@TuesdayFields
Call @Supermodel_1971 and tell her you've got a surprise.

@StellaCavill
Which is?

@TuesdayFields
I don't know yet, but working on it . . .

@StellaCavill
What did you get @Mum? Imitation is the sincerest form of flattery. I'm claiming lack of imagination. Can I copy?

@TuesdayFields
While the seared scallops at The Wolseley are very nice, I'm not sure I'd fly 3,000 miles across the Atlantic for them.
>> Although such a gesture would go some to placate an irate @Supermodel_1971.

@StellaCavill
Point.

@TuesdayFields
Tell you what, though, I'd have traded an angry @Supermodel_1971 for a glum-faced and frankly depressive @Mum today.
>> Face like a smacked arse.

@StellaCavill
You do have a way with words, Tuesday Fields. Why smacked-arse face? As you keep reminding me, you are the perfect daughter!

@TuesdayFields
I thought I was, but made elementary error selecting somewhere other than @Quaglinos.
>> Then Dad ballsed up by double booking golf, and sisters excelled themselves by being no shows.

@StellaCavill
Sisters 'no shows' on Mother's Day?

@TuesdayFields
Siblings were spending the day somewhere in suburbia with assorted offspring and mother-in-laws.

@StellaCavill
Yawn.

@TuesdayFields
@Mum always bleating on about how important it is for Saskia and Martha to spend time with their in-laws.
>> Then they do and she gets morose.

@StellaCavill
Did you turn it and her mood around?

@TuesdayFields
Eventually. Took a while after a bad start . . .

@StellaCavill
Which was . . . ?

@TuesdayFields
Me and my single self turning up with wet hair and zero make-up. What can I say?
>> It was either turn up on time undone, or turn up late, done.

@StellaCavill
Was she terribly disappointed?

@TuesdayFields
Opening line from @Mum: 'Darling, glad to see you're on time but what are you wearing?
>> I suppose being so unfortunately presented is your little rebellion, but how you'll ever attract a man is beyond me.'

@StellaCavill
More direct than Paxman. Any other pearls of wisdom?

@TuesdayFields
As many as were round her neck.

@StellaCavill
A plethora, then?

@TuesdayFields
Resigned rant followed about how sad it was that I was the only one of her three daughters seeing her on Mothering Sunday. Cue the violins . . .

@StellaCavill
Quite possibly at that moment you were wishing you hadn't bothered either!

@TuesdayFields
Oh I'm not done yet. Or rather @Mum wasn't. Cherry on the cake incoming . . .

@StellaCavill
Standing by, bracing . . .

@TuesdayFields

@Mum: 'Darling, you remember Fenella, don't you? You went to school together. Handsome husband, heart surgeon.

>> She's having her third today, a water birth according to Marjorie in the shop. Isn't that lovely?'

@StellaCavill

Lovely. Hope you reminded @Mum that the people with the most picture perfect lives . . .

>> . . . are the ones who are most likely to indulge in dogging and divorce.

@TuesdayFields

I'll remember to throw that back at her next time.

@StellaCavill

Do, because you know as well as I, as certain as the sun rises in the east and sets in the west there will be 'a next time' . . .

@TuesdayFields

. . . and a time after that . . .

@StellaCavill

. . . and one after that!

@TuesdayFields

Anyway I didn't have the heart to tell @Mum that Fenella has been shagging the gardener for months.

@StellaCavill

How very Lady Chatterley! So this next sprog . . .

@TuesdayFields

. . . could very well be the gardener's and not her heart surgeon husband's at all, yes.

@StellaCavill
Rather begs the question is the grass always greener?! Anyway, how are you in possession of this information and @Mum isn't?

@TuesdayFields
Marjorie in the village shop has a bigger mouth than @Joan_Rivers. Didn't take five minutes for friend from school Sophie to extract the above from her.
>> @Mum just not asking right questions.

@StellaCavill
So @Mum not so Paxman-esque after all, more @KateKingTV. @Mum's line of questioning really should have gone along the lines of:
>> 'Marge, spill, is it really true Fenella Fudgecake is being pruned by Jesse Metcalfe?'

@TuesdayFields
Something like that!

@StellaCavill
Right, enough. What am I getting @Supermodel_1971? You were coming up with genius plan and the clock, lest we forget, is ticking . . .

@TuesdayFields
Tick tock, tick tock, damn clock. Have perfect present for @Supermodel_1971 . . .

@StellaCavill
Well, come on Tuesday, out with it, I am both cash and time poor right now.

@TuesdayFields
Email the @HummingBBakery by her in South Ken with 'that' Vogue cover and they will bake it as a giant red velvet cupcake!

@StellaCavill
But @Supermodel_1971 hasn't eaten cake since, well, 1971.

@TuesdayFields
Well I do have another idea, although I'm not sure you'll go for it and it will require considerable air miles . . .

@StellaCavill
I can do air miles. Well, Will can and he won't notice if I nick some. Where is this heading?

@TuesdayFields
Fly her to NYC. I know it's a bit in your face but you know she'll pick up her room at The Carlyle and any incidentals.
>> You'll just have to do dinner!

@StellaCavill
A bit in your face? How about a lot in your face?! Just like @Supermodel_1971.

@TuesdayFields
I know she can be a nagging old bag but book her on a flight to NY and dinner at The Monkey Bar . . .
>> . . . and I promise you'll find her much more agreeable.

@StellaCavill
I hope you're right. I'll book it – flight and Monkey Bar. May it is. I can hardly contain my excitement.
>> She'll have to make do with Premium Ec. though.

@TuesdayFields
Tight arse.

@StellaCavill
I wish!

@TuesdayFields
Trust doghouse averted with @Supermodel_1971?

@StellaCavill
Yes – and dreading the NYC invasion next month.

@TuesdayFields
Perfect timing for your break any minute with @MerchBanker to prepare yourself then. When you off to soak up sun and rum?

@StellaCavill
We leave a week today. Americans don't really do Easter, so break won't be completely Crackberry free.

@TuesdayFields
Do yourself and that relationship of yours a favour, S, and lock that bone of contention in the hotel safe.

@StellaCavill
I'll try.

@TuesdayFields
Where's @MerchBanker booked?

@StellaCavill
Antigua. Some ridiculous hotel, Jumper something.

@TuesdayFields
Jumby Bay! He's going all out – I wonder why?!

@StellaCavill
Don't. You sound like @Supermodel_1971, who thinks she's arriving in NYC to go to Vera Wang.

@TuesdayFields
No harm in speculating . . . anyway nice place, good spot, full of flash gits.

@StellaCavill
This is my fear. I think I may have created a monster, Will's become fussier about bathrooms than I am. Such a Prince.

@TuesdayFields
Just be grateful his first name's not Hugo. @HugoPr1nce wouldn't countenance going anywhere that didn't provide brand new bedding, daily.
>> Would demand to see the packaging too, as proof.

@StellaCavill
Freak. He and @RedS0ledShoes deserve each other.
>> RT @RedS0ledShoes: 'Busy day! Getting blow dry before going on Eurostar to Parris. So exited!'

@TuesdayFields
Does she mean 'excited'?

@StellaCavill
I think so. Paris is hardly Mississippi in the spelling stakes either.

@TuesdayFields
@PM_TV would have a field day correcting @RedS0ledShoes spelling and grammatical cock ups. You 'exited' about your break away?!

@StellaCavill
Apprehensive. It's make or break, Tuesday. We've still hardly spoken since my birthday.
>> To make things worse all @Supermodel_1971 keeps talking about is rings and carats.

@TuesdayFields
Does she know nothing of the recent hiccups?

@StellaCavill
Nothing.

@TuesdayFields
How so?

@StellaCavill
Haven't told her Will and I are in trouble, could hardly confide in her about the @MichaelAngeloMovie saga . . .
>> . . . she'd have got drunk at Annabel's with the owner of @TheDailyGB and it would have ended up on Page 3.

@TuesdayFields
Does she even know things are tough at Stellar Shoes?

@StellaCavill
No. Nothing. She's always been disparaging about it and I don't want her lording it up all over me that the company's in crisis.

@TuesdayFields
Perhaps you should fill her in on at least some of it? She might surprise you, S, being her only child and all that.
>> Who knows, she might even be able to help.

@StellaCavill
Hinder more like. If I introduce her to @AllThatGlittersIsGold, she'll only try and marry him.

@TuesdayFields
Would that be so very awful? I mean at least you'd be keeping it in the family. Could be cozy . . .

@StellaCavill

She'd come out of the divorce well. He – and by extension I – would not . . .

***

@TuesdayFields

@JakeJacksonLive left for Afghanistan today.

@StellaCavill

Missing him already?

@TuesdayFields

V. funny. @TheBossWUB threw lame leaving party for him last night. We all wished him well whilst quaffing cheap cava.

@StellaCavill

So you went, then?

@TuesdayFields

How could I not?

@StellaCavill

Thought you might have wriggled out of it citing a 'headache'.

@TuesdayFields

Well I figured he is going to war and all that. Least I can do is turn up to shitty send-off drinks.

@StellaCavill

So, come on. Did you do the honorable thing and give him the send-off he deserved?

@TuesdayFields
No! I gave him a quick goodbye hug. Schoolgirl error in that it was in front of @AnchorManTV, who made silly schoolboy whooping noises.

@StellaCavill
That man is so peculiar. Even his pattern baldness is strange. Bet he's got all sorts of skeletons, way he carries on.

@TuesdayFields
Back to the 'hug' – all beyond awkward.
>> @AnchorManTV hollering like a teenage boy discovering what his penis can do for the first time and @KateKingTV flashing me daggers.

@StellaCavill
That would be because @KateKingTV has looked into her crystal ball and seen Tuesday and Jake sitting on the Wake Up Britain sofa . . .
>> . . . K-I-S-S-I-N-G!

@TuesdayFields
Stop it! Surprising as it may be I actually managed a swift and sober exit last night.
>> Which is what I should have done on the 14th February.

@StellaCavill
What was that?

@TuesdayFields
What?

@StellaCavill
That noise?

@TuesdayFields
What noise?

@StellaCavill
The one that sounds like a broken record . . .

@TuesdayFields
Sod off, Stella.

@StellaCavill
So what will @JakeJacksonLive be missing (other than you) while he's being Ross Kemp? What's 'news' from Wake Up Britain world?

@TuesdayFields
Let's see. Well, for one thing @KateKingTV has abdicated all responsibility to cover sport so I'm now officially the 'sports' girl.

@StellaCavill
That's good, surely?

@TuesdayFields
You'd think so, but unfortunately @TheBossWUB is a news man. Last few sport stories I've worked on been biffed for the latest 'hot topics'.

@StellaCavill
How 'hot' were said 'topics'?

@TuesdayFields
Tepid. Recently fallen victim to several debates about more MPs fiddling expenses and one in particular fiddling with his secretary.

@StellaCavill
Presuming plan to replace @KateKingTV and become new darling of morning television has temporarily stalled then?

@TuesdayFields
Until MPs stop taking the state and their secretaries for a ride then, yes, stalled.

@StellaCavill
In which case you could be waiting a while.

@TuesdayFields
Did you see @TheDailyGB piece on Saturday? If not . . .

RT @TheDailyGB: 'Meet Generation X; childless career women who have sacrificed personal fulfillment to make a professional impact.
>> We ask, is it worth it?'

@StellaCavill
Ouch! They are wrong of course. We are working on both having personal fulfillment and impacting professionally.

@TuesdayFields
Trying.

@StellaCavill
Yes, very.

@TuesdayFields
As much as I hate @TheDailyGB it certainly livened up a recent meeting about a meeting when I received this from @Mum:

RT @Mum: 'Darling, Page 12. 'Pistols at Dawn: The Inside Story of Cross Words and Croissants'. Exposé on WUB!
>> Next time your presenters row tell your mother.
>> Terribly embarrassing to have Marjorie point it out at bridge when my own daughter works there!'

@StellaCavill

Poor @Mum. She's right. You should have more care for her social standing.

@TuesdayFields

Poor @TheBossWUB. He cares more about @WUBTV than his own wife and kids.
>> This latest off air drama between @KateKingTV and @AnchorManTV is pushing him to the edge.
>> We're all bracing ourselves for an epic blowout.

@StellaCavill

He needs a holiday.

@TuesdayFields

So do you. Make sure you get the break you need in Antigua with @MerchBanker.

@StellaCavill

Otherwise I'm heading into @TheBossWUB territory?

@TuesdayFields

Fortunately for you, you're about six stone lighter and favour champagne and salads to a diet of fast food and beer . . .
>> . . . but yes, you too could be heading down a one way street to breakdown if you're not careful.

@StellaCavill

On the sound advice of Dr. Fields, I'll bury Crackberry in sand and focus instead on the sun, sea and sex.

@TuesdayFields

Shag away. Doctor's orders!

@StellaCavill

It's been a while. Says it all.

@TuesdayFields
PS. Stumbled across this other day, sums things up pretty nicely I thought: 'Everything will be OK in the end. If it's not OK, it's not the end.'

@StellaCavill
Perfect thought for the day. At least we both know we are some way off 'The End'.

@TuesdayFields
Good, because in case you hadn't noticed I'm nowhere near achieving personal fulfillment or making a professional impact.

@StellaCavill
In case you hadn't noticed, neither am I. Now, more importantly, what to pack? Will's insisting on hand luggage only.

@TuesdayFields
Nasty bastard.

@StellaCavill
I know. Stropping already. I am going to relax on this holiday even if it kills me.

@TuesdayFields
That's the spirit, Stella. Relax, lie back and don't think of balance sheets!

***

@StellaCavill
I've just had to unbury the Blackberry.

@TuesdayFields
Trouble in paradise?

@StellaCavill
It's day two and we still haven't done it yet.

@TuesdayFields
What! OK let's run through the checklist, make sure you've not forgotten any essentials . . .
>> . . . bearing in mind your boyfriend made you travel like a hobo.

@StellaCavill
Fine, shoot.

@TuesdayFields
Champagne, your favourite?

@StellaCavill
Check.

@TuesdayFields
Romantic dinners on the beach, occasionally disturbed by annoying steel drum band?

@StellaCavill
Check!

@TuesdayFields
You did remember your @MYLA_LONDON?

@StellaCavill
Check. So tiny. One of the only things Will and I didn't row about packing.

@TuesdayFields
So you've got all the ingredients for a shagfest, what's the problem?

@StellaCavill
It's been an unmitigated disaster. @MerchBanker got blind drunk on Pina Coladas the first night and was foul all yesterday.
>> He's still sleeping it off today.

@TuesdayFields
You need to seduce him all over again. Get back to where you once were before work got in the way.

@StellaCavill
Or @MichaelAngeloMovie. Am sat on the loo messaging you.
>> If I look at the Crackberry in Will's line of sight he shoots me this accusatory stare that implies my latest tweet is from you know who.

@TuesdayFields
And is it?

@StellaCavill
Yes, but I haven't responded. Which of course means @MichaelAngeloMovie is chasing harder.

@Tuesday Fields
Doubt he does rejection. Not since he got the part of that gawky kid on that cheap US sitcom. What was it called again?

@StellaCavill
I'd forgotten about that. 'Boys Will Be Boys'. I'm recalling stone-washed jeans and neon leg warmers.

@TuesdayFields
And that was the boys! Do you remember Smash Hits calling it 'Boys Will Be Girls'.

@StellaCavill
Heat magazine is but a poor imitation.

@TuesdayFields
Just 17 was my teen porn of choice. Remember the advice page?

@StellaCavill
Yes – of course I do!

@TuesdayFields
'My best friend fancies my dad, shall I tell my mum?'; 'Do all girls get turned on by their teachers or is it just me?'

@StellaCavill
You are disgusting but I'm going to give you a chance to redeem yourself. Come on then, Mrs. Mills, advise me.
>> What am I going to do, T, to liven things up here?

@TuesdayFields
You are going to turn off your Blackberry, head back into the bedroom . . .
>> . . . and remind @MerchBanker of why he fell for you in the first place, Wonder Woman.

@StellaCavill
Think my super powers wore off some time ago. Could it be that he just doesn't care anymore?

* * *

@TuesdayFields
@KateKingTV just asked @JakeJacksonLive what he'd had for breakfast when he was trying to report on the Taliban's latest atrocity.
>> She's got the sensitivity of a rhino.

@StellaCavill
What's @TheBossWUB saying about the job Jake is doing? And @KateKingTV, for that matter.

@TuesdayFields

Significant amount of door slamming. Given the chance @JakeJacksonLive's performance is pretty solid.
>> @KateKingTV's line of questioning however, is shall we say, an acquired taste.

@StellaCavill

In bad taste. How on earth is she still there?

@TuesdayFields

Appeals to Middle England. Kills @TheBossWUB, but she does have a faithful following.

@StellaCavill

Of course! @TheDailyGB readers! Come to think of it I bet @Mum was actually wondering what @JakeJacksonLive had for breakfast.

@TuesdayFields

Consider your case rested:

RT @Mum: 'That boy @JakeJacksonLive is looking terribly thin, Tuesday. Needs to forget this silliness and get back to some home cooking.'

@StellaCavill

Poor @JakeJacksonLive. Being scrutinised for his size and not his war reportage. How is he looking?

@TuesdayFields

Really, really good. Chiselled. He's also rather interestingly taken to wearing t-shirts underneath flak jacket that show off his biceps.

@StellaCavill

And there we were thinking it was only @No1Sportsman who could get away with those.

@TuesdayFields
Silly us, I guess.

@StellaCavill
You didn't tell me about the biceps.

@TuesdayFields
I was trying to blank them out to avoid hormonal temptation.
>> Anyway, he's developing quite the fan base here – his post bag has gone through the roof.

@StellaCavill
Caught yourself thinking, Tuesday Fields?

@TuesdayFields
Maybe. Occasionally. Sometimes. An awful lot.

@StellaCavill
I knew it!
>> You're in deeper than you realised. Somewhat unfortunate on your part that it's taken a war to make you notice what was staring you in the face for months!

@TuesdayFields
Alright, keep your knickers on! I only said I sometimes think about @JakeJacksonLive, he doesn't occupy my thoughts 24/7, Stella.
>> And another thing . . .

@StellaCavill
Let me guess – he's too young. Boring.

@TuesdayFields
It would only end in tears and they won't be his. Now, give it a rest will you?!

@StellaCavill

Fine. So anyone else box-ticking in @JakeJacksonLive's absence?

@TuesdayFields

@No1Sportsman has been texting . . .

@StellaCavill

You have to be f**king joking? OMG Tuesday. Why wait until now to tell me? Is he or is he not your perfect man?

@TuesdayFields

He might be if it wasn't for the Victoria's Secret model girlfriend.

@StellaCavill

Since when has a @VictoriasSecret model been a match for your intellect, articulation and eloquence?

@TuesdayFields

@TyraBanks isn't doing too badly.

@StellaCavill

Smiling with her eyes, AKA 'The Smize', doesn't mean she's going to be the next @Oprah or her protégé @RubyRainerUS.

@TuesdayFields

Except she probably will be. @RubyRainerUS's show has just started being screened here – she's incredible.
>> Bad example.

@StellaCavill

Bad example. So what gives with @No1Sportsman?

@TuesdayFields

He's invited me to Monaco.

@StellaCavill

Hold the phone. Are you serious? Pack me in your suitcase?

>> I've always dreamed of waking up in the Hotel d'Paris, gambling at the casino and propping up the bar at Jimmyz . . .

@TuesdayFields

Come!

>> @TheBossWUB is splashing the cash and sending me to cover the Grand Prix in any case, so no need to accept invitation from @No1Sportsman.

>> Surely a great stomping ground for selling Stellars?

@StellaCavill

Sending @SINternUK to do the Cannes Film Festival so makes sense for her just to buzz up the coast.

@TuesdayFields

Can't I twist your arm? Be much more fun with you there to help me wind up @No1Sportsman and keep me out of his hotel bedroom!

@StellaCavill

Suite I suspect. You can confirm at a later date. Wish I could be there, but remember the small matter of @Supermodel_1971's impending arrival?

@TuesdayFields

Ah, yes. That.

@StellaCavill

To compound the issue, @AllThatGlittersIsGold is threatening to spend all summer at his home in East Hampton here.

>> i.e. threatening to be more hands on.

@TuesdayFields

So you gallivanting up and down the French Riviera is a definite no-no. At least you'll have more support from him if he's on top of you.

@StellaCavill
That's true. It's not easy being the boss. I do feel incredibly isolated here with no @MerchBanker around.

@TuesdayFields
Did he go straight back to Asia after your time away?

@StellaCavill
Yes. I'm worried, T, one night of perfunctory passion does not a relationship solve.

@TuesdayFields
Oh, S, I'm sorry. At least you've got Stellars to keep you busy.

@StellaCavill
Thank God, for as long as people believe the hype I still have Stellars. For now at least.

* * *

@StellaCavill
I'm so angry with Will right now I could scream.

@TuesdayFields
Why? What's he done now?

@StellaCavill
He's only going to Monaco.

@TuesdayFields
What, without you?

113

@StellaCavill
Corporate jolly.

@TuesdayFields
Are bankers still jolly?

@StellaCavill
Admittedly he's claiming it's because he's desperate for clients and those who still have 'serious' cash will all be there.

@TuesdayFields
Why's he not taking you?

@StellaCavill
No WAGS allowed, apparently. Such bullshit.
>> He knows I've always wanted to go and there used to be a time I was viewed as an asset on these jaunts.

@TuesdayFields
Doesn't sound like him. Probably thought with @Supermodel_1971 and @AllThatGlittersIsGold descending . . .

@StellaCavill
I'm not so sure. Will BBM'd me. He only does that when he's too scared to speak.

@TuesdayFields
Where is @MerchBanker right now?

@StellaCavill
Brazil. All about the BRIC's.

@TuesdayFields
BRIC's?

@StellaCavill
Brazil, Russia, India and China.

@TuesdayFields
I like it. Going to throw that acronym into conversation with @PM_TV when he next tries to outfox me with clever drivel.

@StellaCavill
Apparently @PM_TV's got other fights to pick right now. Have you seen the bet he's made with @LordTw1tter?

@TuesdayFields
Yes, @LordTw1tter's charitable foundation is going to do extremely well whoever has the bigger follower count at the end of the year.

@StellaCavill
Hilarious banter between the two of them. What's @PM_TV's favourite hashtag?

@TuesdayFields
#twittertaxiforLordTw1tter

@StellaCavill
That's the one. Like a couple of overgrown schoolboys.

@TuesdayFields
Do you think they really hate each other, or is this just about getting follower counts up?

@StellaCavill
Probably both.

@TuesdayFields
@PM_TV's stock is seemingly ever rising. When that happens it always riles others who are public and powerful.

@StellaCavill
@LordTw1tter isn't doing too badly – how many billion from flogging mobile phones is he on now?

@TuesdayFields
I met him at a benefit with @HugoPr1nce. He's actually disarmingly charming.

@StellaCavill
Must be a power thing. @AllThatGlittersIsGold can talk the talk too. Starting to panic about his imminent arrival.
>> Been desperately stock-taking to check the levels . . . taken.

@TuesdayFields
Speculate to accumulate a little too much during awards season, did you?

@StellaCavill
Looking at the figures I think I was juggling too many balls – might have dropped a few.

@TuesdayFields
Might not be too late. @AllThatGlittersIsGold is just the person to help you catch them in time.

@StellaCavill
Or insist on letting them fall. Christ, must pull myself together immediately. Packed for Monaco yet?

@TuesdayFields
Squishing the Choos into the suitcase right now. Would Blahniks be better?

@StellaCavill
Pack both. A girl needs options in a playground like Monte Carlo! No red-soled ones though. Passé.

@TuesdayFields
Noted.

@StellaCavill
And this time, Tuesday, pack a change of clothes in your carry
on . . .
>> . . . in case you spill the entire contents of the hostess' trolley
over the ones you're wearing. Again.

@TuesdayFields
I'll have you know smartarse, that after the New Year sleepsuit
episode, I'm strictly carry on only now.

@StellaCavill
Like Will. I'm worried, Tuesday. Our relationship is dying a slow
and painful death, I just know it.

@TuesdayFields
Don't overthink just because @MerchBanker is on a boys' trip.
>> @SINternUK and I will keep a close eye on him. You have
nothing to worry about, I'm sure of it.

@StellaCavill
Hope you're right. Pit of the stomach feeling just won't budge.
You know what I'm talking about?

@TuesdayFields
I do. I'm busy panicking about bumping into @HugoPr1nce and
@RedS0ledShoes.

@StellaCavill
They'll be busy gin palace hopping and you will have your hands
full with work and @No1Sportsman.
>> You probably won't even cross paths/racetracks/jetties.

@TuesdayFields
Hope so. @TheBossWUB has got me on a tight schedule.
>> Wants live hits four times an hour from pretty much here,
there and everywhere I can blag my way into. Special weekend
programming.

@StellaCavill
@No1Sportsman's suite count?!

@TuesdayFields
Well, he has got me 'Access All Areas'. I know what you're thinking – don't say it!

@StellaCavill
Moi? I'm not saying a word.

@TuesdayFields
@No1Sportsman and I are both professionals, in Monaco, to
work.

@StellaCavill
Good luck with that. And look after Will.

@TuesdayFields
Will do!

TUESDAY FIELDS

@TuesdayFields: London
Living and loving life in the fast lane.

Monthly Must:
Win over @TheBossWUB with flawless display of live television skills.

Monthly Must Not:
Be lured back to @No1Sportsman's Monaco suite on the promise of another 'exclusive'.

Followers:
Watch this space . . .

STELLA CAVILL

@StellaCavill: New York, New York
Helping men do the Cannes-Cannes.

Monthly Must:
Sell shoes.

Monthly Must Not:
Don't give away shoes.

Followers:
Dwindling.

***

@TuesdayFields
@No1Sportsman and I are head over heels.

@StellaCavill
What?! Since when?!

@TuesdayFields
With wheels! Not with each other, S. Fast cars are the only thing we have in common. That and a mutual appreciation of Monaco.

@StellaCavill
Who doesn't love Monaco? It's fabulous. Apart from its residents, that is. Particularly the Prince – and we're not talking Hugo.

@TuesdayFields
Wonder how many Princesses are locked up in tower blocks here?

@StellaCavill
Half the population. Remember the old adage: in Monaco the orgasms are fake but the jewels are real . . .
>> . . . in St Trop the orgasms may be real but the jewels are fake.

@TuesdayFields
I'd wager the orgasms in St Trop are fake too.

@StellaCavill
The sophistication of the French Riviera. You called @SINternUK yet?

@TuesdayFields
Not. Been busy doing behind the scenes pieces for @WUBTV. Correction, killing myself for @WUBTV.

@StellaCavill
@TheBossWUB pushing the authenticity boundaries again?

@TuesdayFields
Damn right he is. Sometimes I think he exists solely to give @Mum a coronary.
>> He is determined to see me at my most natural and thus most unflattering state on national television.

@StellaCavill
While @Mum is fully aware that to achieve the ultimate 'natural' look takes hours of very careful application?

@TuesdayFields
More so than ever now I'm apparently 'no longer a spring chicken, darling.'

@StellaCavill
Straight men are clueless. Give me a gay boy any day of the week.

@TuesdayFields
Nothing gay about this weekend's interviewees . . .

@StellaCavill
So I hear . . .

@TuesdayFields
Swear once I'm done doing triathlons with @JensonButton, bleep testing with @LewisHamilton . . .
>> . . . and cycling up hills with @alo_official, I'll buzz @SINternUK.

@StellaCavill
You'll find her either buzzing or broken after drama of Cannes.

@TuesdayFields
Sounds traumatic?

@StellaCavill
Apparently @LeoDiCaprio and Matt Damon got in a scrap over my shoes . . .

@TuesdayFields
You're joking? The metrosexual male. A complex creature full of contradictions.

@StellaCavill
Blame David Beckham. He started it.

@TuesdayFields
He did. So much for women being high maintenance.

@StellaCavill
Lucky @SINternUK was there to placate them both and more importantly make sure they attended the premiere both wearing Stellars.

@TuesdayFields
That alone seems to justify the expense of sending her over doesn't it?

@StellaCavill
Let's hope so. After Cannes, she'll go to @F1Monaco. If I can break that market then that's a big bump in sales.
>> You know what those boys are like – they'll buy one in every colour.

@TuesdayFields
There's nothing they love more than breaking in and out the black AMEX.

@StellaCavill
Even if they decide Stellars are not for them they'll at least put their super-yachts crews in them. So what's cooking with @No1Sportsman?
>> All tweets no trousers?

@TuesdayFields
Precisely. If flirting was an Olympic discipline, @No1Sportsman would be going for gold.

@StellaCavill
Don't knock it. He's just trying to be the best that he can . . .

@TuesdayFields
Alright Henry Kelly! Last DM from him will make you snigger:

RT @No1Sportsman: 'Hey baby. What's up? When can I see you? Jimmyz before midnight then my suite at Hotel de Paris?'

@StellaCavill
Doesn't he have a race to drive tomorrow? And a supermodel-ensconced ensuite?

@TuesdayFields
Yes, he does.

@StellaCavill
But the missive is full of questions. In normal sext-type situations, that's a good sign.

@TuesdayFields
He's all hot air. If I gave an inch he'd run a mile, not take it!

@StellaCavill
Well if you really do need rescuing, there's always Will.

@TuesdayFields
So he really came without you, then?

@StellaCavill
Yes. Stopped in NYC long enough to dump his washing and flew out with the boys on the red-eye last night.
>> Beware, brash American bankers incoming desperately trying to drum up some cash for their fund . . .

@TuesdayFields
Well they'll certainly be spending it. Martinis retailing at €50 a pop in Jimmyz, models substantially less.

@StellaCavill
Tuesday. TMI! I really don't want to know what @MerchBanker will be doing with his little black card.

@TuesdayFields
What he does with his little black card is the least of your problems . . . Only joking! It'll be fine, I'm sure that's not his style.

@StellaCavill
I'm not. Keep an eye on Will and @SINternUK for me? @SINternUK is an anecdote waiting to happen. And as for @MerchBanker . . .

@TuesdayFields
Will do after I've completed triathlon, bleep test, hill cycling etc. Until @WUBTV comes off air I'm afraid they are on their own.

@StellaCavill
Oh God.

@TuesdayFields
I wouldn't worry. With Martinis €50 a pop how much trouble can they possibly get in?

* * *

@StellaCavill
You know I said @SINternUK attracted anecdotes . . .

@TuesdayFields
Yes . . . .

@StellaCavill
She just called to say that she almost got arrested last night.

@TuesdayFields
She was clearly having more fun than me, but doing what?

@StellaCavill
All quite innocent, apparently, but she obviously wanted to cover her bases.

@TuesdayFields
Why, what happened?

@StellaCavill
She took off her five-inch heels on the walk home and the police stopped and gave her a warning.

@TuesdayFields
Why? Were the Choos all she was wearing?

@StellaCavill
She assures me on this occasion she was fully clothed. Apparently it's illegal to walk barefoot in the land of the bolting Princess.

@TuesdayFields
I'm breaking out the Blahniks later. Good job they are my most wearable of an otherwise toe crunching shoe wardrobe.

125

@StellaCavill

I've not been out of Wellingtons for a month. NYC having its heaviest month of rainfall of the year. It's May. I am not amused.

@TuesdayFields

Playing havoc with your labels?

@StellaCavill

And my mind. I'm cold, wet and bordering on bonkers.

@TuesdayFields

You won't want to hear that you could fry an egg on the cobbles of Casino Square then?

@StellaCavill

No.

@TuesdayFields

Thought not. On subject of fried eggs, I think mine are shrinking. >> Reflection in the bathroom mirror this morning confirmed they are definitely going south.

@StellaCavill

Mine not big enough to go anywhere. You located my wayward ex-intern and Will yet?

@TuesdayFields

DM'd. Hatched a plan to catch up at Jimmyz later.

@StellaCavill

Wish I could be there.

@TuesdayFields

We wish you could be here! Will twitpic photo of @SINternUK, @MerchBanker and me preceding complete cocktail inebriation.

@StellaCavill
Look forward to it! I think . . .

@TuesdayFields
Last live hit for @WUBTV with @AnchorManTV was a bit of a cock up.
>> On grid with @No1Sportsman, who forgot himself and called me 'darling' on air.

@StellaCavill
Did @KateKingTV simultaneously fake a seizure in the studio to divert attention back onto her? She will have hated that, Tuesday!

@TuesdayFields
Might have been interference on the live link but sure I heard @KateKingTV spluttering something about professionalism or lack of it . . .
>> . . . and @AnchorManTV sniggering . . .

@StellaCavill
Well one thing's for certain, it'll have done plenty to fuel speculation of an already suspected illicit liaison between you and @No1Sportsman . . .
>> . . . I've seen the blogosphere!

@TuesdayFields
Typical. The only liaising I've been doing concerning @No1Sportsman is with his agent about interview do's and don'ts!

@StellaCavill
Shame she didn't brief him on the don'ts!
>> Questions will be asked, Tuesday Fields, about how exactly you secured that 'exclusive' with a supposed 'media reclusive' . . .

@TuesdayFields
No comment.

@StellaCavill

Well if it does make @TheDailyGB you can be sure it won't be in the back pages.

@TuesdayFields

And that @Mum will read it.

@StellaCavill

It could be worse. You could have cast aside your credibility/ integrity/reputation and actually slept with him.

@TuesdayFields

I'm beginning to wish I had. At least then @TheDailyGB wouldn't be printing bollocks.

@StellaCavill

Again. Incidentally, forewarned is forearmed: I see from the online version @HugoPr1nce and his tartlet @RedS0ledShoes are on the Riviera.

@TuesdayFields

Do you think @RedS0ledShoes has an @TheDailyGB snapper on speed dial? No one can look like they've just stepped out of a salon all of the time.

@StellaCavill

Unless they have always just stepped out of a salon, which reading her tweets suggests that she almost always has.

@TuesdayFields

They deserve each other.

@StellaCavill

Well for what it's worth, I'm sure she does tip off the press. @RedS0ledShoes is a media whore for sure.

@TuesdayFields

@HugoPr1nce loves the spotlight but not sure even he's unscrupulous enough to go there.

@StellaCavill

Chances are Tuesday, he doesn't even know.

@TuesdayFields

Dreading bumping into him at the Drivers' Ball tonight. Would rather stick pins in my eyes than ask @RedS0ledShoes who she's wearing.

@StellaCavill

Not a lot apart from the Louboutins would be my guess.

@TuesdayFields

What with @No1Sportsman's indiscretion this morning and the prospect of a face to face with @RedS0ledShoes this evening, today could be my broadcasting last.

@StellaCavill

I'll DM @SINternUK and @MerchBanker immediately. If you're going to go out, you must do so in the company of friends and alcohol.
>> Drink of TV deathbed choice?

@TuesdayFields

Gordon and tonic please.

@StellaCavill

Is there anything else? You're in Monaco for Christ's sake and @MerchBanker's Black Amex is ready . . .
>> . . . and I believe still has enough credit for such emergencies.

@TuesdayFields

Well in that case a bottle of Cristal seems more appropriate . . .

@StellaCavill
Order is in. Enjoy!

* * *

@StellaCavill
Tuesday, are you there? I can't sleep.

@StellaCavill
Tuesday Fields where are you and where is that photo you promised? Want to hear all about last night!

@StellaCavill
Hurry up and DM me back. Will's not picking up.

@StellaCavill
Are you in @No1Sportsman's suite? I bet you are, you minx. Tweet me the second you surface from under his black satin bed sheets.
>> That's an order!

@StellaCavill
OK. It's now 11AM your time. You can't still be with @No1Sportsman.
>> There is no way you'd have squeezed fresh pants and enough make up in your evening bag.

@StellaCavill
Which rather begs the question, where the hell are you?! @SINternUK not picking up either. Was it that big a night?

@StellaCavill
OK I give up. You, @SINternUK and Will are as useless as each other. Off to Starbucks.
>> To my relief @Supermodel_1971 has a busy shopping and surgery schedule here in NYC so our encounters have so far been mainly just coffee.

@StellaCavill
DM me later, OK? I want to know exactly what you all got up to.
My imagination is running riot. And not in a good way.

***

@TuesdayFields
Hello? Stella?

@StellaCavill
There you are! Where the hell have you been, Tuesday Fields?

@TuesdayFields
Not where you think.

@StellaCavill
So not giving @TheDailyGB something to write about which
won't land them in a lawsuit then?

@TuesdayFields
Not.

@StellaCavill
You disappoint me and I have to say, surprise me!

@TuesdayFields
Sorry. Nothing to report here.

@StellaCavill
Nothing at all?

@TuesdayFields
Well not currently, unless you count an empty packet of Nurofen
and the trashed pair of Blahniks in my immediate line of sight.

@StellaCavill

Another night, another pair of Blahniks sacrificed. Sacrilege.

@TuesdayFields

To quote the immortal words of Richard E. Grant, 'I feel like a pig just shat in my head'.

@StellaCavill

At the very least, boarding school gave us Withnail and I.

@TuesdayFields

And introduced us to the Camberwell carrot . . .

@StellaCavill

For which we will be eternally grateful.

@TuesdayFields

Just a damn shame it also gave us deranged housemistresses, pervert science teachers and nits.

@StellaCavill

Yours did that too?

@TuesdayFields

I think it's obligatory for any British fee paying educational establishment to have a quota of weirdos.

@StellaCavill

You mean 'eccentrics'.

@TuesdayFields

Correction. 'Eccentrics'. I need Evian. Have you heard from @SINternUK or @MerchBanker yet today?

@StellaCavill
@SINternUK finally tweeted to say hi and bye. Was dashing for flight back to London, only to be delayed when she arrived at Nice.
>> No sympathy.

@TuesdayFields
What about @MerchBanker?

@StellaCavill
No word from Will. Out of sight, out of mind . . . Well for him, at any rate.

@TuesdayFields
Probably just run out of juice again on his Crackberry. You know what boys are like. One things leads to another . . .

@StellaCavill
And . . .

@TuesdayFields
And they're all out of juice all too quickly.

@StellaCavill
TMI Tuesday!

@TuesdayFields
I didn't mean that! Meant he probably just forgot to put the thing on charge after last night, that's all.

@StellaCavill
Hope those Goldstein Smythe boys didn't lead him too far astray?

@TuesdayFields
To be honest, S, I didn't see him much last night. That I did see was boys behaving badly but not necessarily astray.

@StellaCavill
I know, I just can't help being a worry wart over all things Will. He's not as streetwise as he looks. @Supermodel_1971 hasn't helped.

@TuesdayFields
Must be fabulous being so self-assured – I don't know how she and @Mum do it. What's the oracle in your world been saying now?

@StellaCavill
She took the opportunity over coffee to warn me about the temptations foreign travel presents to the foreign traveller (Will).

@TuesdayFields
What does she know about foreign travel? She's not Alan bloody Whicker.

@StellaCavill
Another boyfriend, another exotic location, another drug-induced haze.
>> She may not be able to remember it all too clearly, but she's lived a life.

@TuesdayFields
1971 was a good time to be a supermodel.

@StellaCavill
So she'd have you believe. To be honest I wasn't paying a whole lot of attention to what she was saying.
>> She was making some pretty strange noises slurping on her skinny-soya-latte.

@TuesdayFields
Slurping? @Supermodel_1971?

@StellaCavill

It's the collagen. She says it's still adjusting. Worse part is she doesn't seem to care how unsightly she is in the meantime.

>> I've never seen her, or her lips, like this before.

@TuesdayFields

You know what this is, don't you? She's at that 'moment' @Mum says @TheDailyGB is always issuing health warnings about.

@StellaCavill

What 'moment'?

@TuesdayFields

The moment in life where, as women, we say, sod it, we're living longer . . .

>> . . . let's get our faces filled and our fat sucked out whatever the cost, pain, humiliation . . .

@StellaCavill

You're right! That's what this is. Her 'moment'. How long does it last?

@TuesdayFields

@Mum says @TheDailyGB says anything between a fortnight and about five years.

@StellaCavill

Five years? You mean @Supermodel_1971 could be dribbling lattes down her Nicole Farhi skirt suits for another four years and 364 days?

@TuesdayFields

According to @Mum, @TheDailyGB says this is a very important time of self-reflection for a woman and those close need to be fully supportive . . .

@StellaCavill
Time of total self-obsession more like.

@TuesdayFields
@Mum keeps dropping surgery chat into conversation when Dad is out of earshot or on the driving range.

@StellaCavill
Will she ever go under?

@TuesdayFields
The surgeon's scalpel? Not a chance.

@StellaCavill
Why not?

@TuesdayFields
Years of fear instilling headlines from @TheDailyGB have, despite the bravado, scared her shitless . . .
>> . . . and, I suspect put paid to any future facial 'enhancement'.

@StellaCavill
Growing old gracefully then?

@TuesdayFields
Supposedly. Not sure I'm going to be taking that route if I'm honest, I've not exactly followed @Mum's path so far in my life.

@StellaCavill
To growing old disgracefully then . . .

@TuesdayFields
To growing old disgracefully with a face full of fillers! @Mum may be chicken but I am not.
>> Shall be willingly nipped and tucked along the way.

@StellaCavill

Ditto. So maybe our mothers are just as insecure as their daughters?

@TuesdayFields

All is not as it seems . . .

@StellaCavill

Mothers aside, where's that wayward photo of you lot in the Med? >> Would cheer me up no end to see my nearest and dearest drowning in champagne . . .

@TuesdayFields

Actually S, there is no photo. @SINternUK and I couldn't locate @MerchBanker before my iPhone died.

@StellaCavill

Not a shred of evidence then of a debauched weekend? How very convenient for you all!

@TuesdayFields

That would seem to be the case.

@StellaCavill

Well I suppose what I don't know/see can't harm me.

@TuesdayFields

Most people prefer it that way, don't you think? Sometimes for the best. Have plane to catch. Must go.

@StellaCavill

Have business to save and boyfriend to locate. Safe flight!

* * *

@TuesdayFields

Holy crap. Fuck. Bollocks. Have flown back into media shit storm!

@StellaCavill
You forgot 'bugger'. What's happened? I mean other than you developing Tourette's?

@TuesdayFields
It's everywhere. And I mean everywhere!

@StellaCavill
What is? For God's sake Tuesday, spit it out! I've got a very important meeting with a tanner to get to (leather, not body spray).

@TuesdayFields
After complaining about no press attention I've now got too much and the wrong sort.

@StellaCavill
What do you mean?

@TuesdayFields
So I thought it might at worst make a diary piece but it's made @TheDailyGB online.
>> Plus the @WUBTV press officer has had a call to say it'll be on page bloody 3 tomorrow.

@StellaCavill
What will be?

@TuesdayFields
@No1Sportsman and me! Weasels picked up on him calling me darling on air, pictured us at the Ball . . .
>> . . . have put two and two together and come up with all sorts of shit. Stella, what the hell am I going to do?

@StellaCavill
Where are you?

@TuesdayFields
Hiding in a toilet cubicle at LHR Terminal 3, arrivals.

@StellaCavill
What on earth, Tuesday?

@TuesdayFields
I know! I panicked. I got off the plane to a flurry of voicemails from the publicist and tweets from @Mum, who's been doorstepped.
>> I'm not sure which I should be more afraid of right now.

@StellaCavill
Rather depends on what you value more, your life or your job?

@TuesdayFields
Can kiss goodbye to job. All that slog, early starts, lousy pay and for what?

@StellaCavill
For plenty! Call yourself a journalist? You're forgetting the facts. There is no affair and no story.
>> Now pull yourself together, T, and stop sounding like one of them.

@TuesdayFields
One of who?

@StellaCavill
An @TheDailyGB reader! You'll be exonerated eventually but first thing's first . . .
>> . . . how to get you out of the ladies at T3 avoiding any awaiting flashbulbs . . .

@TuesdayFields
I was thinking I could just wait until closing and sneak out when it's dark outside.

@StellaCavill

You'll be waiting a while, then. Since when did the world's busiest airport ever close?

@TuesdayFields

Well do you have a better idea, because right now I'll take anything, other than a phone call from @Mum?

@StellaCavill

Actually I do. Give me 5. Don't go anywhere.

@TuesdayFields

Well I was thinking of flushing myself down the loo. Where the hell do you think I'm going to go?!

***

@TuesdayFields

I owe you one, S. You and @SINternUK. Thanks for saving my arse, and for pulling my head out of it.

@StellaCavill

I take it my master plan of Monday continues to work then?

@TuesdayFields

It's Thursday and the papers have got better pictures to print. That @SINternUK of yours most certainly knows how to create a diversion.

@StellaCavill

Told you about the exhibitionist streak.

@TuesdayFields

Well, she streaked and did so brilliantly.
>> Flashbulbs and paparazzi's eyes popping all over the place and none, thanks to her, in my direction.

@StellaCavill
Well, let's face it. Those hacks at arrivals are lucky if they get a smile out of @VictoriaBeckham . . .
>> . . . let alone a full frontal out of a twenty something beauty.

@TuesdayFields
Suspect she'll make a much worthier page 3 in @TheDailyGB than I ever would!

@StellaCavill
Lucky her flight got delayed. Dust settled then?

@TuesdayFields
Just about. @TheBossWUB is considering forgiving me on grounds I got several rating-winning interviews with @No1Sportsman.
>> Not sure he's bothered if a bed was involved or not.

@StellaCavill
How about @Mum?

@TuesdayFields
@Mum taking a little more convincing . . .

@StellaCavill
No? Really?! When you told her you wanted to make headlines I'm sure . . .
>> . . .'Tuesday Has A Field Day Shagging Famous Sports Star' was exactly what she had in mind.

@TuesdayFields
Oh sod off, Stella!

@StellaCavill
You never know. Nothing like your favourite read writing a defamatory piece about your daughter to stop you buying it . . .

@TuesdayFields
Sadly not the case.
>> She refused on principle to have the newsagent deliver @TheReflector and admitted to finding @ThePost a bit tricky in places.

@StellaCavill
So @TheDailyGB lives to fight another day in the Fields household despite slur on its first born.

@TuesdayFields
Yes indeed.

@StellaCavill
What does that young war reporter @JakeJacksonLive think of your infamous carry ons?

@TuesdayFields
Oh God, do you think he'll have heard?
>> Maybe not, since I think it's safe to say he's got more important things to worry about than my love life these days.
>> Small stuff, like staying alive.

@StellaCavill
And @KateKingTV and @AnchorManTV?

@TuesdayFields
United, it would seem for once, in my fall from grace.
>> My national humiliation has somehow resulted in a strange calm permeating the @WUBTV studio.

@StellaCavill
Calm before the storm.

@TuesdayFields
At work, yes.

@StellaCavill

And at home? Has that shit @HugoPr1nce been in touch by any chance after seeing you all over the British tabloids?

@TuesdayFields

How'd you guess?

@StellaCavill

Because he's oh-so predictable. I hope you haven't replied. Tuesday?

@TuesdayFields

Haven't. Not yet anyway.

@StellaCavill

Change his name in your phone immediately to 'He Who Must Not Be Called'. He's toxic.

@TuesdayFields

I just – well I did love him once upon a time . . .

@StellaCavill

In your fairytale mind, Tuesday.
>> Perfect timing with you feeling so vulnerable that he now thinks he can be your knight in shining armour and whisk you off your feet again.
>> See it for what it is, T.

@TuesdayFields

It does sound all too convenient, I admit.

@StellaCavill

Because it is. I didn't want to rub your nose in it but if friends can't, who can? @RedS0ledShoes has covered herself in glory again . . .

RT @RedS0ledShoes: 'Last night was amazing. We roll played.
>> I was Rapunzel, got extensions and everything and
@HugoPr1nce was my Prince Charming!'

@TuesdayFields
And cue the political ambitions of a one-time brilliant but flawed
mind slowly but surely ebbing away . . . and any second chances
with me . . .

@StellaCavill
Thought that would bring you back to earth with a bump – I'm
sorry.

@TuesdayFields
OK. Text deleted. Thanks.

@StellaCavill
And the number?

@TuesdayFields
Now reads 'Don't Dial or Text'.

@StellaCavill
Good. Well this side of the pond my relationship is rapidly
disintegrating.
>> Will's been back for 48 hours and it feels like we've been
rowing for most of them.

@TuesdayFields
Worse than Easter?

@StellaCavill
Much. He's never been this difficult.

@TuesdayFields
Being impossible about everything or specifics?

@StellaCavill
Everything. Snapping. Picking fights. Accusing me of affairs with all of my clients, not just @MichaelAngeloMovie.

@TuesdayFields
Any clues at all, Miss Marple, as to why he's behaving like such a prick?

@StellaCavill
No. Just get the feeling something's happened that he's keeping from me. It's probably work related – it usually always is with me.

@TuesdayFields
Probably.

***

@TuesdayFields
It's just not cricket. Well it's not going to be today anyway. @PM_TV's match, a certified washout.

@StellaCavill
Oh, you're not there, are you? I've seen the tweets. He'd amassed the best line up ever to be seen in Chipping Norton . . .

@TuesdayFields
. . . and it's raining cats and dogs. We're huddled together eating soggy sandwiches in a musty marquee.
>> I'm thinking, does anything work outside of London?

@StellaCavill
Or New York?

@TuesdayFields
Or New York.

@StellaCavill
Can't you find something to occupy yourself, like conduct an impromptu exclusive with an ageing cricketing great or something?

@TuesdayFields
Do you know Stella for the first time in a long time I really can't be arsed.
>> I think I'm going to disappear into a vat of free Pimms instead.

@StellaCavill
What happened to intrepid news hound Tuesday Fields, reporting for duty, whatever the weather?

@TuesdayFields
She had to go; I couldn't sustain her or her lifestyle. Too draining and too unsociable.

@StellaCavill
She'll be back.

@TuesdayFields
Maybe. Tonight though, I choose cricketers, mindless fun and, of course, Gordon.

@StellaCavill
Of course.

***

@TuesdayFields
OMG OMG OMG @KateKingTV has hit the roof.

@StellaCavill
What? Why?

@TuesdayFields
Resigned! She's resigned from @WUBTV. Door of @TheBossWUB's office nearly came off its hinges as it slammed behind her.

@StellaCavill
You mean the sofa spot's up for grabs?

@TuesdayFields
Yes and @TheBossWUB wants to see me. Of course it could mean I'm about to get fired . . .

@StellaCavill
Or more likely, hired. Carpe diem Tuesday Fields.

@TuesdayFields
I'm not ready! Really, I'm not.

@StellaCavill
You're just six months ahead of schedule. That's all.

@TuesdayFields
I'm what?

@StellaCavill
Your New Year's resolution, Tuesday; to occupy the sofa spot by Christmas.
>> i.e. six months from now. Personally you may not be fulfilled yet but professionally you are making an impact!

@TuesdayFields
I was drunk.

@StellaCavill
When?

@TuesdayFields
New Year!

@StellaCavill
Small detail. Tiny. Now go get @TheBossWUB and @KateKingTV's job!

@TuesdayFields
Well she did say as she stormed out, Elnett wafting in her wake, she never wanted to see @AnchorManTV's face again as long as she lived . . .

@StellaCavill
It looks like from now on that pleasure will be all yours.

#JUNE

TUESDAY FIELDS

@TuesdayFields: London
'Courage is grace under pressure'. Ernest Hemingway.
Whatever, Ernest.

Monthly Must:
Get a grip.

Monthly Must Not:
Stuff up the biggest professional opportunity of life to
date.

Followers:
Growing, one by one.

STELLA CAVILL

@StellaCavill: New York, New York
Shoes that fit for every type of Season.

Monthly Must:
Save relationship with @MerchBanker.

Monthly Must Not:
Respond to incessant supply of direct message tweets
from @MichaelAngeloMovie.

Followers:
Dying off, one by one.

***

@TuesdayFields

Pinch punch, first day of the month and all that bollocks.

@StellaCavill

Someone's feeling bright and breezy . . .

@TuesdayFields

Someone's up way too early . . .

@StellaCavill

Weird dreams about @MerchBanker. Something just doesn't seem right.

@TuesdayFields

Why? What's he said?

@StellaCavill

Nothing of note.

@TuesdayFields

Then there can't be anything of note to worry about can there?

@StellaCavill

No. Well, I don't think so.
>> Anyway, if Maggie T. can run a country on four hours sleep I figure I can run a barely-there shoe company on five.

@TuesdayFields

And can you?

@StellaCavill

No. At least not without my good friend, caffeine.

150

@TuesdayFields

Love caffeine. On course for a personal best this end. If I can make it four Americanos before midday, then I'm home and dry.

@StellaCavill

Are you putting as much effort into your new job alongside @AnchorManTV as you are into your coffee drinking, Tuesday Fields?

@TuesdayFields

Almost. Trying to find ways to tolerate the chauvinistic, narcissistic, opinionated old fart but finding it . . . well, tricky.

@StellaCavill

Still being an arse even after I had @SINternUK send over another pair of his favourite brogues? No pleasing some people/men.

@TuesdayFields

Add 'unappreciative' to my list of adjectives which best describe my co-presenter. What an arse.
>> Oh, add 'arse' too, while you're at it.
>> No idea why Susan-the-crap-make-up-artist thinks the sun shines out of his, or how Audrey has put up with him all these years.

@StellaCavill

Next time he requests a pair of 'Stellars', I'll get @SINternUK to hand deliver . . .

@TuesdayFields

Far be it for me to ask you to throw @SINternUK to the wolves but . . . Thanks, S.

@StellaCavill

Pleasure. As you know by now, @SINternUK can more than handle herself and the likes of @AnchorManTV.

@TuesdayFields
God he was a tool this morning, (add 'tool' to list). Refused for me
to do a two-way with @JakeJacksonLive.

@StellaCavill
I'll refrain from making a tawdry joke.

@TuesdayFields
Pre-watershed where you are, would be for the best.

@StellaCavill
So you weren't allowed to speak to @JakeJacksonLive on what
grounds? That you might suddenly declare your undying love for
him live on air?!

@TuesdayFields
No, you fool. On the grounds that 'women don't do war'.
@AnchorManTV is a pompous prig. NB add 'pompous prig' to
list too.

@StellaCavill
Did you give him both barrels? Pardon the pun.

@TuesdayFields
I waited for the break then reminded him how lucky we all were
to be in the presence of such a brave war broadcaster.
>> The gallery started sniggering.

@StellaCavill
Why?

@TuesdayFields
Because, Stella Cavill . . .
>> . . . @AnchorManTV spent most of the Iraq war reporting
from the balcony of his luxury five star hotel room at least thirty
miles from any action.

@StellaCavill
You are joking? The flak jacket was all for show then?

@TuesdayFields
The bloke is a complete fraud and everyone here knows it, just the viewers he's got fooled.
>> Highly likely he's never seen or heard real gunfire despite covering an actual war!

@StellaCavill
Unlike the heroic, manly, devastatingly attractive hero that is @JakeJacksonLive . . .

@TuesdayFields
Well unlike @JakeJacksonLive . . . the coffee machine is calling me! Must go if I'm to hit my midday target.

@StellaCavill
Keep your eye on the target, Tuesday. You and @JakeJacksonLive both. Speak later.

* * *

@TuesdayFields
Smashing daily coffee drinking record out of the park has its drawbacks . . .

@StellaCavill
Let me guess. You've got insomnia?

@TuesdayFields
Bingo. It's almost midnight for God's sake. I've got to get up in three sodding hours.

@StellaCavill
Sounds like the sofa slot has its drawbacks too?

@TuesdayFields

I can see my first big press interview right now . . .

>> Interviewer (fresh faced and glowing): 'what was it that first attracted you to the job?'

>> Me (red eyed with aged skin): 'Umm. Fuck knows'.

@StellaCavill

You could say it was @AnchorManTV?!

@TuesdayFields

Through gritted teeth and with everything crossed maybe. Don't you think they would see through it?

@StellaCavill

Judging by your apparent on air chemistry/lack of it, yes, afraid I do.

@TuesdayFields

Bugger. That obvious? Resolution for today: I will go out of my way to try harder with the old goat.

>> Christ I can't believe it's today already.

>> What can I count to help me sleep, can't see any sheep?

@StellaCavill

Tell you what you could count . . .

@TuesdayFields

What?

@StellaCavill

@PM_TV's twitter followers.

>> I've just checked and being that we're now into day two of June, just, it would seem he's on course to lose his mid-year bet . . .

@TuesdayFields
Seriously? #twittertaxiforPM_TV?

@StellaCavill
While you're busy counting sheep or whatever it is you choose to count, he'll be counting the cost of losing out to @LordTw1tter.

@TuesdayFields
Any minute now he'll be begrudgingly wiring a sizeable cash payment into the @LordTw1tter Foundation bank account.

@StellaCavill
That'll dent . . . the ego if not the bank balance.

@TuesdayFields
Just a bit. Not been the best six months for @PM_TV has it?

@StellaCavill
Let's see. Since NYE . . .
>> . . . his beloved Arsenal has lost a cup final, he's been forced to close his pub twice and his charity cricket day was a complete washout.

@TuesdayFields
When you put it like that . . .

@StellaCavill
Poor @PM_TV.

@TuesdayFields
Do you think @PM_TV has as much trouble as I do sleeping?

@StellaCavill
Doubt it! Bet he sleeps like a baby whatever the weather/headlines/his ratings. Careful.
>> Before you know it you'll start counting @PM_TV's . . .

@TuesdayFields
You just put paid to any fading chance I had of some shuteye.

@StellaCavill
Signing off Twitter might help . . .

@TuesdayFields
Too true. Will do. Shortly . . .

@StellaCavill
I need to stop banging out messages on the Crackberry too. Will's home any minute and I'm setting the scene. Been way too long.

@TuesdayFields
How long?

@StellaCavill
Too long. Beginning to wonder if Will and I would ever shag again what with my workload and the way he's been behaving lately.

@TuesdayFields
Tonight's the night with Will and he doesn't even know it yet . . . Night Stella!

@StellaCavill
Morning Tuesday.

* * *

@StellaCavill
Forget any sort of climax(ing). Anti-climax more like it.

@TuesdayFields
You mean the earth didn't move?

@StellaCavill
Not exactly.

@TuesdayFields
What does not exactly mean?

@StellaCavill
Just that. Might have helped if I'd remembered to switch my Crackberry off and not picked up to @AllThatGlittersIsGold mid bonk.

@TuesdayFields
And who said romance was dead? Stella, for God's sake!

@StellaCavill
I know, I know.

@TuesdayFields
You have to find a way to stop thinking spreadsheets and start spreading something else – for example, legs!

@StellaCavill
Well it's not like I didn't try! Candles, massage oil, I even bought new @MYLA_LONDON.
>> But the one thing I didn't do was turn off my phone.

@TuesdayFields
Couldn't you have at least ignored it this one time?

@StellaCavill
What with Gloria Gaynor bellowing out 'I Will Survive'? Hardly.

@TuesdayFields
Of all the lyrics! Well that's just asking for it . . . (have picked up hairbrush)
First I was afraid, I was petrified . . .

@StellaCavill

(Have picked up TV remote) . . . kept thinking I could never live without you by my side . . .

@TuesdayFields

I know I started it but enough! Consider the picture well and truly painted . . .

@StellaCavill

Now do you see why I had no choice but to pick up? Walking out of doors – hardly conducive lyrics to have sex to, Tuesday!

@TuesdayFields

OK, so you had to answer. Just don't tell me you then HAD to have a conversation?

@StellaCavill

I had a conversation.

@TuesdayFields

What?!

@StellaCavill

I know, I know!

@TuesdayFields

Well what did @MerchBanker say/do while you were banging on to @AllThatGlittersIsGold?

@StellaCavill

Stopped 'banging' me. What he did was what Gloria ordered him to do, walked out the door and didn't turn around. What a mess.

@TuesdayFields

Well not as long as he put some pants on after climbing off you and before leaving the house . . .

@StellaCavill
I'm glad you're finding this so funny, T.

@TuesdayFields
And @MerchBanker will do too, eventually!
>> Anyway so what if he doesn't? You know what, Stella Cavill
– it's like Gloria said, you will survive!

@StellaCavill
Your flippancy has raised a smile but it doesn't end there.

@TuesdayFields
What doesn't?

@StellaCavill
The evening's events . . .

@TuesdayFields
Oh God. How much worse did it get?

@StellaCavill
I kept my phone on, thinking @MerchBanker would reply to one
of my endless apologetic messages.

@TuesdayFields
He didn't?

@StellaCavill
No. And just as I was getting irritated with his lack of response . . .

@TuesdayFields
Don't tell me. I already know! @MichaelAngeloMovie got in
touch?

@StellaCavill

Bingo. And I've been trying not to respond to him recently, but I was so cross with Will, I did.

>> Mid textual banter, @MerchBanker walks back through the door.

@TuesdayFields

Did he know what you were up to?

@StellaCavill

No, but he probably guessed when he saw the expression my face was wearing.

@TuesdayFields

Don't tell me you were in bed?

@StellaCavill

I was in bed. Will walked into the bedroom, clocked my obvious guilt and spent the night on the sofa.

@TuesdayFields

Best laid plans or in this case not laid. Sorry, S.

@StellaCavill

C'est la vie. Another sleepless night – for all the wrong reasons.

@TuesdayFields

Seems like we are all suffering from them at the moment. @Mum in on the act too.

@StellaCavill

@Mum too? Why's she turned insomniac?

@TuesdayFields

I'd have thought that was perfectly obvious, S . . .

@StellaCavill
You?

@TuesdayFields
Me. @Mum reportedly woke up with a start at 2AM.
>> Unable to swiftly shift her concerns, she woke Dad up for a detailed discussion about yours truly.

@StellaCavill
Let me hazard a guess – the motherly concern stems from you plus work equals no grandchildren, yet or ever?

@TuesdayFields
That, as we both know is a great worry but not the reason for her waking my darling dad in a fluster last night.
>> That was something altogether much more serious . . .

@StellaCavill
I'm at a loss. Something in @TheDailyGB?

@TuesdayFields
Connected. She is worried about . . . wait for it . . . my face.

@StellaCavill
What do you mean she's worried about your face?

@TuesdayFields
She thinks the early starts are ageing me.

@StellaCavill
What did you tell her?

@TuesdayFields
The truth. They are! I did also point out that early starts are an occupational hazard when presenting a breakfast show.

@StellaCavill
What did she say?

@TuesdayFields
Only that she'd been looking at pictures of celebrities in @TheDailyGB . . .

@StellaCavill
And . . .

@TuesdayFields
She couldn't understand how they managed to look so 'alert', these 'celebrities' . . .
>> . . . when her own much younger daughter looked like an old hag already. I'm paraphrasing obviously.

@StellaCavill
Obviously. Well done @TheDailyGB.

@TuesdayFields
I suggested some 'celebrities' may have shoved something up their noses to look 'alert', as she put it . . .

@StellaCavill
How did she react to that?

@TuesdayFields
To quote @Mum: 'well darling, all these people look very good on coke'. I'm not paraphrasing!

@StellaCavill
@Mum living in blissful ignorance. I've lost count the number of times @Supermodel_1971 has had to have her nose rebuilt.

@TuesdayFields
Does it function as a nose should after all that work?

@StellaCavill
Barely. If she catches a cold I worry a single sneeze could blow it right off.

@TuesdayFields
At least life with @Supermodel_1971 isn't dull. Dad has a taken up a new hobby.
>> I'm assuming it's just another way to spend more time away from @Mum.

@StellaCavill
Which is?

@TuesdayFields
He's taken to moth catching.

@StellaCavill
Why would anyone want to spend their time catching moths?

@TuesdayFields
Like I said, it gets him out of the house . . .

@StellaCavill
Bit drastic though?

@TuesdayFields
I know. Key is not to show too much interest in his new hobby.

@StellaCavill
Or what?

@TuesdayFields
He thinks you're interested!

@StellaCavill
Poor Dad.

@TuesdayFields
Oh he's alright. Shame about the butterflies, though.
>> I've got a feeling there will be less of them around with Dad and his big moth catching net on the prowl.

@StellaCavill
If @Mum is half as bad as you make out they'll be an endangered species within months.

@TuesdayFields
Endangered? Extinct more like.

* * *

@TuesdayFields
I hate @AnchorManTV. He's a sanctimonious, self-centered shit with a patchy scalp and bad breath.
>> How Susan can spend so long attending to him in his dressing room is beyond me.

@StellaCavill
This list is getting very long – not exactly another glowing character reference, Tuesday.

@TuesdayFields
Not, and with good reason. The wanker completely stitched me up on air this morning, gave me nowhere to go and left me with egg on my face.
>> I hate him.

@StellaCavill

Shame @TheBossWUB didn't bin him at the same time as @KateKingTV. You don't suppose he's giving you a hard time for replacing her?

@TuesdayFields

I honestly have no idea. I've lost count of the amount of career cul de sac's he's taken me down this week.

@StellaCavill

And it's only Tuesday, Tuesday!

@TuesdayFields

Ha. I know. But for @TheBossWUB yelling down @AnchorManTV's earpiece this morning from the production gallery, I might have been toast.

@StellaCavill

Well at least you know @TheBossWUB has your back.

@TuesdayFields

But for how long? He has execs to answer to and the viewing figures have nosedived since @KateKingTV's exit.

@StellaCavill

Has @TheBossWUB said anything?

@TuesdayFields

Not yet, but I do know that he is beyond mad with the whole saga and @AnchorManTV behaving badly is not helping.

@StellaCavill

So how did @AnchorManTV blot your copybook this morning?

@TuesdayFields
@ProducerGabe messed up the item timings in the programme rundown.
>> We found ourselves with an end of the hour, three minute banter window.

@StellaCavill
I take it @AnchorManTV doesn't do small talk?

@TuesdayFields
Well he made it pretty clear he won't with me. With 2.59 left to fill he turned to me wearing a smug look on his face and simply said . . .
>> . . . 'Tuesday, over to you' . . .

@StellaCavill
You're joking?

@TuesdayFields
I wish I was.
>> The fucker then watched in glee as I visibly shrank, contorted and virtually died on air whilst trying, in vain, to recap the top stories.

@StellaCavill
I'm sure it's not as bad as you remember it, T.

@TuesdayFields
Sky plussed it. Trial week and all that. Played it back a hundred times and with every viewing another little part of me dies.
>> Total cringe.

@StellaCavill
What's @TheBossWUB said about it?

@TuesdayFields
He gave @AnchorManTV a bollocking after we fell off air and told him to give me a break . . .
>> . . . but I can see @TheBossWUB starting to wonder why he gave me this break at all.

@StellaCavill
Bet @ProducerGabe was apologetic afterwards. Sounds like a right plank for dropping you in it like that?

@TuesdayFields
He was busy lining up a live link to @JakeJacksonLive, so not all his fault in fairness.
>> I just need to stop stuttering and stumbling and start speaking properly.
>> How hard can it be?

@StellaCavill
Easier said than done. It's live TV – most people would shrivel up and die.

@TuesdayFields
It's literally just reading out loud.

@StellaCavill
Tomorrow is a new day, Tuesday.
>> You can blow your audience away with your ability to string sentences together using words placed in the right order then.

@TuesdayFields
Like you said Stella, easier said than done. Did I tell you that I hate @AnchorManTV? Well I do. Hate him.

@StellaCavill
I think you may have mentioned it, yes.

@StellaCavill

It's quite possible that I may have started something I'm not capable of finishing . . .

@TuesdayFields

I'm listening . . .

@StellaCavill

It's probably all very harmless but what if it isn't?

@TuesdayFields

What?

@StellaCavill

Harmless.

@TuesdayFields

Stella. You're beginning to get on my ever-decreasing tits. Speak English will you?

@StellaCavill

@MichaelAngeloMovie. I can't seem to shake him.

@TuesdayFields

Do you want to?

@StellaCavill

Want to what?

@TuesdayFields

Shake him?!

@StellaCavill

Oh. Yes. Well I think so.

@TuesdayFields
You think so?

@StellaCavill
No. I do. Want to shake him that is.

@TuesdayFields
So what's stopping you?

@StellaCavill
He is. He won't seem to take no for an answer.

@TuesdayFields
That'll be because he's never had to.

@StellaCavill
Until now.

@TuesdayFields
Until now . . .

@StellaCavill
What's that supposed to mean?

@TuesdayFields
What?

@StellaCavill
Dot dot dot . . . as if implying something's been left unsaid.

@TuesdayFields
Well something has, hasn't it?

@StellaCavill
No!

@TuesdayFields
Why can't you just admit you quite like having @MichaelAngeloMovie in your life?

@StellaCavill
Because I don't!

@TuesdayFields
Yes you do Stella Cavill, and it's not just about the shoes either.

@StellaCavill
What do you mean?

@TuesdayFields
Right now you have a never-present boyfriend and an ever-present client, who happens to be hot as hell.

@StellaCavill
What are you trying to say?

@TuesdayFields
Admit it, every time something goes wrong with @MerchBanker, @MichaelAngeloMovie provides the perfect ego boost.

@StellaCavill
I guess . . . Will said he was going to London for three weeks, I felt abandoned, again – so I responded to M. I'm a bad person aren't I?

@TuesdayFields
No, you're human. Along comes an A-list movie star hell bent on getting you into bed and . . .

@StellaCavill
And . . .

@TuesdayFields
And you feel flattered. Who wouldn't? He does want to get you into bed, you do know that?

@StellaCavill
Clarification: shag me senseless then leave me for dust.

@TuesdayFields
Whatever.

@StellaCavill
What are you saying?

@TuesdayFields
I'm saying, choose.

@StellaCavill
What, between Will and @MichaelAngeloMovie?
>> I know we've been having some problems, Tuesday, but you know Will wins that battle every time for me.

@TuesdayFields
Does he?

@StellaCavill
@MichaelAngeloMovie is not a realistic option! Seriously! Why would you even ask me to choose?

@TuesdayFields
Because as Fenella Fudgecake discovered, sometimes the grass is greener.

@StellaCavill
Trust me, Tuesday; it isn't where @MichaelAngeloMovie is concerned. I would never, could never cheat on Will.

@TuesdayFields
And he's not just the safe option? Comfortable appearances can be deceptive.

@StellaCavill
What do you mean? You think Will and I are uncomfortable?

@TuesdayFields
No, don't mean that. Forget I even said anything. You're right. You love @MerchBanker.
>> With @MichaelAngeloMovie it would just be sex.

@StellaCavill
Exactly.

@TuesdayFields
Great sex though. Mind blowing, break-the-bed sex, but just sex.

@StellaCavill
Just sex, Tuesday. Now help me, how the hell am I going to get him off my back?

@TuesdayFields
Haven't a clue. If it was me that's exactly where I'd want to keep him.

@StellaCavill
Tuesday!

@TuesdayFields
Just thinking of the biceps. Or maybe just the sex . . . Sorry.

@StellaCavill
You focus on that while I concentrate on taking the moral high ground.

@TuesdayFields
Good luck with that . . .

* * *

@TuesdayFields
Have you seen it? It's all over Twitter, Stella, I'm trending . . .
Christ, think I've blown it.

@StellaCavill
Last time you tweeted me a message like that . . .
>> . . . you were in the ladies loo in T3 @Heathrow avoiding
paps over reports of a fling with @No1Sportsman.
>> Now what?

@TuesdayFields
Well not that. Not this time anyway.

@StellaCavill
Can an @SINternUK streak solve it, because if it can I can
arrange it right away?

@TuesdayFields
Sadly not. More clothes better than none in this case.
>> At least I wish I'd been wearing more when a gust a wind
chose to target dress and hat simultaneously this morning.

@StellaCavill
What, are you @RoyalAscot?

@TuesdayFields
Yes. Being that I'm the junior presenter with a specialty in all
things sporting I was the obvious choice for @TheBossWUB.
>> Royally stuffed up this time, Stella.

@StellaCavill
So when did this awful thing happen?

@TuesdayFields
During a live cross with the Master of the Horse. He looked as delighted as I did mortified.

@StellaCavill
But I'm presuming you chose to save modesty and reached for dress over hat, Tuesday?

@TuesdayFields
You'd have thought so, wouldn't you, because that would be the logical thing to do.

@StellaCavill
You didn't?

@TuesdayFields
I did. The rest as they say is history, or should be if it weren't for YouTube.
>> 'This is Tuesday Fields reporting from Royal Ascot with no hat and no knickers either!'

@StellaCavill
No knickers?! You didn't mention you weren't wearing any pants!

@TuesdayFields
That's because to call them knickers is probably a bit generous, more of a nude thong.

@StellaCavill
So you may as well have been wearing nothing at all?

@TuesdayFields
Yup and that's exactly how it looks online. Not something I'm particularly proud of.
>> Feel like such a twat after everyone watching @WUBTV this morning got to see mine.

@StellaCavill
What are you trending as? 'Sharon Stone'?

@TuesdayFields
Ha bloody ha. @AnchorManTV basking in my fashion faux pas as I suspect @TheDailyGB will be tomorrow. Cue @Mum.

@StellaCavill
A piece of friendly advice: stop having imaginary flings with @No1Sportsman and start wearing knickers live on air . . .
>> . . . then @TheDailyGB might turn their attention to @AnchorManTV instead. Must have a few skeletons . . .

@TuesdayFields
For sure. Just got to find where those bodies are buried.

@StellaCavill
And start wearing proper pants.

@TuesdayFields
And start wearing proper pants. Fuck.

TUESDAY FIELDS

@TuesdayFields: London
It's now or never.

Monthly Must:
Wear knickers at all times.

Monthly Must Not:
Tell Stella about what really happened in Monaco.

Followers:
Alive and kicking.

STELLA CAVILL

@StellaCavill: New York, New York
Stand your ground.

Monthly Must:
Get some sleep.

Monthly Must Not:
Give up on Stellar Shoes. Or Will.

Followers:
Almost dead.

@StellaCavill
I'm going to kill Will.

@TuesdayFields
What's @MerchBanker wanker done now?

@StellaCavill
I've just been Facebooked by some stupid cow of a girl, who I'm sure stole my milk at school.

@TuesdayFields
Facebook. I don't get it. Isn't there a reason why we keep up with some and not others since school?
>> I mean why 'reconnect' with people we never connected with in the first goddamn place?

@StellaCavill
Point.

@TuesdayFields
Do you know there is actually a fake one of me on there?
>> I mean why would you bother to create a fake me, I'm struggling as it is to make the real me interesting.

@StellaCavill
@RoyalAscot? Need I say more?!

@TuesdayFields
You've already said too much! So what's the deal with the Facebook girl, who you may or may not have gone to school with?

@StellaCavill
Well I figured I'd preempt anyone who might be bored enough to create a fake Stella Cavill account and now I'm wishing I hadn't.

@TuesdayFields
What happened?

@StellaCavill
This 'contemporary' wrote to say she was so sorry about me and Will . . .

@TuesdayFields
What about you and Will?

@StellaCavill
Apparently he was all over some Marlborough bird at Boujis last week. I Googled her.
>> Turns out her claim to fame was organising those sex parties in Portland Place.

@TuesdayFields
Oh God. That doesn't sound good?

@StellaCavill
Christ, @MYLA_LONDON was enough to give Will a heart attack in the early days, let alone glow in the dark condoms.

@TuesdayFields
What have they got to do with anything?

@StellaCavill
Compulsory attire for men at sex parties. Apparently.
>> Anyway, where does the cow get off lying about @MerchBanker getting off? Nasty piece of work.

@TuesdayFields
Stella, there's something I should tell you but I think it's best if I call. Give me 5.

@StellaCavill
No! Don't call, T. I'm in the office with @AllThatGlittersIsGold.
He thinks I'm working. Let's not spoil the illusion. What is it?

@TuesdayFields
It's about Monaco.

@StellaCavill
What about Monaco?

@TuesdayFields
That night. The one you couldn't get hold of Will.
>> Truth is I was with @SINternUK and we . . . we're pretty
sure we saw Will leave Jimmyz with someone, with a girl.

@StellaCavill
Why the hell didn't you tell me this, Tuesday? That was two
months ago!

@TuesdayFields
I went over and over it wondering if I should. I thought it must
have been a one-off, that it might not be worth . . .
>> Oh God, S, I'm so sorry. Obviously now I wish I had.
>> You have every right to want to strangle me. If I were you, I'd
want to strangle me too.

@StellaCavill
You're bloody right I do – I'm furious! How could you do this to
me, Tuesday?

@TuesdayFields
He was paralytic, Stella. Completely sozzled.
>> I figured you had enough on your plate and if I told you it
would only destroy everything you and Will have.

@StellaCavill

Had! Had, past tense. So, what happened? What didn't you tell me that you should have?

@TuesdayFields

He was playing the ice cube game with his banker wanker friends and some assorted tarts.
>> All the boys were at it. I thought that's all it was, just a stupid drinking game.

@StellaCavill

But?

@TuesdayFields

Listen, Stella. Seriously, it was about as meaningful as a kiss and a fumble at one of those Portland Place sex parties you were just talking about.
>> Less so.

@StellaCavill

Why didn't you do anything? And @SINternUK. Iris should have told me. I'm so angry at you both!

@TuesdayFields

Iris did want to say something.
>> She was ready to kick off but I didn't want her causing a scene because she was there representing you and Stellars.
>> I dragged her off to the loo and when we came out they'd gone.

@StellaCavill

Gone? Gone where?

@TuesdayFields

I'm not exactly sure where, but we did see @MerchBanker and the girl he'd been kissing at the table stagger into a cab.
>> I'm so sorry Stella, really I am.

@StellaCavill
Did he see you?

@TuesdayFields
He did earlier in the evening, but he'd been drinking all day, I
don't think it registered.
>> Chances are @MerchBanker wasn't capable of doing
anything more than collapsing.

@StellaCavill
I see. Guess I said I didn't want to know, didn't I.

@TuesdayFields
I thought it was a mindless, drunken one off. Honest to God, I did.
That's why I didn't say anything, S.
>> I didn't for one minute think he was a repeat offender.

@StellaCavill
But it wasn't a one off was it? That cow on Facebook was right
about Will.

@TuesdayFields
Stella, listen, you shouldn't be on your own –
@AllThatGlittersIsGold sitting opposite you analysing his busi-
ness interests doesn't count.
>> Who else is there with you?

@StellaCavill
No one. But it's been that way for a long time. I just didn't realise
until now how true that is.

* * *

@TuesdayFields
Stella?

@StellaCavill
Well, I did it. Confronted Will.

@TuesdayFields
And . . .

@StellaCavill
I'm still shaking, although a slug of Krug has helped a bit.
>> I know there is nothing to celebrate but there was also nothing else in the fridge. The irony.

@TuesdayFields
When did @MerchBanker get back in from London?

@StellaCavill
About three hours ago.

@TuesdayFields
What did you say?

@StellaCavill
I think I'd already said most of it before he got on the plane. Called him – had to leave a voicemail of course, as he wasn't picking up.
>> 'Left word' that I knew about Monaco. About Boujis. And waited.

@TuesdayFields
What happened?

@StellaCavill
I'd packed my things before he arrived. How can I ever trust him again? He asked me to stay.
>> He cried. I cried. But I think deep down he knows it's curtains.

@TuesdayFields
He stuffed up Stella but is there really no way back? Are you sure that's it?

@StellaCavill

Once upon a time in my fairytale world, back in our flat in Islington, I had him pinned as my knight in shining armour.

>> But Manhattan will change a man.

@TuesdayFields

Maybe it has changed you, too?

@StellaCavill

Maybe. We were soulmates, Tuesday, I was so sure of it. But I'm not so sure anymore that we're supposed to end up with our soulmate.

>> Perhaps it's too hard, if you care too much.

@TuesdayFields

So you've left the loft. Where are you staying?

@StellaCavill

Hero of the hour? You won't believe it, but it turns out the ice maiden does have a heart after all. @Supermodel_1971 to the rescue.

@TuesdayFields

She finally stepped up?

@StellaCavill

She did. I'm in an empty brownstone with a fridge full of Krug that belongs to one of her society friends.

>> They're in the Hamptons for the summer.

@TuesdayFields

I knew @Supermodel_1971 would step up. Eventually.

@StellaCavill

She's also wired me a whole wad of money to go and rent somewhere more permanent.

>> I've got no credit rating here so I'll need to put down a massive deposit.

@TuesdayFields
Well at least that's one less thing to worry about. Good old @Supermodel_1971.

@StellaCavill
Less of the old, she'd hate that! Seriously though, for the first time I can ever recall, she's come over all maternal.
>> She's decreed I need somewhere with a doorman.

@TuesdayFields
But of course! Got to hand it to her, she's still got style.

@StellaCavill
Feels like I've been mothering her so long, it's odd to have her look after me for a change.

@TuesdayFields
She's worried about you. So am I.

@StellaCavill
I'm 34 years old – it's humiliating I need her like this.
>> I should be able to stand on my own two feet, Tuesday, with or without a cheating wanker banker boyfriend.

@TuesdayFields
Are you kidding? How many times do I go running to @Mum? That's what they're there for.
>> That and to remind us we are getting older, less fertile and more selfish!

@StellaCavill
So @Supermodel_1971 has come into her own – as has another . . .

@TuesdayFields
@AllThatGlittersIsGold?

@StellaCavill
No. I'm using work as my refuge.
>> Figured @AllThatGlittersIsGold doesn't need to know that I'm falling apart personally when professionally we're so close to cracking up too.

@TuesdayFields
You'll turn it around, S. Personally and professionally.

@StellaCavill
I hope so. Where Stellar Shoes is concerned, right now it's about facing the reality of our situation and fixing it, not just papering over the cracks.
>> Harder than I thought.

@TuesdayFields
So who's looking out for you as well as @Supermodel_1971, if not @AllThatGlittersIsGold?

@StellaCavill
Guess.

@TuesdayFields
Worryingly, I'm not sure I need to. Are you serious?

@StellaCavill
Yes! I can't believe it either but @MichaelAngeloMovie is checking up on me almost hourly!
>> He's even offered me the use of his West Village apartment.

@TuesdayFields
What, with him in it?

@StellaCavill

He says not and anyway he's safely ensconced in Memphis shooting a film with Pacino. I opted for the uptown brownstone.

>> I don't want to owe anyone anything. Or rather, him anything.

@TuesdayFields

Well it's not like you can take the moral high ground with @MerchBanker if you head straight over to @MichaelAngeloMovie's shag pad, is it?

@StellaCavill

Exactly. And I need my space. But I can't say I'm not tempted to do something stupid, Tuesday . . .

@TuesdayFields

Well you know my thoughts on that particular subject . . .

@StellaCavill

Remind me . . .

@TuesdayFields

It's time you had some fun. Caution to the wind and all that.

@StellaCavill

@MichaelAngeloMovie is a great distraction, don't get me wrong.

@TuesdayFields

So what's stopping you?

@StellaCavill

I don't need the love of my life to leave it . . .

>> . . . and then have a one night stand with someone I'm forced to look at/hear about for the rest of time through @TheDailyGB et al.

@TuesdayFields
@MichaelAngeloMovie isn't exactly low profile.

@StellaCavill
You of all people must see where I'm coming from, T?

@TuesdayFields
I am more than familiar with being unwillingly thrust into the media spotlight . . .
>> . . . and also for not being able to get away from a one-night stand so yes, I do.

@StellaCavill
Which begs the question, how is @JakeJacksonLive's heroic wartime turn?

@TuesdayFields
@Mum has reliably informed me @TheDailyGB have given him the ultimate accolade and started referring to him as 'The Housewives Choice'.

@StellaCavill
And to think you thought he wasn't grown up enough to handle being a thirty-something's bit of crumpet.
>> Now he's being touted as the perfect toyboy for cougars everywhere!

@TuesdayFields
Yes, thank you for reminding me, Stella.

@StellaCavill
Well I suspect @Schofe will be quaking in his Stellars about the new kid on the block.

@TuesdayFields
You sent @SINternUK in to This Morning too?

@StellaCavill
Of course. I send her everywhere!

@TuesdayFields
They are everywhere! Stellars' that is.

@StellaCavill
That's the plan. Ubiquitous in the right places . . . Unfortunately I seem to be giving away more than I'm selling.

@TuesdayFields
I don't know, I've seen a few stomping round @Wimbledon.

@StellaCavill
No doubt posh boys and sports stars that @SINternUK has provided freebies to. How is the green and pleasant land that is SW19?

@TuesdayFields
Off sofa and broadcasting live from here this fortnight.
>> According to @TheDailyGB via @Mum it's because I'm not up to scratch on aforementioned settee.

RT @Mum: 'Darling, @TheDailyGB think you lack experience and gravitas but they like your hair. That's something, isn't it?'

@StellaCavill
She's right. That is something!

@TuesdayFields
Not a glowing report, other than for my colourist, on my debut though, is it?
>> Needless to say @AnchorManTV is trying to sabotage my every move.

@StellaCavill

Look on the bright side, T. The Wimbledon gig is a good one.

>> A chance to show the public there's more to you than being @AnchorManTV's bit of fluff.

@TuesdayFields

Unfortunately I'm not even sure I can be considered that anymore.

>> @TheDailyGB seem to have it in for me and @Mum is starting to take it all very personally.

RT @TheDailyGB: 'Are Tuesday Fields', 33, Days Numbered?'

RT @Mum: 'Darling why are they saying your days are numbered? What does that say about me if they say you're done at 33?

>> Your father is out catching silly butterflies again. Speak later, love old dried up Mum.'

@StellaCavill

Poor @Mum. I actually feel a pang of sympathy for her.

>> Listen Tuesday, get your head down this fortnight and with no @AnchorManTV beside you, you'll shine.

@TuesdayFields

That's one consolation. Another is I get paid to gawp at Rafa Nadal's biceps for fourteen days straight.

@StellaCavill

Pervert.

@TuesdayFields

Well given the chance to wash his whites you would, wouldn't you?

@StellaCavill
I'm not so sure. I've always been a Federer girl, post haircut.

@TuesdayFields
No better biceps in the world than those of Rafa.

@StellaCavill
Along with @No1Sportsman. And @JakeJacksonLive. Am I spotting a running theme here?

@TuesdayFields
Stop stirring. And Stella?

@StellaCavill
Yes, Tuesday?

@TuesdayFields
Hang in there.

@StellaCavill
Yes, Tuesday.

* * *

@TuesdayFields
Oh God, I've just seen @HugoPr1nce.

@StellaCavill
What? Where?

@TuesdayFields
@Wimbledon. I was wrapping up my men's final report and he waited.
>> A man who doesn't wait, waited for me to finish pontificating about first serve percentages.

@StellaCavill
Was @RedS0ledShoes there?

@TuesdayFields
No. He was on some corporate jolly with the boys, so had been on the booze. He asked me to join him for one for the road . . .

@StellaCavill
You went for a drink with him?

@TuesdayFields
I have to admit, it was nice to see him.

@StellaCavill
Did you ask him about his live-in girlfriend?

@TuesdayFields
We touched on it. Briefly. He looked so unhappy though, S.

@StellaCavill
So he was evasive?

@TuesdayFields
A little.

@StellaCavill
No surprises there.

@TuesdayFields
When we got back from drinks in the clubhouse the crew had already left. He gave me a lift back into town.

@StellaCavill
You got in a car with him?

@TuesdayFields
It was a Sunday, Stella. Chauffeur-driven, air-conditioned Mercedes or the district line with the Wimbledon masses.

@StellaCavill
So you sat there, in his fuck-me-mobile. Then what?

@TuesdayFields
Then nothing.

@StellaCavill
Clearly not nothing. Did you kiss? If that driver could talk . . . Oh wait . . . he can.

@TuesdayFields
Don't panic, Janet. There'll be an iron clad confidentiality agreement somewhere, I'm sure.

@StellaCavill
I hope for your sake. You're hardly under the radar anymore, T.

@TuesdayFields
Don't remind me. Christ, you've got me thinking – I hope we did evade the photographers.

@StellaCavill
Suspect you got lucky and they got distracted by Nadal's biceps.
>> Back to @HugoPr1nce: please don't tell me he invited you into his flat and that you accepted?

@TuesdayFields
He invited me into his flat. And I accepted.

@StellaCavill
Of course you did.

@TuesdayFields
We kissed. We stumbled into the corridor, making our way to the bedroom . . .

@StellaCavill
Oh Jesus Christ.

@TuesdayFields
And walked smack into @RedS0ledShoes with her mother. Apparently they'd been at a Prom but left early as the music was too old fashioned.
>> For both of them.

@StellaCavill
How the hell did you manage to get out of that one?

@TuesdayFields
@HugoPr1nce said that I was just leaving. So I did.

@StellaCavill
Lucky escape in more ways than one.

@TuesdayFields
Yup. He's clearly not breaking up with her, he just didn't want me to break ties with him. What a twat.

@StellaCavill
You or him?

@TuesdayFields
Both.

@StellaCavill
Have you heard from him since?

@TuesdayFields

Of course not. Like you say, I think he just wanted to check if he still could have me. Well, he can't.

@StellaCavill

I'm sorry, T. Are you OK?

@TuesdayFields

No. But I will be. Are you OK?

@StellaCavill

No. But I will be.

***

@StellaCavill

Bless @PM_TV. I was beginning to think I'd never laugh again.

@TuesdayFields

So was I. Every time I think of it tears stream down my face. Just the most stupid scenario.

@StellaCavill

It was the set up that was so genius.
>> The endless tweets about how he was going to hang with @HughHefner at the Midsummer Playboy Mansion ball.

@TuesdayFields

The twitpics about which pyjamas he was going to wear, each potential pair more hideous than the last.

@StellaCavill

The chatting up of the @HollyMadisons of this world over Twitter.

194

@TuesdayFields
And then he falls off his @SegwayInc on Santa Monica Boulevard. Ha!

@StellaCavill
How is it possible to end up in Cedars Sinai with three broken ribs from one of those?

@TuesdayFields
No idea. But knowing @PM_TV he's probably already picked up an exclusive from someone in a rehab programme there.

@StellaCavill
More likely getting a boob – or moob – job. Which reminds me, I've made a decision about something . . .

@TuesdayFields
Not fake boobs? At least not without me! Have you ever actually felt them?

@StellaCavill
Yes actually. Once. At the place @PM_TV was heading before he ploughed his Segway into a lifeguard tower, the Playboy Mansion!

@TuesdayFields
What were you doing at the Playboy Mansion, Stella Cavill?

@StellaCavill
Giving out free shoes to Playboys of course!

@TuesdayFields
So if it's not to up your bra size what is this big decision then?
>> Don't tell me you're going to jack in being a hot-shot businesswoman for a quieter life as @HughHefner's third wife?

@StellaCavill

No, I'm too old for him. I'm – well I'm thinking of, getting on the proffered @NetJet and going to Memphis.

@TuesdayFields

To visit Elvis? Why do you want to go and see him all of a sudden? You do know he's dead, right?

@StellaCavill

Not to pay homage at Graceland. To see @MichaelAngeloMovie, you muppet.
>> He's sending flowers daily – it's a long time since I've felt this, well, wanted.

@TuesdayFields

And?

@StellaCavill

I figure take a leaf out of Tuesday Fields' book, take a flyer. Or an @NetJet . . .

@TuesdayFields

Because look how well that approach to life has worked out for me, S! Are you really sure about this?

@StellaCavill

You're going to try and talk me out of it aren't you? I can't believe it!

@TuesdayFields

No. As long as you know what you're doing.

@StellaCavill

I always used to. But now – I'm just not sure I care.

@TuesdayFields

Need to feel alive again? Is that it?

@StellaCavill
Yes. Am I mad?

@TuesdayFields
No! The hottest most talented movie star of his generation is flying you to a film set on a PJ after he has spent months flirting with you.

@StellaCavill
Well, when you put it like that.

@TuesdayFields
Some would say it was the most sensible move you've ever made.

@StellaCavill
Some would say it's insane.

@TuesdayFields
The definition of insanity is doing the same thing twice and expecting a different result. Ever shagged a movie star?

@StellaCavill
No!

@TuesdayFields
Then off you go . . .

* * *

@TuesdayFields
It would seem that @PM_TV does not have exclusive rights to public humiliation . . .

@StellaCavill
I thought we discovered that post the knickers at Ascot incident, Tuesday. What could possibly be worse?

@TuesdayFields
Potentially this: I've been assigned the 'fun in the sun' slot for the next fortnight.

@StellaCavill
I'm suspecting you won't be waking up Britain from Portofino?

@TuesdayFields
Correct. Magaluf.

@StellaCavill
Shagaluf! Well I suppose unlike the Playboy Mansion it will contain men who are young enough to get it up.

@TuesdayFields
@TheBossWUB has cited budget restraints and put us in a hotel with plastic sheets.

@StellaCavill
Hotel guests are not expected to have control of their bodily functions?

@TuesdayFields
That would be more hope over expectation.

@StellaCavill
I would have thought Marbella was more appropriate for the @WUBTV target audience?

@TuesdayFields
Marbella box ticked last year and the powers that be thought we should be tightening our belts along with the rest of the nation.

@StellaCavill
In a place renowned for its belt unbuckling. The irony of the situation cannot be lost on @TheBossWUB?

@TuesdayFields

Oh never fear, Tuesday's here. Reporting this time from a hot and distinctly unsavoury hellhole.

>> I've somehow managed to unearth the odd child who's taken too much sun.

@StellaCavill

Good for you. How's the cameraman coping with finding angles that don't have 18-30 strip water games in shot?

@TuesdayFields

Challenging. So, go on, rub it in, when are you off to the Deep South?

@StellaCavill

I'm waiting for the wisecrack . . .

@TuesdayFields

It's coming. Literally.

@StellaCavill

Shut up!

@TuesdayFields

Had Brazilian?

@StellaCavill

Yes.

@TuesdayFields

Legs lasered?

@StellaCavill

Yes.

@TuesdayFields

Spray tan sans paper pants so no visible tan line?

@StellaCavill
All of the above.

@TuesdayFields
So you're really going?

@StellaCavill
I think so, although I'm already feeling guilty and I've not done so much as get on the plane yet!
>> I'm just still so bloody angry – haven't heard a thing from Will.

@TuesdayFields
Any idea where he is?

@StellaCavill
Reports that he's in St Tropez.

@TuesdayFields
Reports?

@StellaCavill
BBM status update. And Facebook. And Twitter.

@TuesdayFields
Stella are you social network stalking your ex? Delete him right now from all forms of media. This minute.

@StellaCavill
Not stalking, it's just he's obviously on all my feeds. What am I supposed to do, delete him? It feels childish.

@TuesdayFields
Self-preservation isn't childish, it's the grown-up thing to do.

@StellaCavill

If truth be told, I'm not sure I'm ready to cut all the cords – I know they're virtual but they feel real.

@TuesdayFields

Are you 100% done and dusted with Will?

@StellaCavill

I will be if I sleep with @MichaelAngeloMovie.

@TuesdayFields

Are you ready for that?

@StellaCavill

Tuesday?

@TuesdayFields

Yes Stella?

@StellaCavill

I've done it. I've just deleted Will. Facebook. Twitter. BBM.

@TuesdayFields

Then you're ready. Wishing you a safe flight, Miss Cavill.

***

@StellaCavill

So it turns out neither @PM_TV nor you have the exclusive franchise on humiliation.

@TuesdayFields

Don't tell me the seduction didn't stick to script? Definitely don't tell me @MichaelAngeloMovie is living a lie and is actually gay?!

@StellaCavill
Well, let me set the scene . . .

@TuesdayFields
OMG I'm right aren't I? @MichaelAngeloMovie is gay!!!

@StellaCavill
He's not gay. Hold your horses. Where was I? Oh yes, in @MichaelAngeloMovie's trailer . . .

@TuesdayFields
Which I'm guessing is bigger than 99% of London/Manhattan apartments right?

@StellaCavill
Right.

@TuesdayFields
Plasma screens?

@StellaCavill
Seven. Also one and a half bathrooms, a gym and a spiral staircase leading to a second floor bedroom with a king size bed.

@TuesdayFields
What could possibly go wrong?

@StellaCavill
Well, I arrive. No time for chit chat. Just kissing, lots of kissing and then off come the clothes . . .

@TuesdayFields
You realise you're sounding just like one of his cheesy rom coms?

@StellaCavill

Maybe movie stars don't know how to live any other way. So, the situation progresses at speed . . .

@TuesdayFields

Not too speedy I hope? It would be disappointing for him to finish before you began.

@StellaCavill

Well, we're just in the moment . . .

@TuesdayFields

Which moment?

@StellaCavill

THAT moment. Well technically speaking THE moment had passed.

@TuesdayFields

Oh THAT moment. And then what?

@StellaCavill

Well if you'd just give me a chance I'll get there . . .

@TuesdayFields

Go on . . .

@StellaCavill

@MichaelAngeloMovie had been ignoring all these the calls and knocks on the door requesting his presence on set . . .

@TuesdayFields

For obvious reasons . . .

@StellaCavill
Exactly. So, the knocks keep coming, @MichaelAngeloMovie keeps ignoring and the director does what any director would do.

@TuesdayFields
What did he do?

@StellaCavill
He walks straight on in.

@TuesdayFields
The director walks in on you in flagrante? You cannot make this up. @MichaelAngeloMovie didn't think to lock the door?

@StellaCavill
Apparently not. I could have died a million times over in THAT moment and the one that followed. I can't decide which was worse.

@TuesdayFields
How do you know it was the director? Did he shout 'cut'?

@StellaCavill
Glad you find it all so amusing. Remember the excited short director with the bald head at the Oscars? The one who won?
>> He was the guy who walked in!

@TuesdayFields
Haha! So apart from getting caught in the act, how was it/he?

@StellaCavill
If I'm honest, not as advertised.

@TuesdayFields
I need details.

@StellaCavill

@MichaelAngeloMovie came quicker than an @NetAPorter express delivery.

>> Which when it's a new pair of shoes or a dress is ideal, but when it's sex . . .

@TuesdayFields

Later rather than sooner, please gentlemen.

@StellaCavill

Well, it didn't help that during the whole thing, not that it lasted long, all I could think about was Will.

@TuesdayFields

Christ, @MichaelAngeloMovie must have been really terrible.

@StellaCavill

To make matters worse, while I was sitting in the trailer rearranging myself, my phone buzzes. Message from none other than @MerchBanker.

@TuesdayFields

No way!

@StellaCavill

Yes way! Long rambling text about how childish I was being with my deletions . . .

>> . . . followed by one apologising for having a go at me when I didn't reply to the first.

@TuesdayFields

Little did he know you were mid dalliance with an A-list movie star who suffers from premature ejaculation. What did you do?

@StellaCavill
Well @MichaelAngeloMovie didn't seem to care one bit about my humiliation.

@TuesdayFields
Shit?

@StellaCavill
Quite. In the end it was the movie director who played the hero. He snuck me into a set car with minimum fuss.
>> I think we can assume he's seen it all before . . .

@TuesdayFields
So where are you now?

@StellaCavill
I'm at the airport. Flying back coach. Looking at my Blackberry and wondering.

@TuesdayFields
Wondering what?

@StellaCavill
I should ignore him, right?

@TuesdayFields
The movie star or the ex?

@StellaCavill
Will. I think it's fair to say @MichaelAngeloMovie and me are done.

@TuesdayFields
Every good thing must come to an end, even if it's a premature one.

@StellaCavill

A bit of me feels relieved. Those movie types are otherworldly. Well the actors are.

>> The directors, on the other hand, are actually rather nice.

@TuesdayFields

Maybe you could heel him next?

@StellaCavill

Good idea. I'll send my knight in shining Armani, this guy Jerry Reuben, a pair of my best selling Stellars to say thank you . . .

@TuesdayFields

You're a class act, Stella Cavill.

@StellaCavill

But not a first class one right now. Off to curl up in coach. Not like I've got any other option.

@TuesdayFields

You've got plenty. Just sadly not where @DeltaAirlines economy class is concerned.

#AUGUST

TUESDAY FIELDS

@TuesdayFields: London
Happy Birthday to me, Happy Birthday to me, Happy Birthday to Tuesday Fields intrepid news hound, Happy Birthday to me!

Monthly Must:
Wave goodbye once and for all to bad men and welcome decent ones with open arms.

Monthly Must Not:
Cry about being a year older but not wiser.

Followers:
Suddenly a lot less than @JakeJacksonLive's.

STELLA CAVILL

@StellaCavill: New York, New York
'It is better to die on your feet than to live on your knees.'

Monthly Must:
Get out of personal and professional rut.

Monthly Must Not:
Rot.

Followers:
Not dead yet.

@StellaCavill
Happy 21st!

@TuesdayFields
Ha bloody ha. Seeing as it is my birthday and @Mum is throwing me a family-only party I think I'm well within my rights to cry if I want to.

@StellaCavill
Be my guest.

@TuesdayFields
Wish you were mine. Tonight's going to be a tiny little bit of hell spent amongst goody two shoes sisters and brash brother-in-laws.

@StellaCavill
Where's @Mum booked for the big occasion?!

@TuesdayFields
Where do you think?

@StellaCavill
Quags it is then!

@TuesdayFields
Again.

@StellaCavill
Again.

@TuesdayFields
@Mum has done me a small favour ahead of the festivities.
>> Given me the heads up that Dad has been spending more time than normal with the 'net' . . .

@StellaCavill
I'm presuming that doesn't mean he's on Twitter?

@TuesdayFields
Correct.
>> My moth-obsessed father has been single handedly decimating the butterfly population of Hampshire in order to give me a truly unique gift.

@StellaCavill
Oh God.

@TuesdayFields
So it looks like I'll have to accept whatever is coming my way, which I can only assume is a framed picture of several of his finest catches.

@StellaCavill
When did you get so lucky?

@TuesdayFields
Do you know I think it was round about the same time I met you.

@StellaCavill
Any idea what you'll get from @Mum?

@TuesdayFields
Probably something from @NigellaLawson's new range . . .
>> Although I'm not sure the domestic goddess is @Mum's favourite anymore, suspect jealousy is to blame . . .

RT @Mum: 'Nigella is drooling again darling, all over the rocky road squares she has just made.
>> Your father's eyes are on stalks. They're all the same darling, these men, all the same.'

@StellaCavill

A woman scorned. Forget her putting money in @NigellaLawson's pocket.

@TuesdayFields

I'm predicting then a couple of @JamieOliver mixing bowls, the odd saucepan, maybe even a whisk if I'm really lucky to stir things up with . . .

@StellaCavill

Like you need one of those to stir things up! Why the fixation with kitchenware for presents anyway?

@TuesdayFields

Think @Mum thinks as long as I'm in my Kensal Rise 10 x 5 kitchen cooking, I'm not out searching for Mr. Wrong.

@StellaCavill

Might explain why you're such a poor chef?!

@TuesdayFields

Truth is with my hours I can't go out and do any searching at all. >> @Mum will probably be suggesting I hand in my notice next in order to secure my long term future (bag Mr. Ordinary).

@StellaCavill

You know how proud she is deep down. You'll be all she talks about at the golf club.

@TuesdayFields

I'm really not so sure.

@StellaCavill

Well at least @Mum's not suggesting you're ready for tweaking like @Supermodel_1971 did on my last birthday. >> And the one before that, and the one before that too.

@TuesdayFields
So technically speaking, according to @Supermodel_1971, you are significantly overdue for a nip and tuck?

@StellaCavill
In her (twice-lifted) eyes I am considered well past my surgery sell by date.

@TuesdayFields
Swap?

@StellaCavill
What?

@TuesdayFields
Mothers?

@StellaCavill
Any day! Although I must acknowledge that mine is not all bad. She has been an incredible support since @MerchBanker and I split.
>> @Supermodel_1971 is the reason I have a roof over my head, after all.

@TuesdayFields
And how often is she reminding you of that?

@StellaCavill
She's being very well behaved, all things considered.

@TuesdayFields
Well, as for this singleton, not a boy in sight tonight, but one did record a special message for me this morning on @WUBTV . . .

@StellaCavill
Am I about to fall in love with @JakeJacksonLive all over again?

@TuesdayFields
Join the queue, and I don't just mean behind me!
>> His death defying reportage is making him something of a
hero with housewives pretty much everywhere.

@StellaCavill
The boy becomes a man – how are things in war torn Afghanistan?

@TuesdayFields
Pants for people who live there but evidently working wonders for
@JakeJacksonLive's career. @TheDailyGB all over him like a
rash.

@StellaCavill
Thought that paper had it in for anyone young, ambitious and
aspirational?

@TuesdayFields
Hmm. Interesting shift in policy has occurred. It seems to have
changed tack since it claimed to have found 'TV's Hot New
Talent'.

@StellaCavill
Wonders will never cease. He is getting some serious attention
then?

@TuesdayFields
@TheDailyGB ran this yesterday:

RT @TheDailyGB: 'Jake Jackson, 24, is winning the battle for
housewives hearts with his slick presentational style and heroic
broadcasts. His is a real success story . . .'

@StellaCavill
OMG. He'll be 'counting them out' then 'counting them back'
next!

213

@TuesdayFields

I know. It's all starting to get a bit much. Profile pieces in the press etc.

>> I mean the irony is he hasn't any real grasp that any of this is happening.

@StellaCavill

Well he will when he eventually touches down on UK soil. Imagine the reception he's going to get.

@TuesdayFields

Quite the star.

@StellaCavill

Isn't he just? Who'd have thought it eh?! So the message he sent you, what did it say?

@TuesdayFields

So he gathered the troops and right down the lens they belted out Happy Birthday to me!

>> Got @AnchorManTV bristling and @TheBossWUB high fiving.

@StellaCavill

Sounds like a result all round. @AnchorManTV still not letting you have any airtime with @JakeJacksonLive bar a birthday sing song?

@TuesdayFields

Nope. Not. If my day is going to end as badly as I think it might, at least it started well thanks to @JakeJacksonLive.

>> How very unlikely . . .

@StellaCavill

Not really, Tuesday. For someone as sharp as a tack you can be wonderfully naive.

@TuesdayFields
What do they say about ignorance?

@StellaCavill
It's bliss?

@TuesdayFields
Quite. An evening of crap chat and dead flattened butterflies beckons. Bye!

* * *

@StellaCavill
I just saw @JakeJacksonLive, live on American telly. @ABC News no less!

@TuesdayFields
Yes I heard yesterday he'd be filing reports for them now and again. @TheBossWUB desperate for the extra cash.

@StellaCavill
Well @JakeJacksonLive fits right in on the box stateside with his all American chiselled looks – and those biceps!

@TuesdayFields
Don't remind me, S.

@StellaCavill
Now, how was the dreaded birthday dinner last week? As bad as you thought it would be?

@TuesdayFields
In a word, yes. However, the upside to an otherwise unenviable evening is I've discovered that I've got physic powers.

@StellaCavill
How so?

@TuesdayFields
Well it was just as I pictured it; crap chat and dead flattened butterflies.

@StellaCavill
What about the @JamieOliver cookware?

@TuesdayFields
I was wrong on that, Delia's actually. As I suspected @NigellaLawson is in the doghouse for being such a prick tease.

@StellaCavill
@Mystic_Meg can breathe a sigh of relief then that you won't be taking her job.

@TuesdayFields
Hang on, let me consult my crystal ball. It says: for now my friend, for now . . .

@StellaCavill
I know we already agreed to swap mothers. While we're at it, fancy swopping lives?

@TuesdayFields
Love to. Where do I sign?

@StellaCavill
Right now I'd be happy to sign it all away.

@TuesdayFields
OK, but I'm warning you – August in London feels like April should. @WeatherWoman and I are this close to coming to blows.

@StellaCavill
What over?

@TuesdayFields
A recent string of terrible forecasts, which have left me without a mac and an umbrella in one too many rainstorms.

@StellaCavill
Perhaps she's trying to sabotage your well-styled flowing locks?

@TuesdayFields
Well-sprayed split ends don't you mean? Do you know what, I am starting to think she might be one of them.

@StellaCavill
One of whom?

@TuesdayFields
You know, 'them'.

@StellaCavill
Not following. Who are they exactly?

@TuesdayFields
Women who don't like other women.

@StellaCavill
Ah, met a few of those along the way.

@TuesdayFields
So what's going on, S? Must be something up for you to want to swap NYC for dreary old London.

@StellaCavill
Put it this way, being there would mean I wouldn't have to be here which at this very moment in time would be heaven.

@TuesdayFields

Heaven? You sure about that? You do know that with my life you get @Mum and moths in frames too?

@StellaCavill

Can't have the rainbow without the rain . . .

@TuesdayFields

So says Dolly Parton. So, serious for a second, where are you and what can possibly be so bad?

@StellaCavill

I'm at @AllThatGlittersIsGold's Hamptons hideaway for what can only be described as crunch talks.

@TuesdayFields

Oh shit. When did this happen?

@StellaCavill

He flew in from Washington on Friday. Got a call from his PA summoning me to East Hampton immediately.

@TuesdayFields

So aforementioned hideaway is actually right in the middle of the entire New York Summer social scene.

@StellaCavill

Quite. Four hours on the @HamptonJitney with a stale muffin, to arrive and discover that he is not a happy bunny.

@TuesdayFields

How bad?

@StellaCavill

He wanted to pull the plug on Stellars right there and then. Cut his losses.

@TuesdayFields

You can't be serious? Did you talk him round?

@StellaCavill

I tried everything. Best I could do is buy myself and Stellar Shoes a few more weeks, but that's all he's prepared to give me.

@TuesdayFields

A few weeks?

@StellaCavill

I know. You're thinking, what's the point aren't you?

@TuesdayFields

I'm thinking it's just . . . a few weeks. Well, it's not much time is it, S?

@StellaCavill

Translation: it's not enough time.

@TuesdayFields

Do you think it is?

@StellaCavill

Of course not. When it comes to Stellar Shoes I may be deluded but I'm not stupid.
>> I know it's not nearly enough time but I was willing to take whatever stay of execution I could.

@TuesdayFields

And that was it?

@StellaCavill

That, Tuesday, was it. The beginning of the end.

@TuesdayFields
Do you know what, Stella, you haven't worked this hard just to give up the fight because @AllThatGlittersIsGold says so.

@StellaCavill
You really think so?

@TuesdayFields
I know so. This ultimatum marks something but not necessarily the end. Anything can happen in a few weeks, you'll see.

@StellaCavill
I hope you're right, Tuesday.

@TuesdayFields
When am I not?!

@StellaCavill
I'm also hoping that was a rhetorical question.

@TuesdayFields
It was. Don't answer. Anyway you don't have time, you've got a business to save, so go and save it.

***

@StellaCavill
And I thought I had problems – have you heard about our good friend @PM_TV?

@TuesdayFields
Not lately. What's he done this time?

@StellaCavill
He's in hospital!

@TuesdayFields
Bloody hell. Again? Why?

@StellaCavill
Word has it he was spending the weekend in Malibu with an assortment of friends/hangers on and fell asleep in the sun.

@TuesdayFields
Since when has falling asleep in the sun necessitated another overnight stay in Cedars Sinai?

@StellaCavill
Apparently he's only gone and given himself third degree burns!

@TuesdayFields
OMG. What an idiot.

@StellaCavill
I know. What was he thinking?

@TuesdayFields
Well he does have rhino skin . . .

@StellaCavill
Evidently not when placed directly in plus 30 degrees centigrade.

@TuesdayFields
You know what's funny, I mean once he's recovered?

@StellaCavill
What?

@TuesdayFields
Every gossip rag in town is bound to speculate on whether he's had a chemical peel or not . . .

@StellaCavill

Ha! You're right. One silly decision to apply Hawaiian Tropic oil instead of factor 50 will cause him no end of grief.

@TuesdayFields

Looks like @PM_TV is going to be left red faced with this one.

@StellaCavill

Very good, Tuesday Fields, very good. So much more than a pretty face.

@TuesdayFields

I like to think so. It's not going to be a comfortable couple of weeks for him, that's for sure. Physically and publicly.

@StellaCavill

Do you think we should do something to ease the pain?

@TuesdayFields

Like what? It's a bit late for sun tan cream, don't you think?

@StellaCavill

How about we send him something, cheer him up a bit while he's convalescing?

@TuesdayFields

Like what? Chamomile lotion?

@StellaCavill

No Tuesday, not chamomile lotion.

@TuesdayFields

OK, how about a photo frame of dead butterflies. I've got one of those I could spare? No wait, I know! I've got it.

@StellaCavill
Finally. What?

@TuesdayFields
Let's send him @Mum. I could do with a break from her relentlessly banging on about how wonderful @JakeJacksonLive is.

@StellaCavill
And there you were thinking she'd hate the idea of you and a younger man/boy.

@TuesdayFields
She hasn't gone so far as to ask why I can't bring a nice boy/man like him home, but she's getting dangerously close.

RT @Mum: 'Oh darling, what a hunk that war reporter is on your show, Jake something isn't it? You haven't mentioned him before. Marvellous cheekbones.'

@StellaCavill
You're right. She is but a whisker away from demanding you bring @JakeJacksonLive out to the country for Sunday lunch!

@TuesdayFields
Well even if she does suggest it at least it's a way off. He's not even in this country, let alone the Home Counties.

@StellaCavill
He's all over TV screens here all of a sudden. Good Morning America, evening news, you name it. Even profiled in @People this week.

@TuesdayFields
What are you doing reading @People? Shouldn't it be @FinancialTimes finding new investors?

@StellaCavill
Trying to distract myself from the complete lack of new investors.

@TuesdayFields
Wish @Mum's nose would get out of @TheDailyGB.

@StellaCavill
Is it still spreading infertility panic attacks among mothers like ours? Or rather, yours.

@TuesdayFields
It's @JakeJacksonLive. If he carries on making the first five pages of @TheDailyGB I can guarantee @Mum won't be able to resist suggesting him for the gene pool.

@StellaCavill
You would have such beautiful children . . .

@TuesdayFields
Shut up, Stella! Where were we on @PM_TV's get well soon gift anyway?

@StellaCavill
I think you suggested sending him @Mum.

@TuesdayFields
Oh yes, I did. How very generous of me.

@StellaCavill
Selfless.

@TuesdayFields
So if not @Mum, which I still maintain is the best idea I've ever had, then what?

@StellaCavill
Fruit basket?

@TuesdayFields
Cuddly toy?

@StellaCavill
Good book?

@TuesdayFields
St Tropez body mousse?

@StellaCavill
You are not taking this seriously, Tuesday Fields.

@TuesdayFields
Yes I am. I'm taking it very seriously. Thought @PM_TV might like to even his skin tone out, that's all.

@StellaCavill
Last chance to offer up something useful before I decide for us both. Now, what's it going to be?

@TuesdayFields
OK . . . how about the promise of an exclusive Stateside interview with @JakeJacksonLive when he does finally return home?

@StellaCavill
That's more like the Tuesday Fields I know and love! That would get @PM_TV smiling again, but are you sure you can deliver it?

@TuesdayFields
I'll probably have to sleep with @JakeJacksonLive to secure it, but needs must! I do miss those biceps.
>> If it makes @PM_TV happy then of course I'll fall on my sword, or Jake's for that matter . . .

@StellaCavill
Didn't you once accuse @RedS0ledShoes and @HugoPr1nce of being media whores? I thought so. How a few months can change everything . . .

@TuesdayFields
But in my case I'd being doing it for a greater cause than for my own advancement. Big difference Stella, big difference.

@StellaCavill
Huge. Also a stark reminder of how generous and giving you are when you want to be.

@TuesdayFields
I'm not going to lie to you, it won't be easy and I doubt I'll enjoy it but this is what friends are for, right?

@StellaCavill
Right. @PM_TV will love you forever and me, by association, when I break the good news.
>> I'll let him know via his PA, publicist, agent or some other minion tomorrow.

@TuesdayFields
Hope he doesn't smile too hard and crack his chemical peel face, sorry, 'sunburn' . . .

* * *

@StellaCavill
@PM_TV is in love.

@TuesdayFields
Who with?

@StellaCavill
You, me, @JakeJakesonLive.

@TuesdayFields
Oh God.

@StellaCavill
You're not about to renege on your offer are you, Tuesday?

@TuesdayFields
No . . .

@StellaCavill
Good. You better not be or you're in deep trouble with me and @PM_TV.
>> He is besotted with your toyboy war reporter. Smitten. A bromance is born.

@TuesdayFields
Find me someone who doesn't want to sleep with @JakeJacksonLive!

@StellaCavill
@PM_TV's obviously drugged up to the eyeballs reading @People and watching @GMA.
>> Not seen him this excited about an interview since he secured Obama!

@TuesdayFields
Oh, don't be so ridiculous, Stella.

@StellaCavill
I'm serious. I also sense he could do with a bump in the ratings.

@TuesdayFields
Well we all have an @TheBossWUB and an @AllThatGlittersIsGold to answer to.

@StellaCavill
You were also on the money about his face . . .

@TuesdayFields
What about his face?

@StellaCavill
It did crack when I broke the news to him via Skype this morning.
Smile followed immediately with a yelp and doctors rushing to his aid.

@TuesdayFields
Knew we should have sent him @Mum instead!

@StellaCavill
So while I was breaking news this side of the Atlantic, have you
told @JakeJacksonLive what you've committed him to yet?

@TuesdayFields
You know what, I think I'll save it until he's back home. Buy
myself a bit more time to figure out how I tell him.

@StellaCavill
I thought you had already decided how?

@TuesdayFields
Hands up. I'd spent the night with Gordon. I'm feeling less brave
and sexy about the whole thing today.

@StellaCavill
Don't you dare back out of this, Tuesday, @PM_TV is counting
on you!

@TuesdayFields
I won't. Promise. Even if it costs me my self-respect.

@StellaCavill
What self-respect?

@TuesdayFields
Looks like I'll have a while to build up to the big moment in any case. @JakeJacksonLive is going into rebel territory tomorrow.

@StellaCavill
That sounds serious?

@TuesdayFields
It is. @TheBossWUB having high powered talks with channel execs here and in the US brainstorming about how to keep him safe etc.

@StellaCavill
Sounds dangerous, Tuesday?

@TuesdayFields
Yup. @AnchorManTV did his best to underplay the whole thing on air today. Made out it was no big thing. Tosser.

@StellaCavill
Like he'd ever go deep undercover.

@TuesdayFields
Deep under the covers to hide maybe.

@StellaCavill
Cowering in the corner of his five star hotel suite miles away from any imminent danger.

@TuesdayFields
How well you know @AnchorManTV!

@StellaCavill

@AnchorManTV does a pretty job of hanging himself these days. Too arrogant for his own good.

@TuesdayFields

Matter of time and certain he'll come a cropper way he's going. Couldn't happen to a nicer person . . .

@StellaCavill

I'm sure.

@TuesdayFields

Can see @TheBossWUB starting to panic about @AnchorManTV becoming a liability.

@StellaCavill

Has he said anything to you about it?

@TuesdayFields

Hell no, but I can tell he's fretting.
>> In this morning's meeting about a meeting, @AnchorManTV and him had a set to about our 'and finally' item, a piano-playing rabbit.

@StellaCavill

Did you really just type 'piano-playing rabbit'?

@TuesdayFields

Sadly, yes. Try taking viewers effortlessly from Afghanistan to Leeds where you'll find Pinky the piano playing rabbit.

@StellaCavill

Was that @AnchorManTV's argument because, I have to be fair, I've got some sympathy with him on this one?

@TuesdayFields
No! Would you believe the BAFTA winning broadcaster was backing Pinky for more airtime, not less, at the expense of @JakeJacksonLive!

@StellaCavill
But why?

@TuesdayFields
Good old fashioned classroom jealousy!
>> He's writhing with anger at how many column inches @JakeJacksonLive is getting – and now it looks like he's breaking America.

@StellaCavill
Broken America, I say. What's @TheBossWUB's take?

@TuesdayFields
Panicking.
>> Think he thought @AnchorManTV's green-eyed monster routine was funny at first but now he's terrified it's all going to bubble over on air.

@StellaCavill
And what do you think?

@TuesdayFields
I think he could be right.
>> Off the back of @JakeJacksonLive's live link today, @AnchorManTV made some cheap gag about him looking like he needed a good bath.

@StellaCavill
I'm sure he'd love nothing more than a good bath being that he's in a filthy warzone. What a See You Next Tuesday.

@TuesdayFields
Don't bring me into this!

@StellaCavill
See You Next Thursday then!

@TuesdayFields
You think you're in hell with Stellar Shoes and @AllThatGlittersIsGold making demands?
>> Well, at least you don't have to sit next to the Neanderthal man for a day job.

@StellaCavill
That's true. Let's hope I'm still agreeing with you come the end of September. By then any job would be better than no job.

@TuesdayFields
I wouldn't be so sure! How Audrey can have had three children by @AnchorManTV is beyond me.

@StellaCavill
On second thoughts . . . Yours is an unenviable task but some-one's got to keep the old goat in check and @TheBossWUB from having a coronary.

@TuesdayFields
No pressure then, on either of us.

@StellaCavill
None whatsoever, Tuesday, none whatsoever.

* * *

@StellaCavill
Are you sitting down?

@TuesdayFields
Not right this minute. On my way to meet @Mum for lunch.
Late.

@StellaCavill
Quags?

@TuesdayFields
Course. Prawn cocktail to start then dish of the day followed by
crème brulee.
>> No deviating from the set menu. What would be the point?

@StellaCavill
Presuming going with the flow is preferable for quiet life?

@TuesdayFields
I'm 34 years old, have flat, car and Sky television and yet still
@Mum feels the need to order for me.

@StellaCavill
So you're not sitting down?

@TuesdayFields
Not yet.
>> Long time on my backside coming so walking, well now
breaking into a gentle jog/sweat in effort to get there on time and
avoid early lecture.
>> Have been warned:

RT @Mum: 'Darling do not be late for lunch please. I'm meeting
Maggie Horton at Fortnum's later for tea.
>> Also have to fit in a hair appointment and Harrods food hall.'

@StellaCavill
Busy @Mum!

@TuesdayFields
So as you will have detected, no time to sit, let alone tweet, can it wait?

@StellaCavill
Well now here's the thing, no not really . . .

@TuesdayFields
Really?

@StellaCavill
Really.

@TuesdayFields
Well I'd better slow back down to a walk and you better tell me what's so important.

@StellaCavill
Good job you're in a rush because if you weren't I'm not sure I'd be able to just blurt this out ordinarily.

@TuesdayFields
Well come on then, Stella. Blurt it out. This better be worth making me late for @Mum.

@StellaCavill
Oh it is, trust me. It's about @SINternUK and @AnchorManTV.

@TuesdayFields
Oh God. What about them? He hasn't tried it on has he?

@StellaCavill
No, he hasn't tried it on.

@TuesdayFields

Well that's a relief, because if he had you'd have put me right off my prawn cocktail. What has he done, then?

@StellaCavill

@SINternUK delivered our latest brogues to him yesterday afternoon and he sort of revealed himself . . .

@TuesdayFields

I thought you said he hadn't tried it on?! Oh God now I do feel sick. How? What happened? Is @SINternUK OK?

@StellaCavill

Calm down, Tuesday. @SINternUK is fine.
>> He didn't try it on but it appears he did try something else on, in fact quite a lot of stuff according to @SINternUK.

@TuesdayFields

Spit it out Stella. What are you talking about?

@StellaCavill

@SINternUK knocked on his dressing room door first but, on no answer, just walked right in and caught @AnchorManTV in full drag!

@TuesdayFields

You've got be kidding me? No frigging way. She can't have done. He's been happily married to Audrey for about a hundred years.

@StellaCavill

Well Audrey may want to check her underwear drawer for missing items.

@TuesdayFields

Are you sure? Is @SINternUK sure?

@StellaCavill

I think the sight of @AnchorManTV wearing stockings, four-inch heels and red lipstick was pretty convincing . . .

@TuesdayFields

OMG. Stella this is unbelievable, scandalous, @TheDailyGB front page news.
>> If this got out it would be game over for @AnchorManTV, no question.

@StellaCavill

No question. What though, if anything, are you going to do with this information?

@TuesdayFields

I hate @AnchorManTV with a passion, but not enough to end his career just because it would make my life easier.

@StellaCavill

Glad to hear you have your moral compass back, even if @AnchorManTV's is all at sea.

@TuesdayFields

I'm not sure I've been terribly moral with @JakeJacksonLive. In the bedding or the avoiding.

@StellaCavill

Nothing that can't be fixed. So what are you going to do about @AnchorManTV?

@TuesdayFields

I'm not sure. This needs some careful consideration Stella.

@StellaCavill

Certainly food for thought . . .

@TuesdayFields
I've suddenly lost my appetite.

@StellaCavill
It's Quags – you'd have lost it by the time the prawn cocktail arrived anyway. Love to @Mum.

#SEPTEMBER

TUESDAY FIELDS

@TuesdayFields: London
Getting over being a year older and not wiser.

Monthly Must:
Confront @AnchorManTV about cross dressing.

Monthly Must Not:
Keep daydreaming about @JakeJacksonLive.

Followers:
Blossoming.

STELLA CAVILL

@StellaCavill: New York, New York
Catwalkers don't get the cream.

Monthly Must:
Let @Supermodel_1971 be maternal. Just this once.

Monthly Must Not:
Let @AllThatGlittersIsGold pull the plug on Stellar Shoes. Yet.

Followers:
Pushing up daisies.

@StellaCavill

I'm hungover and it's all @PM_TV's fault. Nothing to do with me. I'm clearly entirely blameless.

@TuesdayFields

Did he bring out the big wines? Let me guess, trying to impress?

@StellaCavill

Bingo. It's NY fashion week so dinner party attendees were beautiful but starving . . .

>> then there was me; token girl with the ability to string a sentence . . .

@TuesdayFields

. . . together. Assuming others not the sharpest scissors in the manicure set?

@StellaCavill

Precisely.

>> Models don't just look different, they are different. I suppose if I looked like them I wouldn't bother using my brain cells either.

>> I mean, what would be the point?

@TuesdayFields

Don't let @Supermodel_1971 hear you say such things.

@StellaCavill

Why do you think I'm typing it? She's still struggling to work out her new brick of a phone and she had me set up her Twitter account.

@TuesdayFields

No chance she'll be able to access tweets without you before at least September 2020?

@StellaCavill
None. Sick of models and modelisers. Rather stick pins in my eyes than spend the night with either.

@TuesdayFields
Don't mind dipping in and out of Fashion Week as long as it is just dipping. Seen any of the 'runway' shows yet, S?

@StellaCavill
Against my better judgment went to a couple at Lincoln Center. Mortifying. I fell out of a Choo on my way in.
>> Some random in my wake picked it up and put it back on for me.

@TuesdayFields
How very Cinderella and Prince Charming! Handsome?

@StellaCavill
Gay. Clearly.

@TuesdayFields
Well if I recall Prince Charming was as camp as Christmas . . .

@StellaCavill
Trust me, this one was not for turning.

@TuesdayFields
Sure?

@StellaCavill
Positive. Shortly after helping me back into my shoe he made a beeline to have his picture taken with Dolce & Gabbana.

@TuesdayFields
What does that prove?

@StellaCavill

Nothing except before he minced off he insisted on borrowing my compact to check his face and add bronzer to accentuate his cheekbones.

@TuesdayFields

Circumstantial evidence . . .

@StellaCavill

Pretty conclusive I'd say.

@TuesdayFields

My gaydar is so unreliable right now. Can't seem to get a reading on gay, straight or both at the moment.

@StellaCavill

Dating?

@TuesdayFields

Not. Going to bed at 8PM and getting up at 3AM is proving problematic for the old love life. I can't think why . . .

@StellaCavill

Glass half full, at least you don't feel like death warmed up today . . .

@TuesdayFields

No, I just feel dead. At least if I had a hangover there's a small chance an indiscretion would have accompanied it.

@StellaCavill

If it makes you feel any better, I've had to call in and say I'm working from home. Thank God @AllThatGlittersIsGold is in Washington today.

@TuesdayFields

What's he doing there?

@StellaCavill

The man has fingers in every pie. Which segues nicely back to dinner with @PM_TV and the entourage.

@TuesdayFields

I presume you're using the term 'dinner' loosely. NB Models present. Did you eat almost everything they didn't?

@StellaCavill

Almost! Same goes for the grog.

>> The need to drown my sorrows combined with competitive spirit got the better of me and I ended up taking @PM_TV on.

@TuesdayFields

@PM_TV has many shortcomings but height and girth aren't two of them. Presumably he drank you under the table, Miss Cavill?

@StellaCavill

Correct. And I ended up spilling the beans about Stellars' straits and how @AllThatGlittersIsGold is on the verge of pulling the plug.

@TuesdayFields

So what did the old sage have to say?

@StellaCavill

He took a second to compute then said in his best Professor Higgins, 'by Stella, I think I've got it'.

@TuesdayFields

Not like he doesn't know how to rise like a phoenix from the ashes. So did he, have it?

@StellaCavill

Have what?

@TuesdayFields
The answer, stupid!

@StellaCavill
I'm unconvinced. He said he'd work on it and get back to me with a plan. When your last hopes rest with @PM_TV, you know you're in trouble.

@TuesdayFields
Don't underestimate him. If anyone can bounce back from disaster, it's @PM_TV. He's done it how many times?

@StellaCavill
True, but I'm not counting any chickens just yet.

***

@StellaCavill
You confronted @AnchorManTV yet?

@TuesdayFields
Not yet. Every time I think about it, I want to vom.

@StellaCavill
Think about him wearing nylons or think about confronting him?

@TuesdayFields
Both. What makes it worse is he is still behaving like a pig. If he wasn't I might consider a stay of execution.

@StellaCavill
You wouldn't?

@TuesdayFields
I might. No, you're right, I wouldn't. It's just finding the right moment to have it out with him.

@StellaCavill
Can I make a suggestion that it isn't while you're live to the nation?

@TuesdayFields
Can you imagine?
>> 'After the break we'll be finding out what it is about wearing women's clothing that my co-host @AnchorManTV finds so appealing . . .
>> . . . See you in three.'

@StellaCavill
It would boost the ratings.

@TuesdayFields
And send @TheBossWUB round the bend. Not sure he's got the constitution to defend a cross dressing TV stalwart publicly or privately.

@StellaCavill
Not exactly defensible behaviour for a breakfast telly host, I suppose?

@TuesdayFields
Not. Although judging by today's segment put forward by @AnchorManTV and that originated in @TheDailyGB . . .
>> . . . I might have to bite the bullet and confront him sooner rather than later . . .

@StellaCavill
What pearls of wisdom has he found in that rag to regurgitate to the masses?

@TuesdayFields
Stress incontinence in older mothers.

@StellaCavill

Oh God. @Mum would have had a field day with that. Presumably iPhone on silent for said segment?

@TuesdayFields

Absobloodylutely. Voicemail she left was . . . interesting.

@StellaCavill

How bad was it?

@TuesdayFields

The segment or the voicemail?

@StellaCavill

I am assuming the voicemail was bad, how did the piece play out?

@TuesdayFields

@AnchorManTV suggested this was one for me as inevitably I would be inflicted by it if I had a child sometime soon . . .
>> . . . what with already being 34+ etc. Bastard.

@StellaCavill

Bastard!

@TuesdayFields

Bit optimistic of him, I thought. Need to find someone to have sex with first.

@StellaCavill

Ha.

@TuesdayFields

Anyway, it gets worse.

@StellaCavill

How can it get worse?

@TuesdayFields
Next up on the show, post segment on stress incontinence in older mothers, was guess who?

@StellaCavill
No?

@TuesdayFields
Yes. None other than @JakeJacksonLive.

@StellaCavill
Who you're still not allowed to speak to on air?

@TuesdayFields
Correct. Anyway, @AnchorManTV made one of his ill-humoured 'jokes' to @JakeJacksonLive at the top of their slot.

@StellaCavill
How on earth did he manage to link stress incontinence in older mothers to a warzone?

@TuesdayFields
In a word, badly. @AnchorManTV 'jested' about @WUBTV's amazing breadth . . .
>> . . . pointing out to @JakeJacksonLive how seamlessly we were going from my future anatomical concerns to Afghanistan.

@StellaCavill
Christ. What did @JakeJacksonLive say?

@TuesdayFields
Actually he put @AnchorManTV back in his box.
>> Suggested tactfully that this was not the time or the place for getting cheap thrills from making cheap quips.

@StellaCavill
God, how apt. Hope it hit home.

@TuesdayFields
Doubtful. @AnchorManTV's skin makes a rhino's look softer than a baby's bottom.

@StellaCavill
So @JakeJacksonLive to the rescue . . .

@TuesdayFields
As @AnchorManTV keeps reminding me, I'm 34+. I should be able to rescue myself, shouldn't I?

@StellaCavill
You do most days. Today just wasn't one of them.
>> Be grateful for small mercies, at least you're not like me and still being rescued by your mother!

@TuesdayFields
It just feels wrong. I don't think I want to be rescued.

@StellaCavill
Are you throwing a diva strop?

@TuesdayFields
Maybe. Just a little one. But I don't want to be rescued Stella, not now, not ever!

@StellaCavill
Well I think it's romantic, especially if it's a handsome war correspondent doing the rescuing.

@TuesdayFields
Well there is that – but you know what this means?

@StellaCavill
What?

@TuesdayFields
I'm going to have to reassert myself, which means telling @AnchorManTV all I know.

@StellaCavill
As they say, knowledge is power . . .

@TuesdayFields
. . . and I intend to use it. Night, S.

@StellaCavill
Night, She-Ra. I mean, Tuesday.

***

@TuesdayFields
Did it!

@StellaCavill
@AnchorManTV? I really hope you didn't.

@TuesdayFields
Not him you idiot but I did do 'it', I confronted him, straight up.

@StellaCavill
How? What? When? Where? Who?

@TuesdayFields
Cornered him in his dressing room after today's programme. Can you believe he was actually putting more make-up on?
>> Most men can't wait to wipe the stuff off.

@StellaCavill
Um, given what we both know, yes, I can believe it. Go on . . .

@TuesdayFields
So, I began by making the point that I couldn't give a toss what he did in his private life but others might . . .
>> . . . i.e. @TheBossWUB and viewers of @WUBTV.

@StellaCavill
That must have pricked up his ears. Then what?

@TuesdayFields
I told him I cared about his career.

@StellaCavill
But you don't.

@TuesdayFields
No, but I was being nice. Tactical.

@StellaCavill
Come again?

@TuesdayFields
Realistic. The advertisers like him, Stella. Truth is Wake Up Britain needs him. The last thing the station needs right now is a scandal.
>> Especially after the @KateKingTV debacle.

@StellaCavill
Fair enough. Now get to the bit where he's forced to defend wearing stilettos, will you?!

@TuesdayFields
I told him there was no easy way to say this but I knew the secret he was hiding . . .

@StellaCavill
And he said . . .

@TuesdayFields
He said he was mortified that I'd found out he was shagging Susan, the middle-aged, completely useless make-up artist!

@StellaCavill
You're kidding?

@TuesdayFields
Nope!

@StellaCavill
No reference whatsoever to cross-dressing?

@TuesdayFields
None!

@StellaCavill
Priceless!

@TuesdayFields
I know. So now I know he's been messing around on his wife Audrey as well as wearing her clothes!

@StellaCavill
This is too much. Does he know you know?
>> Not about Susan, but about wearing Audrey's clothes and, come to think of it, probably Susan's too?

@TuesdayFields
He does now. I thought while @AnchorManTV and I were sharing . . .

@StellaCavill
Bet that threw him. So what did he say?

@TuesdayFields
It wasn't so much what he said, more the colour he went.
>> Or rather the colour his shirt collar went after he'd sweated profusely all over it.

@StellaCavill
You got him, Tuesday.

@TuesdayFields
Apparently so. Predictably, once the reality of his situation had sunk in the begging began.

@StellaCavill
How very macho.

@TuesdayFields
Well as we know he is all man . . . Not.

@StellaCavill
So what did @AnchorManTV say?

@TuesdayFields
He asked if we could put the whole sorry business and details of his sordid secrets behind us.
>> I agreed to – if he'd just cut me some slack on set.

@StellaCavill
Sounds like you let him off lightly.

@TuesdayFields
Let's hope he keeps sight of that over the coming days.

@StellaCavill

So from now on you'll be permitted to cross live to @JakeJacksonLive . . .

>> . . . despite @AnchorManTV's previous protestations about you not being up to the task?

@TuesdayFields

Yup. Roll on Monday morning . . .

@StellaCavill

. . . and a conversation with @JakeJacksonLive! Where exactly is the boy wonder these days anyway?

>> I haven't watched the news properly for weeks.

@TuesdayFields

Deeply embedded somewhere in Afghanistan.

@StellaCavill

Deeply embedded, eh?

@TuesdayFields

As @JakeJacksonLive will tell you, Stella Cavill, this is not the time or the place for humour.

>> Actually I think he may have got himself in a bit of a pickle. Didn't check in as expected today.

@StellaCavill

When he gets word you'll be on the end of the live link on Monday, I'm sure he'll surface.

@TuesdayFields

Oh shut up, Stella. Let's hope he does.

* * *

@StellaCavill
Smiling . . .

@TuesdayFields
Why? Not that you shouldn't be but you haven't been much of late. New apartment?

@StellaCavill
No, although thoroughly enjoying being an uptown girl.

@TuesdayFields
Consider yourself an Upper East Side cliché.

@StellaCavill
I am actually Midtown. It's perfect. I have a doorman, I'm walking distance to window shopping at Bergdorf's . . .
>> . . . and since Will's life is downtown I have considerably reduced the danger of bumping into him.

@TuesdayFields
Any word from @MerchBanker?

@StellaCavill
Radio silence. Odd, isn't it, how the most important person in your life goes from everything to, well, nothing.

@TuesdayFields
No such thing as a platonic relationship between a man and a woman.

@StellaCavill
You really believe that?

@TuesdayFields
How many of your ex-boyfriends do you still talk to?

@StellaCavill

Seems a waste though, doesn't it?

>> I mean when you've been through so much with someone then piff paff poof, they're gone, out of your contacts and your life.

@TuesdayFields

Piff paff poof?! Who do you think you are, The Great Soprendo?

@StellaCavill

Why is it we always end up reminiscing about childhood TV personalities?

@TuesdayFields

Because we are stuck in a nostalgia rut. Just don't get bogged down in fond memories where @MerchBanker is concerned.

>> Those rose-tinted spectacles are responsible for warping realities time and time again.

@StellaCavill

He's probably shacked up with some 22-year-old model anyway.

@TuesdayFields

What, Will? A modeliser?

@StellaCavill

One man for every ten women here in NYC, and beautiful ones too. Odds are stacked in his favour, Tuesday.

@TuesdayFields

Stop speculating. Torturing yourself won't get you anywhere, least of all where you need to go, which is forwards.

@StellaCavill

When did you get so wise?

@TuesdayFields

Just recently. Nice of you to notice. So what is making you smile then? @PM_TV left word about his master plan yet?

@StellaCavill

No, but he's being very cryptic. Said I've got to go to a taping of his show next week.

@TuesdayFields

What for?

@StellaCavill

He won't say. I've tried to find out who @PM_TV's interviewing, but nothing forthcoming.

@TuesdayFields

He wouldn't tell you?

@StellaCavill

Said it was best I didn't know. Google drew a blank so the info must be on lockdown.

@TuesdayFields

Maybe he's found you a new man?

@StellaCavill

I'd rather he'd found me a way to save Stellar Shoes. Can't believe it's curtains at the end of the month unless I work a miracle.

@TuesdayFields

Don't write off @PM_TV yet. So come on, your smile, who's responsible if not @PM_TV?

@StellaCavill

The funniest new follower. Some character called @BugsBunnyMovie.

@TuesdayFields

Other sorts of rabbits raising a smile I get, but this one, what's so special about him?

@StellaCavill

He's hilarious. Keeps tweeting me jokes. Nothing dodgy, just plain old, simple, funny.

"RT @BugsBunnyMovie: 'Before you criticize someone, you should walk a mile in their shoes.

>> That way, when you criticize them, you're a mile away and you have their shoes.'

@TuesdayFields

Correction. Stellar Shoes!

@StellaCavill

Suspecting an American, with the 'z' – and that's a Jack Handey quote. So older.

@TuesdayFields

How can you be sure he's not some nutter?

@StellaCavill

I can't be. Not even sure he is a 'he'. Might be a 'she' for all I know, but I suspect not by the tone.

>> Wisecracks are interspersed with compliments.

@TuesdayFields

So some random person, masquerading as a cartoon rabbit, is rampantly stalking you and you're flattered?

@StellaCavill

Yes.

@TuesdayFields
You're mad.

@StellaCavill
Well, whatever. @BugsBunnyMovie's amusing me.

@TuesdayFields
So you replied to this @BugsBunnyMovie? Please say you're not following him back? Is he now DM'ing you?

@StellaCavill
Calm down, Tuesday Fields. No, I'm not following him.
>> You know I have a strict policy of only following (dis)reputable people that I've met or verified organizations I approve of.

@TuesdayFields
Or men that you are stalking . . . @MichaelAngeloMovie.

@StellaCavill
Or men that I'm stalking . . . @No1Sportsman right back at you.

@TuesdayFields
So @BugsBunnyMovie is following you, you are not following him – is he aware that you are aware that he/she even exists or no?

@StellaCavill
As of this morning yes.
>> I read an article by Twitter founder @Jack and he says tweeting back occasionally to random followers is a good way to accumulate more.
>> Apparently word spreads you're accessible.

@TuesdayFields
How accessible?

@StellaCavill
Not that accessible! Here's the weird thing about Bugs, though . . .

@TuesdayFields
What, other than a grownup pretending to be a cartoon character?

@StellaCavill
No, the strange thing about @BugsBunnyMovie is it took me forty minutes to compose a 140 character tweet back.

@TuesdayFields
Is that supposed to mean something?

@StellaCavill
Put it this way, responding to @MichaelAngeloMovie never required that level of brainpower.

@TuesdayFields
Speaking of which, whatever happened to @MichaelAngeloMovie?

@StellaCavill
Whatever happened to @No1Sportsman?

@TuesdayFields
Touché.

***

@StellaCavill
I'm in love with @PM_TV.

@TuesdayFields
Expand and fast before I jump to all sorts of hideous conclusions.

@StellaCavill

So I arrive at the studio as instructed wondering what I'm about to walk into, when I walk into, well @RubyRainerUS.

@TuesdayFields

The @RubyRainerUS? Humanitarian campaigner, global TV icon, agony aunt and general modern day Saint?

@StellaCavill

That would be the one.

@TuesdayFields

OMG Stella. Even @Mum now watches @RubyRainerUS. 50+, childless, single yet somehow she's cultivated being a heroine to @TheDailyGB readers.
>> Remarkable.

@StellaCavill

I know! @Forbes even went so far as to put her second in list of the top 100 most influential women, second to guess who?

@TuesdayFields

Who?

@StellaCavill

Only Oprah bloody Winfrey!

@TuesdayFields

Blimey. Funny story about Oprah bloody Winfrey. Actually less story, more another of @Mum's famous gaffes . . .

RT: @Mum 'Tuesday, Opera Wimpey is talking to Dr. Phil about boyfriends with baggage.
>> Why are they worried about men's luggage? Is this what they call dumbed down television? Ghastly. Mum.'

@StellaCavill

I don't know what part of that anecdote I like more, @Mum calling @Oprah 'Opera Wimpey' or the fact that she thinks baggage means luggage.

@TuesdayFields

Suddenly Wake Up Britain looks frightfully high-brow.

@StellaCavill

I wouldn't go that far, darling.

@TuesdayFields

So what happened when @PM_TV met @RubyRainerUS, I mean after the director said 'cue'?

@StellaCavill

@PM_TV did what he does best and made her cry.

@TuesdayFields

Not again? Losing track of the number of celebrities caught on camera blubbing like babies on his watch.
>> Grown men, women, power houses of entertainment, politics and business. No one is safe.

@StellaCavill

Not even Opera Wimpey's protégé @RubyRainerUS.

@TuesdayFields

Not even her. Tell me, did he reach out and place his hand gently on her arm whilst probing about childhood abandonment issues?

@StellaCavill

How did you guess?

@TuesdayFields

You can take the hack out of Fleet Street but you can't take Fleet Street out of the hack.

>> Classic interviewing technique. Brilliant when used on the vulnerable.

@StellaCavill

You're as bad as he is!

@TuesdayFields

What can I say? I've learnt from the best.

@StellaCavill

Not @AnchorManTV?

@TuesdayFields

No you idiot, I was talking about @PM_TV. Studied his style for years. I'd never own up to that of course.

@StellaCavill

Of course.

@TuesdayFields

So, let's be clear about this – @PM_TV lures you to the studio to introduce you to @RubyRainerUS? But why?

@StellaCavill

You're supposed to be the journalist, you figure it out . . .

@TuesdayFields

Holy shit! That's @PM_TV's grand plan.

>> All he needs to do is make the introduction, big you up a bit and hey presto you're on her show promoting Stellar Shoes . . .

>> . . . to an audience of millions. That's brilliant!

@StellaCavill
Isn't it?!

@TuesdayFields
I think I might love @PM_TV too.

@StellaCavill
Who'd have thought he could be quite so, well, thoughtful. I spent most of the day pinching myself to check I wasn't dreaming.

@TuesdayFields
Rock on @PM_TV. Heart of a hack but also of gold.

@StellaCavill
I know. What's more as @PM_TV ushered @RubyRainerUS off set and in my direction, he referred to me as the 'smartest young entrepreneur I know'.

@TuesdayFields
Promise me you didn't do what I did on my first day on the @WUBTV sofa and freeze on the spot?

@StellaCavill
Didn't have time to, thank God. Actually you'd be rather impressed.
>> Left the jumping up and down like a demented moron till I was safely out of sight afterwards.

@TuesdayFields
So what happens next, @RubyRainerUS's new best friend?

@StellaCavill
Tweeting to you and booking flight to LA simultaneously.
>> Turns out @RubyRainerUS's doing a show all about entrepreneurial women, of which I am now considered one!

@TuesdayFields

Get you, Nicola Horlick, although Horlick does have about eight kids so really you're just below her in the high achievement rankings.

\>> But still, good work you!

@StellaCavill

Thanks, T. Stella Cavill coming to a showbiz sofa near you sometime soon . . .

@TuesdayFields

I'll notify @TheBossWUB. Make him aware of the next big thing in sofa chat stateside.

@StellaCavill

Oh God, no! Don't. My bravado couldn't be more of a front. I'm terrified.

@TuesdayFields

Swap that for excitement immediately. When is the big day anyway?

@StellaCavill

Next month. I'm so nervous. Anything more than an audience of five and I'm rendered speechless. @RubyRainerUS + entourage was about my limit.

@TuesdayFields

The good news is @RubyRainerUS is already on your side. Loves a working girl.

@StellaCavill

You may want to rephrase that . . .

@TuesdayFields

Put it this way. Last thing she is going to do is stitch you up.

\>\> First thing she's going to do is put Stellar Shoes where it should be, firmly on the map.

@StellaCavill

Do you really think so?

@TuesdayFields

Think? Know so. After that airing @AllThatGlittersIsGold will be putting his house and everything else on you.

@StellaCavill

@AllThatGlittersIsGold has now granted Stellars a stay of execution until Christmas. I live to fight another day . . .

@TuesdayFields

Good times are a coming Stella Cavill, you'll see.

@StellaCavill

And are things better your end? How's the king of the TV stitch up, our good friend now we know all his dirty secrets, @AnchorManTV?

@TuesdayFields

Behaving better, actually. He was fully prepared to let me interview @JakeJacksonLive the other day but it never happened.

\>\> Someone pulled the plug on it – but it wasn't @AnchorManTV, which is something, I suppose.

@StellaCavill

@AnchorManTV finally seeing the error of his ways?

@TuesdayFields

Thanks to the wonder that is @SINternUK. She'll have her work cut out with that flood of orders you'll be getting post @RubyRainerUS.

@StellaCavill
She better!

@TuesdayFields
How will you cope?

@StellaCavill
Let's cross that bridge when I come to it. I haven't really thought about it . . .

@TuesdayFields
Liar.

@StellaCavill
You're right I am lying. So shoot me!

@TuesdayFields
Then what would men the world over do for footwear? You really haven't thought this through at all have you Stella?

@TuesdayFields
Trust me, Tuesday, I have. I really have.

* * *

@StellaCavill
Tuesday, I've just seen it trending worldwide. Where are you? Pick up your phone.

@TuesdayFields
Can't. In newsroom doing live hits on air. Not a clue what's happening or where @JakeJacksonLive is.

@StellaCavill
What the hell happened?
>> I know you said @JakeJacksonLive was going into enemy

territory, but didn't he have guides, security, the army to protect him?

@TuesdayFields

His 'fixer' screwed him over. Double crossed him, sold him to the Taliban apparently along with his local cameraman and sound guy.

@StellaCavill

Jesus.

@TuesdayFields

I knew something was up, Stella. Had a gut feeling when he didn't show for Monday's live link.
>> Figured not even @AnchorManTV was capable of sabotaging that.

@StellaCavill

How are you bearing up?

@TuesdayFields

Other than feeling physically sick about the whole thing I'm muddling through. Just. Problem is we don't even know if he's still alive.
>> Not a word from the kidnappers.

@StellaCavill

@JakeJacksonLive's a western journalist, a household name in both the US and UK – he's far too valuable to harm, he's a commodity.
>> Whoever has him will want to use that to get what they want.

@TuesdayFields

And what the hell is that?

@StellaCavill
God knows. But they'll find him. I'm sure they will.

@TuesdayFields
The worst part so far is, because the office know that he and I are close, they took a straw poll on who should ring his Mum.

@StellaCavill
And you drew it?

@TuesdayFields
It's all very sad, Stella. Turns out @JakeJacksonLive is all she has. His dad died young and she brought him up more or less all by herself.
>> Lovely lady, so horrible for her.

@StellaCavill
This gets worse.

@TuesdayFields
I know. Christ what if he's dead?

@StellaCavill
He's not. Think only positive thoughts and just focus on doing your job while others do theirs to find him.

@TuesdayFields
I'm not sure I can keep it together.

@StellaCavill
You can and you will. In the meantime I'll give @AllThatGlittersIsGold a call, see if he or any of his Washington contacts can help.

@TuesdayFields
Thanks, S. This is a nightmare and what makes it so much more awful is I've been such an arse.

@StellaCavill
What about?

@TuesdayFields
@JakeJacksonLive. All this time I've been trying to bury my feelings towards him.
>> Right now he could be being buried and I'll never get to tell him any of it.

@StellaCavill
Any of what?

@TuesdayFields
How I feel Stella! How I feel. The thing is, I know it sounds mad but, I think I might be in love with @JakeJacksonLive . . .

@StellaCavill
Durr! Tell me something I don't know. You'll get him back and the chance to tell him all of this, I know you will.

@TuesdayFields
I can't believe it's taken me a war, a kidnapping and a possible murder for me to finally see what was right in front of me all this time.

@StellaCavill
I can. Now keep calm and carry on. I'll make that call.

TUESDAY FIELDS

@TuesdayFields: London
Putting on a brave face.

Monthly Must:
Think only positive thoughts about @JakeJacksonLive's plight.

Monthly Must Not:
Think negative thoughts about @JakeJacksonLive's plight. Not at all. Not ever.

Followers:
Increasing, thanks to rubber necking brigade. Sickos.

STELLA CAVILL

@StellaCavill: New York, New York
The best foot forward.

Monthly Must:
Conquer panic attacks brought on by the prospect of @RubyRainerUS appearance.

Monthly Must Not:
Vom all over @RubyRainerUS and other guests on show.

Followers:
Possible upturn imminent . . .

* * *

@StellaCavill
Any news?

@TuesdayFields
Nothing. We don't know where @JakeJacksonLive and his crew are.
>> Am permanently on call to do hits throughout the day but my
current updates is – we know nothing.

@StellaCavill
Exhausted?

@TuesdayFields
Nothing compared to what Jake's going through. We don't even
know if he's alive, S.

@StellaCavill
Of course he is, Tuesday. @AllThatGlittersIsGold continues to
be hopeful which says a lot, trust me.

@TuesdayFields
Suspect he's just trying to put a positive spin on the situation to
make you, and subsequently me, feel better.

@StellaCavill
@AllThatGlittersIsGold? He never puts a positive spin on
anything, ever. This leopard is not about to change its spots.
>> If he's hopeful, we should be.

@TuesdayFields
I wish I could believe you.

@StellaCavill
If he's sure, it's because his contacts in Washington are. They'll
find @JakeJacksonLive alive and well. They have to.

@TuesdayFields

I hope so. God Stella, why was I such a bitch? Karma is coming back to bite me on my ever increasing backside.

@StellaCavill

Tuesday, you weren't cruel, just aloof.

@TuesdayFields

I was. I was a total cow bag. You know it and so do I.

@StellaCavill

@JakeJacksonLive doesn't think it though. He knows you were just being an insecure idiot. He'd forgive you in an instant given the chance.

@TuesdayFields

I'm worried neither of us will get that chance. I just – there's so much I want to say. .

@StellaCavill

And you will. With all that's going on, is @AnchorManTV behaving a little at least?

@TuesdayFields

Strangely yes. He's being the perfect gentleman. Think he's even surprised himself.

@StellaCavill

Stuff like this only serves to remind you life's too short for petty squabbles and one-upmanship. Even @AnchorManTV can see that.

@TuesdayFields

He came in this morning with purple hair. I howled with laughter. First time I've found myself doing that recently.

@StellaCavill
Something tells me that wasn't the reaction he was looking for?

@TuesdayFields
No, but at least it lightened the mood. Clearly moved on from Audrey's underwear drawer and now rooting around in her bathroom cabinet.

@StellaCavill
Why doesn't that surprise me?

@TuesdayFields
Here's the thing though, Stella, he was more than happy to admit he'd cocked up and read the instructions wrong.
>> Left the colour on for 60 minutes instead of 60 seconds!

@StellaCavill
Presumably he didn't go on air with purple hair?

@TuesdayFields
Susan, the make-up woman whose face has been stuck in permanently mortified mode ever since their dalliance came to light . . .
>> . . . hid it with a coating of black hair-thickening spray.

@StellaCavill
I bet he looked a fright. Unlikely @TheDailyGB won't pick it up.
>> What is it about middle-aged men growing old disgracefully
– or at least with bad dye jobs?

@TuesdayFields
The Just for Men brigade . . .

@StellaCavill
Why do they do it? It's not like it makes them look any younger.

@TuesdayFields

On the contrary, it makes them look so much older.

>> As much as I'd love to tell @AnchorManTV how ridiculous his hair colour is, now's not the right time. Not when we're finally getting on.

@StellaCavill

Funny how a crisis pulls people together, isn't it?

@TuesdayFields

Bit like 'panic passion'. People end up shagging people they ordinarily wouldn't go near with a barge pole in times like these.

@StellaCavill

You're not about to go to bed with @AnchorManTV and risk him walking away with your La Perla are you?

@TuesdayFields

What do you think?! I'm deeply protective over my La Perla!

@StellaCavill

You know what you need?

@TuesdayFields

News?

@StellaCavill

That and . . . a new pair of patents to keep @AnchorManTV onside now you've got him where you want him.

@TuesdayFields

Send them immediately.

@StellaCavill

Incoming. I'll carry on bugging @AllThatGlittersIsGold too. See if he can shed any light on @JakeJacksonLive's predicament.

@TuesdayFields
Please, S. I never was any good at patience and right now no news is not good news.

***

@TuesdayFields
Distract me. I need to think about something, anything but @JakeJacksonLive six feet under or worse.

@StellaCavill
I know you're going through it at the moment but what could possibly be worse than six feet under?

@TuesdayFields
Stop picking holes and distract me, will you?
>> I keep looking at my Twitter feed in hope, but all I'm getting is news about @KimKardashian's lipstick line.

@StellaCavill
Would something on Jake's whereabouts really go on Twitter first?

@TuesdayFields
Unless it was hushed up for some reason. Where all news breaks these days.

@StellaCavill
How the world's changed.

@TuesdayFields
Listen to yourself! Next you'll be doing an @Mum and reminding me I'm not getting any younger . . .

@StellaCavill
Well, you're not!

@TuesdayFields
Pot, kettle . . .

@StellaCavill
Thanks.

@TuesdayFields
Sorry, S. If you think about it . . . Twitter, well it's sort of responsible for us too, isn't it?

@StellaCavill
What do you mean?

@TuesdayFields
Well would we be friends if it weren't for Twitter?

@StellaCavill
I guess maybe not . . .

@TuesdayFields
Pen pals for the 21st century . . .

@StellaCavill
A transatlantic friendship separated by an ocean . . .

@TuesdayFields
. . . but united by a social network!

@StellaCavill
When did we start completing each other's sentences?

@TuesdayFields
I think sometime around June.

@StellaCavill
Christ alive. Anyway, cyber pal, I need your help, see it as a welcome distraction from all the worrying you're doing over @JakeJacksonLive.

@TuesdayFields
Happily. Hit me with it.

@StellaCavill
My first foray into television – we tape @RubyRainerUS tomorrow. I feel sick with nerves about it.

@TuesdayFields
I am crap cyber pal, completely forgot. Sorry Stella. Isn't that filmed out of LA? Where are you?

@StellaCavill
JFK. About to jump on @VirginAmerica.

@TuesdayFields
Don't you mean you're about to go disco dancing 35,000 feet up?

@StellaCavill
Typical @RichardBranson. Meddling with tradition. What's so wrong with regular strip lighting on planes anyway?

@TuesdayFields
I think you just answered your own question. I rather like the pink and purple glow.
>> Reminds me of heady days stumbling out of some club at 6am in Ibiza.

@StellaCavill
Now who's sounding old?!

@TuesdayFields
Word of warning, S.
>> Don't get too caught up on the instant messaging between seats unless you're 100% certain the person on the other end is worth it.

@StellaCavill
Speaking from experience?

@TuesdayFields
Had a minor issue shaking off someone sporting a Branson-esque beard on landing at LAX a while back.

@StellaCavill
Are you 100% sure it wasn't actually @RichardBranson?! Never been into facial hair. Doesn't agree with my sensitive skin.

@TuesdayFields
Stubble rash poses way too many uncomfortable questions about exactly where your face has been.

@StellaCavill
Moving swiftly on – what were you doing in LA anyway?

@TuesdayFields
Endlessly traipsing round agents and production companies. City of angels, my arse. More like city of self-obsessed wannabes.

@StellaCavill
So Hollywood's gravitational force not pulling you towards it, Tuesday Fields?

@TuesdayFields
Not. Baggage reclaim at LAX being remodelled, sign overhead read, 'It's not just the people here who are under construction'.
>> I mean what sort of a place brags about that?

@StellaCavill

LA makes me feel old too. And in need of surgery. Let's agree never to move there.

@TuesdayFields

You won't get any argument from me on that. So how you feeling about your TV debut being beamed live into 80 million American homes?

@StellaCavill

Terrified. Everything I've ever worked for is at stake. I cannot cock this up, Tuesday.

@TuesdayFields

You won't. Just be yourself and the rest will take care of itself.

@StellaCavill

Just be myself? A jibbering, teetering-on-the-brink wreck?!

@TuesdayFields

OK, not that. I meant the you before the fear of appearing on @RubyRainerUS took hold.

@StellaCavill

Easier said than done.

@TuesdayFields

What you wearing? Block colours work best.

@StellaCavill

One step ahead of you. @RubyRainerUS's producers gave me the heads up on that, gone for my fallback @DVF purple number.

@TuesdayFields

Old ones are the best ones . . .

@StellaCavill
So long as it's only dresses you're referring to, I agree. Producer says I'll pop right out.
>> I pretended to know what she was talking about. What was she talking about?

@TuesdayFields
She means you'll stand out without confusing the camera.
>> Much better because you want the viewer to concentrate on what you're saying, not wearing, Stella.

@StellaCavill
No I don't!

@TuesdayFields
Yes you do! This is a once in a lifetime opportunity for you to sell your shoes to the world, Stella Cavill.

@StellaCavill
What if I can't? What if it doesn't work?

@TuesdayFields
It will work. A few minutes of TV time can change everything. Look at Susan Boyle.

@StellaCavill
It's hardly the same thing, Tuesday. She's a global sensation.

@TuesdayFields
And that's exactly what your shoes could be if you play your cards right, look the part and don't speak like a blithering idiot.

@StellaCavill
@PM_TV's pre-warned me to speak in my finest Queen's English and very, very slowly.

@TuesdayFields

Bang on. You don't want an audience of 80 million not being able to understand a word you're saying.

@StellaCavill

It's not really that many, is it?

>> Oh dear God, I feel sick, again. Took @PM_TV an age to learn to stop gabbling in front of Hollywood A-Listers.

>> I've got one seven minute segment.

@TuesdayFields

That'll be enough! And anyway . . . @PM_TV . . . for 'gabbling' read 'fawning'.

>> It's only because he's madly in love with pretty much every single one of his interviewees, male or female.

@StellaCavill

True!

@TuesdayFields

How is @PM_TV? Haven't had a proper catch up with him since the 'sunburn' incident.

@StellaCavill

Been all virtual communication for me too – I've only seen him lately on my TV.

>> God he looks a sight for sore eyes some days. I can help him with his shoes, but the rest of it . . .

@TuesdayFields

Still wearing those hideous ties?

@StellaCavill

Someone needs have a word in his ear about block colours being preferable to multi colour.

@TuesdayFields

That's unfair – @PM_TV follows block colour rule to the letter. Regularly teams brown jackets with solid lime green shirts, you know that.

@StellaCavill

Do you think there's a chance he's colour blind? I wouldn't want to make fun of him if he's actually got a problem.

@TuesdayFields

Like he doesn't make fun of those who can't spell on Twitter! What if they're dyslexic?

@StellaCavill

Point.

@TuesdayFields

Thing is right now, Stella, you don't feel like you could ever be critical or joke about @PM_TV again, do you?
>> His recent display of good-hearted generosity has clouded your judgment!

@StellaCavill

How did you guess?
>> Right now I have nothing but love for the man. @PM_TV's the reason why I'm on @RubyRainerUS and may manage to salvage Stellar's.

@TuesdayFields

Did he tell you he sent me a note about @JakeJacksonLive?

@StellaCavill

No. Did he allude to knowing anything about you two? I've said nothing, I promise.

@TuesdayFields

He doesn't know a thing. Sent message to me to pass onto the Wake Up Britain team.

@StellaCavill

And the office really doesn't suspect?

@TuesdayFields

They suspect but they don't know.
>> No one knows about @JakeJacksonLive and me, except you. They assume we were close but the rest of it – not a clue.

@StellaCavill

Are close, Tuesday.

@TuesdayFields

Are close. Safe travels and good luck tomorrow, Stella Cavill. Rooting for you from across the pond!

@StellaCavill

Argh, don't remind me. Palpations again.

@TuesdayFields

Breathe, speak slowly and most importantly sell, sell, sell!

* * *

@TuesdayFields

So, how did it go? The @RubyRainerUS show? Dying for a debrief . . .

@StellaCavill

Well I did it! Went by – so fast! Once we were on set that is. The preparation seemed to be interminable, mind you.

@TuesdayFields
American TV in the HD age. Crude calculations suggest you would have to be in hair and make up for several hours at least. Right or wrong?

@StellaCavill
Right! Hours. And I'm an utter fidget at the best of times.

@TuesdayFields
On a scale of 1-10, 1 being @PM_TV, 10 being @JoanCollinsOBE, how big was your hair?

@StellaCavill
11! I did my best to pat it down in a restroom just before we went on, but with little success. Amazed I could fit through the studio doors.
>> As for the make up . . .

@TuesdayFields
Applied with a trowel?

@StellaCavill
Caked. I looked like something out of Priscilla, Queen of the Desert.

@TuesdayFields
Funny thing about telly is somehow it hides a multitude of sins. You'll see. It'll have looked great on screen.
>> Trust me, I'm a TV presenter.

@StellaCavill
Meanwhile in real life I found wrinkles I didn't know I had yet.

@TuesdayFields
Welcome to my world.

@StellaCavill

I don't know how you do it, day in day out. The whole experience was terrifying. I walked out needing more than just the one stiff drink.

@TuesdayFields

Problem for me is, Gordon isn't really a viable option at 9AM, unless of course I did have a problem. Which I don't, yet!

@StellaCavill

After that ordeal there was only one thing for it. I'm tweeting from the airport bar.

@TuesdayFields

Ha! So come on, S, stop procrastinating, tell me how did it go, the show?

@StellaCavill

Bit out of body really.
>> Good news was, the only other woman in fashion was a designer doing affordable clothes for the larger lady – @FTF_tweet.

@TuesdayFields

Growing market in the US.

@StellaCavill

Literally. Did you know 1 in 3 Americans are obese with ever expanding numbers?

@TuesdayFields

Know? No. Guessed? Yes. Any word on your website getting ever expanding sales post @RubyRainerUS?

@StellaCavill

Hold your iPhone. @AllThatGlittersIsGold is calling – give me ten and I'll let you know . . .

***

@TuesdayFields

That's ten and then some! Well, what did he say . . . ?

@StellaCavill

Website crashed!

@TuesdayFields

Oh no! Stella, I'm so sorry, what terrible timing.

@StellaCavill

Crashed with hits, Tuesday! Looks like we're going to sell out of stock!!!!!

@TuesdayFields

Stella – that's amazing!!!

@StellaCavill

Just got to keep the momentum up now.

@TuesdayFields

Keep the momentum up? I wouldn't worry about that. Sounds like you're full steam train ahead . . .

@StellaCavill

@RubyRainerUS has put us on her site for 24 hours following the broadcast so that should help. Niche to mainstream, here we go . . .

@TuesdayFields

Here's hoping @AllThatGlittersIsGold will drown you in Cristal to celebrate.

@StellaCavill

Not out of the woods yet, but things suddenly looking considerably better. He said the phone was ringing off the hook – can you believe it?!

@TuesdayFields

Yes. Until now I think you're the only one that couldn't. Well you and @AllThatGlittersIsGold. He'll be eating his words.

@StellaCavill

Speaking of success stories, why didn't you tell me about the love letters?

@TuesdayFields

Love letters?

@StellaCavill

From @TheDailyGB to Tuesday Fields . . . kept quiet about those, TF.

@TuesdayFields

How do you know about that?

@StellaCavill

Couldn't sleep last night for nerves and needed something to send me off . . .

>> . . . so figured I'd trawl through @TheDailyGB online and guess what I found?

@TuesdayFields

A piece on yours truly?

@StellaCavill

Not just the one either! Turns out they think you are, wait for it . . .

>> RT @TheDailyGB: 'a breath of fresh air. Viewing figures on @WUBTV have rocketed thanks to Tuesday Fields, 34 . . .

>> . . . and her inimitable style of broadcasting'.

@TuesdayFields
I love the way they always have to crowbar my age in.

@StellaCavill
And house prices, they're terribly keen on including them, too. Anyway, congrats – looks like you've turned it right around, T.

@TuesdayFields
It's only because @AnchorManTV isn't trying to stitch me up every five minutes anymore that suddenly I don't look quite terrible.

@StellaCavill
We both know it's not just that. @Mum must be chuffed?

@TuesdayFields
Admittedly she couldn't wait to get to the golf club after the latest @TheDailyGB piece.

@StellaCavill
About time the two of us had a bit of good fortune. Wish we could celebrate together Tuesday Fields. Maybe New Year?!

@TuesdayFields
Seems fitting doesn't it? It's just . . .

@StellaCavill
You don't feel like celebrating?

@TuesdayFields
I really don't.

@StellaCavill
They'll find him. They will.

@TuesdayFields
God I hope so. I really do.

* * *

@TuesdayFields
When were you going to tell me?

@StellaCavill
When was I going to tell you about what?

@TuesdayFields
I couldn't sleep last night so . . . I looked at your Twitter account.
STELLA?!!!

@StellaCavill
I know! Can't quite believe it myself.
>> Every time I press refresh I gain another tranche of followers.
Since @RubyRainerUS it's been ridiculous.

@TuesdayFields
I wasn't talking about the number of followers Stella . . .

@StellaCavill
You weren't?

@TuesdayFields
Nope . . .

@StellaCavill
Oh . . .

@TuesdayFields
We need to talk . . .

@StellaCavill
We do?

@TuesdayFields
Stop pretending you don't know what I'm referring to. Your '@' twitter mentions – discuss!

@StellaCavill
I'm not sure what you can possibly mean?!

@TuesdayFields
You know exactly what I mean . . . @BugsBunnyMovie!!!

@StellaCavill
What of him?

@TuesdayFields
Don't do that.

@StellaCavill
Do what?

@TuesdayFields
Make out he doesn't matter.

@StellaCavill
He doesn't.

@TuesdayFields
Judging by the amount of tweets back and forth between you and the rampant rabbit, clearly he does!

@StellaCavill
So we've been tweeting – so what?

@TuesdayFields
I see he liked the purple DVF number you were wearing on @RubyRainerUS.

@StellaCavill
He thought I 'popped'.

@TuesdayFields
And I saw the incessant jokes . . .

@StellaCavill
They're funny, no?

@TuesdayFields
And the begging for you to follow him back?

@StellaCavill
He was very persuasive . . .

@TuesdayFields
Stalkers tend to be! Are you out of your mind?

@StellaCavill
Well here's the thing – and I was waiting for the opportune moment to tell you.

@TuesdayFields
I don't believe you.

@StellaCavill
I didn't want to bother you. You've got more important things to think about.

@TuesdayFields
All the more reason for you to keep my spirits up and my mind off what I can't change.

@StellaCavill

Alright. Consider myself told.

@TuesdayFields

So you are following Bugs. Why?

@StellaCavill

Did you look at who his followers were?

@TuesdayFields

I saw he had about 30, while he was following at least three times that many.
>> In Twitter-world, he's about as cool as @JCRClarksonesq's jeans.

@StellaCavill

Quality not quantity – that 30 happens to include a mutual 'friend' . . .

@TuesdayFields

What common denominator could you possibly have with @BugsBunnyMovie?

@StellaCavill

@MichaelAngeloMovie.

@TuesdayFields

What?! Hang on – the biggest film star in the world and your ex squeeze is following @BugsBunnyMovie?

@StellaCavill

'Ex-squeeze'?
>> That's stretching the truth a bit far! Anyway, just a shame I can't ask aforementioned film star why he's following @BugsBunnyMovie.

@TuesdayFields
Still no speaks after the in flagrante director moment?

@StellaCavill
Still.

@TuesdayFields
You think you met @BugsBunnyMovie with @MichaelAngeloMovie?

@StellaCavill
Maybe.

@TuesdayFields
But you only met @MichaelAngeloMovie twice? I say 'met' . . .

@StellaCavill
Shut up Tuesday. And it was more than that.

@TuesdayFields
Four?

@StellaCavill
More! Well. Anyway, I thought we agreed morals don't count with movie stars so stop your preaching Miss Fields!

@TuesdayFields
Wouldn't dream of it – but I'm still confused, who is @BugsBunnyMovie?

@StellaCavill
Well him knowing @MichaelAngeloMovie certainly narrows the field down considerably.

@TuesdayFields
You don't think it's . . .

@StellaCavill
I think it might be.

@TuesdayFields
Surely not?

@StellaCavill
I know it's crazy, but there was really only person it could be . . .

@TuesdayFields
The bald, slightly chubby director?

@StellaCavill
The triple Oscar, four time Emmy, seven time Tony award winning director . . .
>> . . . who was incredibly gallant after possibly the most humiliating moment of my life, you mean?

@TuesdayFields
There is that.

@StellaCavill
Naturally I couldn't help myself and Googled aforementioned director, Jerry Reuben.

@TuesdayFields
What gives?

@StellaCavill
It turns out he has an exclusive three picture deal with Warner Bros.

@TuesdayFields
So @BugsBunnyMovie is Jerry Reuben. Who'd have thought it?

@StellaCavill
I haven't confronted Jerry/Bugs yet – do you think I should?

@TuesdayFields

Not yet. Get him to reveal more about himself before you 'fess up to what you think you know.

@StellaCavill

I'm 99% sure it's him.

@TuesdayFields

Not certain then?

@StellaCavill

Not. For the foreseeable, I'll carry on calling him Bugs and appear to be none the wiser.

@TuesdayFields

Hang on a sec, you're not thinking Bugs is a potential, are you? Seriously Stella?

@StellaCavill

I don't know. Maybe I'm deluded but there's something there . . .

@TuesdayFields

Is it the 'naked' truth?

@StellaCavill

Don't remind me. Brain over brawn every time for me, T. Say what you want about @MerchBanker, but he was clever.

@TuesdayFields

Yes but he had brawn too . . .

@StellaCavill

When we started out, not so much, though.
>> I know there's probably limited potential with @BugsBunnyMovie on that front – but he's bright and very funny, Tuesday . . .

@TuesdayFields
Well on the plus side the ones that don't look like George Clooney do tend to work harder in bed.

@StellaCavill
Because they have to?

@TuesdayFields
Just that.

@StellaCavill
Not if they've won three Oscars. Then they can have any Barbie doll in town.

@TuesdayFields
Ah, but you can't have a conversation with Barbie. Well you can try, but she won't give you much back.
>> What does @PM_TV do whenever he's around models and the like?

@StellaCavill
Invite me along to provide the conversation.

@TuesdayFields
Exactly.
>> When @MerchBanker eventually figures that out he'll come running back with his tail between his legs begging for you to take him back too.

@StellaCavill
You think so?

@TuesdayFields
I know so. Problem for him is by then you won't want him because you'll be hopelessly devoted to someone else.

@StellaCavill
So I'm forgiven for entertaining and following back @BugsBunnyMovie?

@TuesdayFields
When I said you'd be head over heels with AN-other than @MerchBanker I wasn't referring to @BugsBunnyMovie, Stella . . .

@StellaCavill
I know YOU weren't . . .

***

@StellaCavill
Guess what @PM_TV's just topped?

@TuesdayFields
Not himself?

@StellaCavill
He may want to after this – @GQ_magazine's worst dressed poll . . . again.

@TuesdayFields
Told you those ties would be the death of him!

@StellaCavill
Just the ties?

@TuesdayFields
And a lot more besides. Well, if he will wear speedos at Sandy Lane he only has himself to blame.

@StellaCavill
At least he's consistent in his appalling sartorial choices.

@TuesdayFields
The irony is none of the garb @PM_TV wears is cheap, he spends a small mortgage on that stuff.
>> But as we've said before S, money can't buy you class.

@StellaCavill
Or style. If he would just scale it all down a bit . . .

@TuesdayFields
What, like not pair pink shirts with purple suits and paisley ties?

@StellaCavill
I don't know why he camps it up quite so much. He'd run a mile if a friend of Dorothy's came calling.

@TuesdayFields
I doubt that.

@StellaCavill
He would! You know he would!

@TuesdayFields
Run from a friend of Dorothy's yes, but a mile? @TheDailyGB's done a feature on successful Brits abroad. Obviously @PM_TV was in it . . .

@StellaCavill
And . . .

@TuesdayFields
Well let's just say he doesn't look like he's been running anywhere much lately.

@StellaCavill
So not only has he been named GQ's worst dressed male, but he's also being lambasted for sudden weight gain?

@TuesdayFields

Evidently being a star has its drawbacks.

>> You remember that, Stella Cavill, while you're making millions and hanging out with @RubyRainerUS and co.

@StellaCavill

She's now emailing me!

@TuesdayFields

What?

@StellaCavill

I think @RubyRainerUS wants to be my friend. Can you believe it?

@TuesdayFields

Actually, I can. Well just don't go forgetting the rest of us, that's all I'm saying on the subject.

@StellaCavill

Likewise @TheDailyGB's new favourite sweetheart. Who'd have thought it?

@TuesdayFields

Not me and certainly never @Mum. Making the most of it while I can, S, Christ knows what's around the corner . . .

#NOVEMBER

TUESDAY FIELDS

@TuesdayFields: London
Finding solace in work, Gordon and chocolate.

Monthly Must:
Locate @JakeJacksonLive with or without
@AllThatGlittersIsGold's help.

Monthly Must Not:
Rise to @Mum and remember she knows not what she
says.

Followers:
Escalating.

STELLA CAVILL

@StellaCavill: New York, New York
You can still have your feet on the ground and wear
good shoes.

Monthly Must:
Make the most of a meteoric surge in shoe sales.

Monthly Must Not:
Put all eggs in Bugs' basket – until 100% certain about
him anyway.

Followers:
Immense improvement.

***

@StellaCavill
Any word about Jake?

@TuesdayFields
Nothing.

@StellaCavill
Hang in there, Tuesday. Remember no news is good news.

@TuesdayFields
You sound like @TheBossWUB. I can see he's beside himself with worry about @JakeJacksonLive but typically, playing it down.

@StellaCavill
Well he's got the ship to steer. He knows everyone will be taking their cues from him and he doesn't want to invoke mass panic.

@TuesdayFields
I guess I just know @TheBossWUB well enough to know that he blames himself sending Jake into a warzone before he was 'ready'.

@StellaCavill
@JakeJacksonLive may be young but he's not stupid. He'll find a way out of this situation whatever it is, wherever he is.

@TuesdayFields
I just wish we had some idea where that bloody well is.
>> Even @AnchorManTV expressed genuine concern earlier. Told me it happens to the best of them.

@StellaCavill
Does he include himself in that analysis?

@TuesdayFields
Before I discovered his wicked side he might have, now he wouldn't dare.

@StellaCavill
Want something to take your mind off @JakeJacksonLive's plight?

@TuesdayFields
Anything.

@StellaCavill
@Supermodel_1971 is flying over to NYC for a long weekend shopping trip.

@TuesdayFields
Well it could be worse . . .

@StellaCavill
How?

@TuesdayFields
She could be coming for a lot longer than a 'long weekend'!

@StellaCavill
Point. But I don't have the time to entertain her every whim, Tuesday. I am simply too busy taking orders!

@TuesdayFields
OMG. How many? Is Stellar Shoes taking over the world and more importantly if it is can I come along for the ride?

@StellaCavill
Yes and yes!!!

@TuesdayFields

Well thank the Lord (or rather @PM_TV and while we're at it) for @RubyRainerUS, for showing men everywhere the light.

>> I assume you're coping with the surge in interest just fine?

@StellaCavill

Well @SINternUK has had to fly over from London to hire and train three new bodies.

@TuesdayFields

Do you think you'll have to move her over to NYC permanently?

@StellaCavill

No, I need her in the UK and besides I can't see anyone or anything ever tearing her away from SW3.

@TuesdayFields

If she's really brave then one day I guess she might make it to Knightsbridge or even Belgravia . . .

@StellaCavill

Like I say, it would take quite something or someone to extract her from @KingsRoad!

@TuesdayFields

Presumably she's gone into organizational overdrive?

@StellaCavill

She's no walking cliché, that's for sure.

>> What a turn around, it seems my preparations for liquidation have had to be shelved in favour of expansion!

@TuesdayFields

And all thanks to @PM_TV and his master plan.

@StellaCavill
@PM_TV master planner extraordinaire!

@TuesdayFields
Clearly he was so busy planning Stellar Shoes' recovery he completely forgot about his own.

@StellaCavill
What you talking about?

@TuesdayFields
His follower count, have you seen it of late? Dwindling . . .

@StellaCavill
With all this extra work it's as much as I can do to log on and catch up with you, my London friend . . .
>> . . . let alone look at what's going on with @PM_TV's fan base.

@TuesdayFields
Aren't you the busy bee?

@StellaCavill
That sounded terrible. Sorry.

@TuesdayFields
You'll be asking for water at room temperature in your new boardroom on Park Avenue before long . . .

@StellaCavill
It wasn't that bad!

@TuesdayFields
It is only a matter of time. @RubyRainerUS has a lot to answer for.

@StellaCavill

Yes, namely thousands of dollars' worth of new orders, but I take your point. Now what's up with @PM_TV? Tell me, am all yours.

@TuesdayFields

Really?

@StellaCavill

Really.

@TuesdayFields

You're not in the middle of a conversation with @SINternUK multitasking?

@StellaCavill

Not.

@TuesdayFields

You are, you liar!

@StellaCavill

Fine – guilty as charged. How on earth did you know that?!

@TuesdayFields

I told you, I have psychic powers.
>> Or rather the ability to predict hideous birthday surprises and know when my friend Stella Cavill is two-timing me with @SINternUK!

@StellaCavill

Right, have sent @SINternUK packing. Promise I'm all yours. Shout.

@TuesdayFields

@LordTw1tter has upped the ante. Offering prizes money can't buy for all those willing to 'unfollow' @PM_TV.

@StellaCavill

How underhand is that?

@TuesdayFields

Very unsportsmanlike.

@StellaCavill

Grown men behaving like boys, again.

@TuesdayFields

Problem is, that whenever @PM_TV rises to the bait and challenges @LordTw1tter back . . .

>> . . . it accelerates the numbers and not in a positive direction.

@StellaCavill

So @PM_TV's NYE resolution to meet the million mark looking less likely?

@TuesdayFields

Yup and rumour has it in the @WUBTV office that @PM_TV's American network is starting to wriggle in their support for him.

@StellaCavill

Oh God. It's worse than we both thought then?

@TuesdayFields

The odd interview with the @RubyRainerUS's of this world notwithstanding, it seems our @PM_TV has got issues with his demographic.

@StellaCavill

There must be a way to lure the viewers in and make them stay.

@TuesdayFields

What he needs is a really good story . . .

>> . . . a reason for people to care about watching instead of all this showbiz crap and blowing smoke up Mariah Carey's arse.

@StellaCavill
What you're saying is that he needs a big exclusive with someone the world wants to hear from?

@TuesdayFields
Don't you say it, Stella.

@StellaCavill
He'll be home in no time.

@TuesdayFields
He better be. Earth calling @JakeJacksonLive, no one wants to play hide and seek anymore, come out come out wherever you are. Please Jake.

***

@TuesdayFields
RT @Mum: 'Tuesday darling, @TheDailyGB doing a 2for1 at the best Conrans. Lunch at Quags then Christmas shopping after? >> We'll have such fun! Mum x'

@TuesdayFields
Such fun. Last bloody thing I feel like. When you rolling out the red carpet for yours?

@StellaCavill
@Supermodel_1971 touches down in a few hours. After that I can kiss goodbye to my life as I know it. Well, for a few days anyway.

@TuesdayFields
Just be grateful it's only a few days. Different proposition when they're on the doorstep.

>> Can't you get @AllThatGlittersIsGold to take her to lunch or something?

@StellaCavill
There's an idea. He is in NY and seriously getting under my feet. Would kill two birds.

@TuesdayFields
You never know, they might hit it off . . .

@StellaCavill
I've kept them apart this long but now all I care about is them keeping each other entertained . . .
>> . . . and out of the office long enough for me to manage the madness.

@TuesdayFields
While you're not watching who knows what might happen . . .

@StellaCavill
Tuesday, stop winding me up. It's only lunch . . .
>> . . . and thanks to your speculating about what might happen between @AllThatGlittersIsGold and @Supermodel_1971 I'm going to struggle to eat mine!

@TuesdayFields
Just don't say I didn't try telling you what could happen . . .

@StellaCavill
It won't. I hope.

@TuesdayFields
Hope springs eternal.

@StellaCavill
I don't want to think about it. Tell me, what's @Mum said about @JakeJacksonLive going MIA?

@TuesdayFields

Well she doesn't know what you know and I'm not about to tell her either.

>> However, like most British housewives she's 'very troubled' by the whole episode.

@StellaCavill

Do you think she suspects anything's going on between you and our absent war reporter/hero?

@TuesdayFields

God no. Last week she asked me if I was a lesbian. Naturally the seed of doubt had been sown by @TheDailyGB.

@StellaCavill

But a fortnight ago they loved you. And now you're a lesbian?!

@TuesdayFields

Yup!

RT @Mum: 'Darling, @TheDailyGB has done a survey. It's terribly shocking. Are you a lesbian? @TheDailyGB seems to think you might be.

>> You're not, are you darling? Mum'

@StellaCavill

They didn't single you out?

@TuesdayFields

Half page picture on page 3, again. Caption read 'Tuesday Fields: Single, 30-something, but is she as straight as she says she is?'!

@StellaCavill

And the survey?

@TuesdayFields
Some crappy findings about an increase in the number of girls turning lipstick lesbians post 30.

@StellaCavill
If only they knew.

@TuesdayFields
Knew what?

@StellaCavill
What a whorebag you really are!

@TuesdayFields
Charming! Slut . . .

@StellaCavill
Well if anything at least it confirms what we always knew.

@TuesdayFields
Which is?

@StellaCavill
How fickle the media world can be.

@TuesdayFields
Have to hand it to @TheDailyGB, though, they've done a pretty good job of painting a fairly accurate picture of @JakeJacksonLive.

@StellaCavill
How're they reporting his capture there?

@TuesdayFields
In a word, thoroughly.

@StellaCavill
Same stateside, just seen a bulletin on morning telly.

@TuesdayFields
Very early morning telly.

@StellaCavill
@JakeJacksonLive's kidnapping seems to have really caught the public's imagination here.
>> Naturally everyone is hoping for a happy outcome . . .

@TuesdayFields
Praying . . .

@StellaCavill
@AllThatGlittersIsGold is onto it, Tuesday.

@TuesdayFields
When he's not wining and dining @Supermodel_1971. Surprised he's got the time for anything else.

@StellaCavill
Don't. @AllThatGlittersIsGold has not got to where he is without being able to juggle women and work.

@TuesdayFields
So why haven't you dared introduce him to @Supermodel_1971 until now?

@StellaCavill
Because my mother is a different breed to most.

@TuesdayFields
I thought you were comfortable with the idea of her distracting him so you could get on?

@StellaCavill

It's a woman's prerogative to change her mind. You of all people should know that Tuesday Fields, mentioning no names @JakeJacksonLive . . .

@TuesdayFields

Any word from @AllThatGlittersIsGold on @JakeJacksonLive, S? Anything at all?

@StellaCavill

Not yet, but he assures me he is on the case.

@TuesdayFields

I hope so. Just applying war paint/brave face for next bulletin. Show must go on and all that.

@StellaCavill

Speaking of faces, not sure how long mine will be in its current incarnation.

@TuesdayFields

Concerned that @Supermodel_1971 will spend most of her time here trying to convince you it's time for surgery?

@StellaCavill

Or at least a little (read, a lot) of Botox! @Supermodel_1971 has ways of making you look younger, or rather her doctor does . . .

@TuesdayFields

Oh sod it. If it shuts her up. What's a bit of poison in the face between mother and daughter?

@StellaCavill

Tuesday! I'll let you know which filler I plump for . . .

@TuesdayFields
Beware the nasty prick won't you? I'm talking about the needle, not @Supermodel_1971's surgeon . . .

@StellaCavill
I'll be keeping both at arms length.

@TuesdayFields
We'll see . . . On air in five then lunch with @Mum. We'll be talking lesbianism, @JakeJacksonLive and Dad's dead moths.
>> Almost as painful as an injection. Almost . . .

* * *

@TuesdayFields
Next year when I say I'm going Christmas shopping with @Mum, remind me of this moment will you?

@StellaCavill
Which moment?

@TuesdayFields
This one. The one where I tell you if I ever, ever, say I'm going Christmas shopping with @Mum, you shoot me.

@StellaCavill
Harrods food hall isn't what it used to be?

@TuesdayFields
I wish I knew. We didn't get that far. We did, however, get to Camberwell, although sadly not with our self-respect in tact.
>> Well, not @Mum's anyway.

@StellaCavill
Did you treat her to any of their famous carrots?!

@TuesdayFields
Wish I frigging had.
>> Might have stopped the tirade of abuse she threw at a parking
warden, car pound man and . . . the duty officer at the local nick . . .

@StellaCavill
You are joking? And I thought @Supermodel_1971's company
was proving painful!

@TuesdayFields
I made the mistake of suggesting @Mum park her car on the
street and not as usual, the Hilton NCP.
>> Failed to see bay had been suspended, cue tow truck . . .

@StellaCavill
Oh bugger.

@TuesdayFields
It wouldn't have been so bad if they hadn't carted the bloody
thing off to a car pound in the arse end of nowhere.

@StellaCavill
Why Camberwell?

@TuesdayFields
That's exactly what @Mum said to the parking warden except
she didn't put it quite that nicely.
>> I never thought I'd hear @Mum use the 'C' word and I don't
mean 'Camberwell'.

@StellaCavill
She didn't?!

@TuesdayFields
And the rest . . .

@StellaCavill
What would @TheDailyGB say?

@TuesdayFields
Well actually they might have quite a bit to say.
>> @Mum made such a massive tit of herself at the pound the guy in charge of it called the police.

@StellaCavill
What?

@TuesdayFields
Dad had to break away from moth catching and come and get us from the station.
>> @Mum detained and cautioned for using foul and/or abusive language to a police officer!

@StellaCavill
You're kidding?

@TuesdayFields
Wish I was.

@StellaCavill
How is @Mum?

@TuesdayFields
Right now, not feeling very clever. Throwing my name into the mix has come back to bite her too.

@StellaCavill
Cringe! Why did she have to do that?

@TuesdayFields
You might well ask. I could have died when I heard the fatal words:

>> 'Do you know who my daughter is? Wake Up Britain will do an exposé on you people!'

@StellaCavill
@Mum!

@TuesdayFields
Thanks to her tirade, she is not only having to attend anger management courses for the next six weeks, but she's about to become famous.

@StellaCavill
Oh no . . . Not @TheDailyGB?

@TuesdayFields
I did try and warn her before she tore the head off the duty sergeant . . .
>> . . . that being the mother of a daughter on the telly carried a small amount of tabloid interest.

@StellaCavill
And what did she say?

@TuesdayFields
She wasn't exactly listening. Inevitably the press has found out about @Mum's wayward behaviour and @TheDailyGB is all over it.

@StellaCavill
So tomorrow's front page?

@TuesdayFields
Could well be @Mum unless some seriously mega breaking news story usurps her.

@StellaCavill
I'm sorry Tuesday, but I'm literally crying with laughter!

@TuesdayFields
Well stop. Immediately! So that was my day, how was yours?

@StellaCavill
Less painful than yours but not entirely painless if you catch my drift . . .

@TuesdayFields
Caught. Face frozen?

@StellaCavill
In time.

@TuesdayFields
Well with @Supermodel_1971 for a mother, it was only a matter of time, I suppose.

@StellaCavill
It's weird, T. I was trying to make expressions in the mirror this morning but nothing doing.

@TuesdayFields
Presumably if something had moved you'd have grounds for suing the surgeon?

@StellaCavill
Excuse-moi. I haven't completely morphed into an American.

@TuesdayFields
Not completely but let's FACE it you're well on your way.

@StellaCavill
Very good, Tuesday. If I could frown, I would.

* * *

@TuesdayFields
Hold the front page, @Mum is on it!

@StellaCavill
Oh God. Howling with laughter. Headline?

@TuesdayFields
'Morning Anchor's Mum, 64, Cautioned by Cops'.

@StellaCavill
They've played it down, then? And true to form they have included her age as well. She must be loving that.

@TuesdayFields
Especially since she's been celebrating turning 59 for the past five years.

@StellaCavill
That sounds familiar. @Supermodel_1971 will be getting me to change her name to @Supermodel_1981 one of these days.

@TuesdayFields
I keep telling @Mum it'll be tomorrow's fish and chip paper, but she's not buying it. Every copy in the village shop however . . .

@StellaCavill
Presuming she sent your dad out at first light to beat the rush?

@TuesdayFields
The upside is he won't be short of newspaper this winter to start a fire with.

@StellaCavill
But can he buy the silence of the villagers I wonder?

@TuesdayFields

Sadly not. Nothing he can do to stop Marjorie mouthing off. It's like giving R-Patz fresh blood.
>> She'll dine out on this for months.

@StellaCavill

At least @Mum might not believe everything she reads in @TheDailyGB from now on.

@TuesdayFields

Every cloud . . . @Mum's national humiliation is dominating my day. What's new with you, pillow cheeks?

@StellaCavill

Glad to see in all the drama you've not lost your sense of humour. Actually, the strangest thing happened today . . .

@TuesdayFields

What, other than you suddenly not being able to move your face?

@StellaCavill

Other than that, yes.

@TuesdayFields

So if not that, what then?

@StellaCavill

So @Supermodel_1971 insisted I drop her at JFK this afternoon . . .
>> . . . apparently any regular yellow cab driver fails to provide the appropriate level of help with bags . . .

@TuesdayFields

That doesn't strike me as being particularly weird, especially where @Supermodel_1971 is concerned.

@StellaCavill

It was what happened as I was waving her off which spooked me.

@TuesdayFields

I was going to say Stella, because it's not like @Supermodel_1971 is somebody who is ever going to travel hand luggage.

@StellaCavill

Well, if you give me a chance, I'll tell you!

@TuesdayFields

Sorry. It's this business with @Mum, it's wound me right up. I'll try and keep calm. You carry on . . .

@StellaCavill

So as I'm turning on my heels and making for the exit who should be heading in the opposite direction and right for me?

@TuesdayFields

What are we talking here, blasts from the past?

@StellaCavill

Exactly that.

@TuesdayFields

@MichaelAngeloMovie? Doesn't he only fly if it's on an @NetJet though?

@StellaCavill

Not @MichaelAngeloMovie. @MerchBanker!

@TuesdayFields

OMG. What are the chances?

@StellaCavill

I know. I know. @MerchBanker thinks it's fate.

@TuesdayFields

He thinks it's what?

@StellaCavill

Fate. At least that's what he wrote in the text he just sent me.

@TuesdayFields

Back up Stella. OK, why is he now texting you? You haven't heard from him in an age and now he's texting you?

@StellaCavill

Our impromptu airport encounter was more than a little bit awkward, so I suppose @MerchBanker felt the need to clear the air.

@TuesdayFields

Clear the air? Fog it up a bit more like with a bloody big confusion cloud!

@StellaCavill

It's alright, Tuesday. I feel strangely calm about the whole thing. I'm not going there again. Not now.

@TuesdayFields

Not ever, Stella. You've got bigger fish to fry.

@StellaCavill

All I know is that me going back to @MerchBanker would be – well – going back.

@TuesdayFields

Suddenly that weirdo @BugsBunnyMovie doesn't seem so bad after all.

@StellaCavill

Ay there's the rub. Because @BugsBunnyMovie isn't all bad. In fact quite the contrary . . .

***

@StellaCavill
New Year's Eve. Any thoughts? We really ought to make a plan.

@TuesdayFields
It's six weeks away, Stella.

@StellaCavill
Doesn't feel that way. @SINternUK has been on my case about making a plan since September!

@TuesdayFields
I thought she'd have better things to do, like manage a million new orders?

@StellaCavill
Told you she was a good multi-tasker. She's been doing such a slick job and the new employees she's trained are so on the case . . .
>> . . . that I'm wondering how long it will be until @SINternUK confirms what I'm starting to suspect.

@TuesdayFields
And what is that?

@StellaCavill
That I'm no longer needed 365/24/7 in my own company.

@TuesdayFields
After the year you've had with Stellar Shoes, please tell me that's a good thing?

@StellaCavill
It is. I'm just at a loss to know what to do with all the spare time that's coming my way, been forever since I had even an hour off.

321

@TuesdayFields
You could come and sit next to @AnchorManTV and read out loud while I stay in bed and catch up on a year of sleep?

@StellaCavill
Your job is not that easy. You know that and so do I so stop doing yourself down. Now, what are we going to do for New Year's Eve?

@TuesdayFields
I'm too tired to think about what I'm doing tomorrow, least of all for New Year. Can't we just leave it to @PM_TV to make a plan for us?

@StellaCavill
Not right now. He's all consumed with getting his ratings and his follower count up. Clock is ticking . . .

@TuesdayFields
Know how that feels . . .

@StellaCavill
Christmas is coming and @PM_TV is in danger of losing out to @LordTw1tter in more ways than one.

@TuesdayFields
He'll come up with something to stem the flow of followers to @LordTw1tter . . .
>> . . . and once he does you know he'll throw all his resources into planning something special for NYE.

@StellaCavill
His twitter followers are one thing but what about his slumping TV audience? @PM_TV needs that BIG interview Tuesday.

@TuesdayFields
Sadly I'm not sure he can rely on me to deliver @JakeJacksonLive . . .

@StellaCavill
And I had you down for being a glass half full kinda gal.

@TuesdayFields
Just struggling to find any positives. @AnchorManTV found me
blubbing after the show today. Put his arm round me.
>> Which would have been welcome if he hadn't stunk of B.O.

@StellaCavill
Well at least he's showing a softer side.

@TuesdayFields
He is. He's also passed over Audrey's bras in favour of a girdle.

@StellaCavill
How do you know that?

@TuesdayFields
He told me. Worryingly I've become something of a confidante
since our confrontation. Funny how things turn out isn't it?

@StellaCavill
I'm not sure this year is done with either of us just yet . . .

@TuesdayFields
I hope you're right, Stella.
>> There are things to say and do before the curtain comes down.
And I see you're saying them, at least to @BugsBunnyMovie . . .

@StellaCavill
Those are just the tweets you can see . . .

@TuesdayFields
Oh, I see! I do!

@StellaCavill
He's suggested dinner. I'm thinking about it. Well, drinks.

@TuesdayFields
Really?

@StellaCavill
Really.

@TuesdayFields
This is my fault.

@StellaCavill
What is?

@TuesdayFields
@MichaelAngeloMovie, the Botox and now you entertaining the idea of @BugsBunnyMovie.

@StellaCavill
What are you talking about?

@TuesdayFields
If I hadn't kept telling you to throw caution to the wind, then you wouldn't be considering drinks with a cartoon character!

@StellaCavill
If you hadn't told me to throw caution to the wind I'd probably still be with @MerchBanker and Stellar Shoes would be but a distant memory.

@TuesdayFields
Hmm, maybe . . .

@StellaCavill
Definitely.

@TuesdayFields
So does this mean you're actually going to meet
@BugsBunnyMovie?

@StellaCavill
I think it does.

@TuesdayFields
OK, but if at any point you think he might not be who you think
he is then tweet me immediately.

@StellaCavill
You can be sure of it. First things first, I've got to confirm he is
who I think he is.

@TuesdayFields
Jerry Reuben. Who knew?

***

@TuesdayFields
Am I dreaming? It's 2AM so I figure I could be– tell me I'm not
dreaming, Stella.

@StellaCavill
It's like I said on the phone just now. It's true. @JakeJacksonLive.
He's alive, Tuesday, he's bloody well alive!

@TuesdayFields
Holy crap! I just can't believe it.

@StellaCavill
Believe it! @AllThatGlittersIsGold says @TheBossWUB has the
finer details and will be calling you any minute with more.

@TuesdayFields
He will? What happened?

@StellaCavill

@AllThatGlittersIsGold just rang me – he's come up trumps. He's even spoken to @JakeJacksonLive himself!

@TuesdayFields

Tell me everything and don't leave anything out!

@StellaCavill

One of @AllThatGlittersIsGold's contacts pulled some strings with the embassy in Kabul . . .
>> . . . so he was the first person @JakeJacksonLive spoke to when he and his crew were rescued earlier tonight!

@TuesdayFields

Rescued? Again, what happened?

@StellaCavill

@AllThatGlittersIsGold says most of it is being kept under wraps, something about governments not wanting to answer any tricky questions.

@TuesdayFields

Understandable. What of @JakeJacksonLive though, how is he?

@StellaCavill

As well as can be expected according to @AllThatGlittersIsGold.
>> Managed to convince a captor to give him back his Blackberry. Promised him safe exit out of Afghanistan if he helped him.

@TuesdayFields

It still worked? But they've been gone two months. Surely the battery was dead?

@StellaCavill

Apparently their kidnappers had been using it. Wonders will never cease.

>> @JakeJacksonLive apparently triggered an alarm by tapping out a code on his phone.

@TuesdayFields
What code?

@StellaCavill
I don't know. One that meant the good guys could find them I guess. Some sort of GPS tracker hidden in his mobile.

@TuesdayFields
I just can't believe it, Stella.

@StellaCavill
Well, believe it.
>> Your handsome war reporter is safe, the hero of the hour, and will be home in no time at all! Typical of @AllThatGlittersIsGold.

@TuesdayFields
What do you mean?

@StellaCavill
Well it's like you said. Twitter normally first with breaking news stories these days. How many can claim beating them to the scoop?

@TuesdayFields
@AllThatGlittersIsGold is a star, Stella. I'm so grateful to him. Thank you, S. But now what?

@StellaCavill
What do you mean now what?

@TuesdayFields
It's just, well, before Jake left I kept banging on about him needing to grow up and now I feel like the big kid.

@StellaCavill

Reacquaint yourself with your good friend Gordon and for once take some of your own advice. Speaking from experience, it's not all bad.

@TuesdayFields

You're right Stella. You're right. Going to hunt down Gordon . . .

@StellaCavill

Maybe not right now, Tuesday. You're on air in less than four hours!

@TuesdayFields

You're right. There is that. Last thing I need is to go on air 'tired and emotional'. Hold on, the phone's going . . .

***

@StellaCavill
@TheBossWUB?

@TuesdayFields

Yup! Confirming @JakeJacksonLive's alive, safe and well!

@StellaCavill

Told you so. So do you know when @JakeJacksonLive will be back in the country?

@TuesdayFields

Not yet but I'll be there waiting whenever, wherever S!

@StellaCavill

Just don't involve @Mum. She attracts all the wrong headlines . . .

@TuesdayFields
Of that you can be quite sure. To think I was cursing you for waking me up with that phone call. Thank you, thank you, thank you, Stella!

@StellaCavill
Happy to be of service. Oh, and by the way there's something else that @TheBossWUB may not know and therefore won't have told you . . .

@TuesdayFields
What?

@StellaCavill
He sends you all his love.

@TuesdayFields
@AllThatGlittersIsGold? Send mine back won't you and say thank you for me, Stella.
>> Next time he's in London drinks are on me at the recently reopened Ferret and Trouserleg!

@StellaCavill
Now that's a date he won't be able to refuse but I didn't mean @AllThatGlittersIsGold, although he was the one who heard it from the horse's mouth . . .

@TuesdayFields
Then who?

@StellaCavill
@JakeJacksonLive . . .

#DECEMBER

TUESDAY FIELDS

@TuesdayFields: London
Tis the season to be jolly tra la la la la la la la lahhhhhhhh hhhhhhhh!

Monthly Must:
Carefully plan T3 reunion with @JakeJacksonLive so as to look completely carefree.

Monthly Must Not:
Let @Mum forget she made @TheDailyGB front page news this year.

Followers:
Who cares?

STELLA CAVILL

@StellaCavill: New York, New York
Santa's little helper.

Monthly Must:
Get used to the new me – and my new face sans frown.

Monthly Must Not:
Go backwards, only forwards in life and love.

Followers:
I've lost count!

@StellaCavill

Have you figured out how you're going to do it yet?

@TuesdayFields

Do what?

@StellaCavill

Greet your war hero @JakeJacksonLive, of course. Not like you haven't had the time to plan it!

@TuesdayFields

Thought of nothing else. According to @TheBossWUB he's being debriefed in Germany before he can fly home for good.

@StellaCavill

And to you! Have you spoken to him yet?

@TuesdayFields

Not yet, which does makes me wonder what the hell he and his crew must have been through if the secret services are quite so involved.

@StellaCavill

Sounds like @AllThatGlittersIsGold got to Jake just before the lockdown then. Now why doesn't that surprise me?

@TuesdayFields

Do you think your moneyed backer is actually just CIA, investing in random shoe companies as a convenient front?

@StellaCavill

Wouldn't put anything past him.

@TuesdayFields
@Supermodel_1971 seems to have found a way to break down his barriers . . .

@StellaCavill
My mother is one in a million. Speaking of mums, has @JakeJacksonLive's been in touch again?

@TuesdayFields
Yes but she hasn't been able to speak to him yet either – she's convinced it's because Jake needs patching up.
>> I hope she's not right, but I fear she might be.

@StellaCavill
The worst is over.
>> Whatever's gone on, @JakeJacksonLive will have some story to tell. @PM_TV will be beside himself if he doesn't get the scoop, you know.

@TuesdayFields
He'll have to join the queue.

@StellaCavill
Surely you can help him jump it?

@TuesdayFields
I plan to. Right after Jake tells @WUBTV and me first. Anyway, in the meantime, how's the rampant rabbit?

@StellaCavill
Date night tonight. God, T, I hope I'm doing the right thing. @BugsBunnyMovie's suggested cocktails at The Mandarin Oriental.

@TuesdayFields

That's acceptable. Keep your phone handy and make sure he doesn't roofie your drink.

@StellaCavill

I hardly think a triple Oscar, four time Emmy and seven time Tony award winning director, is going to bother putting rohypnol in my cocktail.

@TuesdayFields

I wouldn't put anything past an ageing Hollywood director, and neither should you.

@StellaCavill

You're not helping my nerves, Tuesday.

@TuesdayFields

At least its just drinks and you can bolt after one if necessary.

@StellaCavill

Booked in a dinner with @AllThatGlittersIsGold as a failsafe and he knows if I'm late to call in the cavalry.

@TuesdayFields

He's good at that.

@StellaCavill

I think I'm getting more savvy in my old age . . .

@TuesdayFields

Less of the old.

@StellaCavill

Age is nothing but a number. Which is fortunate for Jerry, as he's got to be 50+.

@TuesdayFields
@JakeJacksonLive could be his son.

@StellaCavill
Again, you're not helping. Back to the date . . .

@TuesdayFields
Having such a concrete, albeit sensible, exit strategy, does beg the question what happens if you fancy more than just the one drink?

@StellaCavill
You mean him? @BugsBunnyMovie?

@TuesdayFields
Well him or maybe just another drink?

@StellaCavill
Isn't that what second dates are for?

@TuesdayFields
With Stellar Shoes selling out of, well, shoes, I'm amazed you've got the time for even a first date. He must be worth it.

@StellaCavill
Well now I've got what's known in the world of commerce as 'employees' there are others to do the hard work so I don't have to!

@TuesdayFields
See you are Wonder Woman after all.

@StellaCavill
Quite the transformation, isn't it? This time last year I was on my uppers and Stellar Shoes was going under . . .

@TuesdayFields

That's not all that's changed . . .

@StellaCavill

Been some twelve months, hasn't it?

@TuesdayFields

The question is how to send it off . . .

@StellaCavill

I have a sneaking suspicion @PM_TV has the matter in hand . . .

@TuesdayFields

After the year he's had, I suspect he'd like nothing more than to see in a new one. Where though?

@StellaCavill

Rumour has it a certain drinking house has turned into a gastro-pub with @CelebChef – or rather one of his minions – cooking up a storm.

@TuesdayFields

The Ferret and Trouserleg? Yes it has! Where I was going to take @AllThatGlittersIsGold for his part in saving @JakeJacksonLive, but NYE there?

@StellaCavill

I know it's not @PM_TV's usual upper class establishment, but it would be fun . . .

@TuesdayFields

You'd come over?

@StellaCavill

God knows I've been trying, but now I'm struggling to find a reason not to!

@TuesdayFields
The Ferret and Trouserleg it is then. 364 days on from when we first met . . .

@StellaCavill
And from when we last saw each other . . .

@TuesdayFields
It's a date!

@StellaCavill
Speaking of which, I have one to get ready for. Tweet you on the other side . . .

* * *

@TuesdayFields
So . . .

@StellaCavill
Wobbled.

@TuesdayFields
Who? You or @BugsBunnyMovie?

@StellaCavill
Me. Not sure I can.

@TuesdayFields
What?

@StellaCavill
Go there.

@TuesdayFields
With @BugsBunnyMovie? He is Jerry Reuben I take it?

@StellaCavill

Yes. And Jerry is clever, articulate, witty, funny, smart, solvent, i.e. all the things I look for in a future husband, but . . .

@TuesdayFields

But . . .

@StellaCavill

It's just the rest of it, more specifically, him. How superficial am I?

@TuesdayFields

Like one of those modelisers you love to hate so much.

@StellaCavill

What is wrong with me, Tuesday?

@TuesdayFields

It's perfectly understandable you should want to spend the rest of your life with someone . . .

>> . . . who the mere sight of doesn't make you feel physically sick, Stella.

@StellaCavill

Tuesday! It's not that bad. I'm just, well, unsure . . .

@TuesdayFields

Is it the baldness because if it is, that can be easily rectified. Look at Wayne Rooney. Proper stud muffin since his op.

@StellaCavill

If this year has taught me anything it's to have an open mind . . .

@TuesdayFields

But not open legs, well not until at least date three . . .

@StellaCavill
What would @Mum say if she heard her daughter talking like that? Wash your mouth out, Tuesday Fields!

@TuesdayFields
@Mum is more liberal than you'd think . . .

@StellaCavill
@Supermodel_1971 is more liberal you'd ever want to be, as I fear @AllThatGlittersIsGold is finding out . . .

@TuesdayFields
Saw that coming a mile off . . .

@StellaCavill
She's turned my impenetrable financier into her white knight. He's whisking her off to a romantic hideaway for New Year's Eve. >> Quite the fairytale.

@TuesdayFields
Young love . . . @Mum and Dad getting on better too. >> He's given up catching moths and spending his days chasing @Mum around the golf course instead.

@StellaCavill
Speaking of happily ever afters, don't tell a soul, but @SINternUK has bagged her prince . . .

@TuesdayFields
Really? What will the establishment say about those photos of her starkers at Heathrow?!

@StellaCavill
Sure she can talk anyone into thinking she's a 'breath of fresh air'.

@TuesdayFields

This is just the start. Expect she'll convince them to let her rule one day too.

@StellaCavill

Or at least till Kingdom come. @SINternUK will be in charge of Stellars soon as well, just given her some stock options.

\>> She deserves it and I can't afford to lose her.

@TuesdayFields

If this all ends the way it should, there will obviously be a fabulous royal wedding. Can I be your plus one?

@StellaCavill

I'll think about it.

@TuesdayFields

@AnchorManTV singing her praises again this morning. I think he's still a little bit in love with her.

@StellaCavill

Aren't they all?

@TuesdayFields

Bizarre though, isn't it, considering she was effectively the one who outed him?

@StellaCavill

Suppose in a weird way he's grateful for the wake up call.

@TuesdayFields

Have to hand it him, since being found wearing nylons and heels he's been nothing but the perfect gent.

@StellaCavill

The irony is not lost . . .

@TuesdayFields
And he's back on track with Audrey. Apparently she's reconciled herself to the fact her husband's a cross dresser.

@StellaCavill
What's happened to the make-up woman he was carrying on with, Susan wasn't it?

@TuesdayFields
Finally sacked for all the right reasons – well she was absolutely crap at her job- so gone from @WUBTV and from temptation.

@StellaCavill
@TheBossWUB must be relieved @AnchorManTV and you have buried the hatchet?

@TuesdayFields
I thought @TheBossWUB was going to have a heart attack with everything that happened this year @WUBTV . . .
>> . . . but he seems pleased as punch with the way things have turned out.

@StellaCavill
Thanks to @JakeJacksonLive's heroics in Afghanistan and @AnchorManTV and you pulling it back from the brink after @KateKingTV left.

@TuesdayFields
Think he thought @WUBTV was a goner, but the budget's just come through for next year . . .
>> . . . and he's jumping round the office like he's on happy pills.

@StellaCavill
Are you sure he isn't?

@TuesdayFields

Not totally. Cashflow isn't the only thing making him smile, @KateKingTV is coming back . . .

@StellaCavill

What? Why?

@TuesdayFields

Apparently she's eaten a sizeable amount of humble pie and wants back into the fold.

@StellaCavill

But what about you, T? You've made that sofa job your own. She can't just barge on back and take it from you?

@TuesdayFields

I'm not going anywhere. @KateKingTV is to be our new Los Angeles correspondent!

@StellaCavill

Wow. She'll bust some balls in Hollywood.

@TuesdayFields

If I'm right in saying, I do believe @PM_TV's are first on the list . . . .

@StellaCavill

I almost feel sorry for @PM_TV.

@TuesdayFields

He'll survive, he always does. So have you decided?

@StellaCavill

Decided what?

@TuesdayFields

On whether date two with Jerry is a viable option?

@StellaCavill

In two minds. When I do decide, you'll be the first to know . . .

***

@StellaCavill

So, date two.

@TuesdayFields

Don't you dare drip feed, Stella Cavill. Spill. Now.

@StellaCavill

This is Twitter. It's all about the drip feed.

@TuesdayFields

Shut up and get on with it.

@StellaCavill

The date went well. Better actually than I thought it would or could.

@TuesdayFields

So can you and will you? Or have you already done so.

@StellaCavill

Not yet . . .

@TuesdayFields

Sounds like you might?

@StellaCavill

A box at The Met on the opening night of Bohème and I'd have to have a heart of stone not to melt a little.

342

@TuesdayFields
Stella Cavill, I do believe you may have met your match!

@StellaCavill
We'll see. Starting to realise that @MerchBanker was lacking, not least in the humour department.

@TuesdayFields
He ended up lacking in a few departments.

@StellaCavill
Jerry's just got things figured out I suppose.

@TuesdayFields
That's the benefit of dating an older man, S. There've got to be some pluses right?!

@StellaCavill
Right! Maybe I'm just finally growing up.

@TuesdayFields
You carry on, if you don't mind I'm going to continue to regress a little while longer.

@StellaCavill
And we all know why that is, don't we? That's a rhetorical question.

@TuesdayFields
Good because I wasn't going to do you the satisfaction of answering it.

@StellaCavill
In other news, Jerry says @MichaelAngeloMovie has gone to Iceland. I thought it was only mums who did that?

@TuesdayFields

For one who frequents Quags, and she does, @Mum would never be caught dead in Iceland.

@StellaCavill

But apparently @MichaelAngeloMovie would, well not the supermarket but the country. @BugsBunnyMovie says he's there saving whales.

@TuesdayFields

Yawn. You're well out of that one.

@StellaCavill

I thought you'd say that.

@TuesdayFields

Presumably he'll return green as grass and within a couple of weeks be back lounging around some swanky set in a luxury trailer?

@StellaCavill

You know him so well!

@TuesdayFields

No, you do!

@StellaCavill

Of which our mutual friend @BugsBunnyMovie is well aware . . . In saying that, he does seem to see the funny side of the whole awful affair.

>> Fortunately.

@TuesdayFields

We've established he's got a sense of humour, Stella, but what I want to know is, do you want to rip his clothes off?

344

@StellaCavill

In a fog of champagne and Puccini last night it occurred to me that I think I might want to . . .

@TuesdayFields

You think you might want to?

@StellaCavill

Put it this way, he's a grower not a show-er.

@TuesdayFields

Known a few of those in my time . . .

@StellaCavill

You and me both. Where is @JakeJacksonLive anyway?

@TuesdayFields

Still in Germany. @TheBossWUB is planning his return for next week and guess who he's assigned to interview him at T5?

@StellaCavill

No?

@TuesdayFields

Yes. So much for a romantic reunion away from prying eyes.

@StellaCavill

Oh God. Can't @AnchorManTV do it?

@TuesdayFields

@TheBossWUB has made his mind up. He wants chemistry . . .

@StellaCavill

He'll get that and a lot more besides!

@TuesdayFields
@Mum has already weighed in with the inevitable lunch invite,

RT @Mum: 'Darling, @TheDailyGB says that nice boy Jake is back soon. Sure he could do with one of my Sunday roasts. >> Why don't you bring him home? Mum x'.

@StellaCavill
You did say it would be a matter of time – at least you now know she approves.

@TuesdayFields
There is that.

@StellaCavill
I see from @TheDailyGB online that the one she would never have sanctioned, @No1Sportsman, has won Sports Personality Of The Year. Again.

@TuesdayFields
Philanderer of the year is more appropriate, but then I suppose that would have broadened the shortlist considerably.

@StellaCavill
Considerably. Ah Tuesday, the men we have loved or almost loved this year . . .

@TuesdayFields
The one who we can thank for bringing us together, other than @PM_TV, has got his comeuppance alright.

@StellaCavill
So I see from the online @TheDailyGB. Something about @RedS0ledShoes shagging @HugoPr1nce's personal trainer?

@TuesdayFields

Yup. Word has it in the @WUBTV newsroom he's sold his story. >> The trainer that is, who unlike the chauffeur I'm not so sure would have had a confidentiality agreement . . .

@StellaCavill

Oh my word. The things he'll have seen . . .

@TuesdayFields

The things he'll reveal . . .

@StellaCavill

My stomach's just turned. Surely this is the beginning of the political end for @HugoPr1nce?

@TuesdayFields

'fraid so.

@StellaCavill

Well it couldn't happen to a more deserving prick.

@TuesdayFields

You took the words right out of my mouth.

@StellaCavill

While we're on the subject I've an update on @MerchBanker . . .

@TuesdayFields

I was starting to wonder if you'd shipped banker wanker off somewhere.

@StellaCavill

I didn't, but Goldsmith Smythe has.

@TuesdayFields

Where?

@StellaCavill

Shanghai. Permanent move because the only dependable markets seem to be emerging.

@TuesdayFields

Not far enough.

@StellaCavill

That's what @Supermodel_1971 said.

@TuesdayFields

I knew we had more than just you in common.

@StellaCavill

You were right, though. Will did try to win me back. Briefly. In a text.

@TuesdayFields

In a text? How very romantic.

@StellaCavill

Told me it was me or Shanghai, so I chose China for him.

@TuesdayFields

He could at least have picked up the phone.

@StellaCavill

I really have moved on, haven't I? I'm not sure I was ever sure that I could.

@TuesdayFields

I was. So when is date three with @BugsBunnyMovie then?

@StellaCavill

Saturday. When is @JakeJacksonLive back?

@TuesdayFields
Tomorrow.

@StellaCavill
Ready?

@TuesdayFields
Ready. You?

@StellaCavill
Ready.

***

@StellaCavill
So . . .

@TuesdayFields
So . . .

@StellaCavill
Was it everything you dreamed it would be?

@TuesdayFields
Was it better than you thought it would be?

@StellaCavill
I'm not sure where to start.

@TuesdayFields
Neither am I.

@StellaCavill
It was better than I thought it would be.

@TuesdayFields
It was everything I dreamed it would be.

@StellaCavill
So . . .

@TuesdayFields
So . . . I waited for what seemed like forever for the doors to arrivals to open and then they did and there he was, @JakeJacksonLive.

@StellaCavill
I was ready earlier than I've ever been for a date.
>> Seemed like an eternity waiting for the buzzer to go and then it did and there he was, @BugsBunnyMovie.

@TuesdayFields
Carrying just a rucksack on his back and looking gaunter than ever @JakeJacksonLive stood there, in arrivals, and absorbed the mania.

@StellaCavill
I'm not sure if it was the cut of his suit, but @BugsBunnyMovie seemed somehow more handsome than normal standing on my doorstep last night.

@TuesdayFields
I watched on, the incessant flashing of photographers' lightbulbs hurting my eyes.
>> And then I eventually found his, and @JakeJacksonLive found mine . . .

@StellaCavill
A look shared between two people can tell a thousand words. @BugsBunnyMovie's eyes went straight through me.

@TuesdayFields
It's hard to put it into words isn't it? That feeling you get . . .

@StellaCavill
The expectation.

@TuesdayFields
The anticipation.

@StellaCavill
The knowing.

@TuesdayFields
Love?

@StellaCavill
Maybe. Just maybe.

* * *

@TuesdayFields
@TheBossWUB just broke the good news, @JakeJacksonLive's return brought in the biggest viewing figures of the year!

@StellaCavill
Tuesday your interview is everywhere; it's making headlines all over the world! I'm surprised @TheBossWUB isn't worried.

@TuesdayFields
Why should he be worried? I don't think I've ever seen him so happy.

@StellaCavill
American networks will be coming calling.

@TuesdayFields
Do you think I'm going to lose @JakeJacksonLive?

@StellaCavill

No, silly – they'll be coming for you both.

@TuesdayFields

We'll see. Trying to keep mine and @JakeJacksonLive's feet firmly on the ground. Well, on my bedroom floor, anyway.

@StellaCavill

Shouldn't think @JakeJacksonLive will resist being grounded for a while, especially not by you, Tuesday Fields!

@TuesdayFields

No need for us to leave the flat after @Mum sent an @WaitroseUK Duchy hamper . . .

@StellaCavill

She is making an effort. The Prince of Wales' produce, no less.

@TuesdayFields

@Mum loves the Prince. Thinks he's misunderstood by the masses.

@StellaCavill

Don't tell her @SINternUK is stalking his son or she'll be shopping for a hat next in an effort to meet the Dad.

@TuesdayFields

In other news, @Mum's back to reading our favourite rag, so any day now @TheDailyGB inspired tweets will restart.

@StellaCavill

That didn't last long! Don't tell @Mum, but I sort of missed them.

@TuesdayFields

@Mum hysterical after @TheDailyGB's front page today posed the question:

RT @TheDailyGB: 'Tuesday Fields, 34, and Jake Jackson, 24. The new Richard and Judy?'

@StellaCavill
Can @TheDailyGB not do better than that?

@TuesdayFields
Apparently not. How're things with @BugsBunnyMovie?

@StellaCavill
I don't want to jinx it, but everything is great, T. Last night he pulled strings and took me for drinks at the Guggenheim – just us. >> We had the run of the place!

@TuesdayFields
Makes @MerchBanker and @MichaelAngeloMovie look a bit crap, doesn't he?

@StellaCavill
Just a bit.

@TuesdayFields
So does this have legs, Stella Cavill, you and Bugs?

@StellaCavill
We'll see. Is it the real deal with you and Jake?

@TuesdayFields
We'll see . . .

***

@TuesdayFields
Well that didn't last long.

@StellaCavill
What? Not you and @JakeJacksonLive? Is everything ok?

@TuesdayFields
Oh yes, we're fine. I meant keeping Jake's feet on terra firma.

@StellaCavill
Why? Where is he?

@TuesdayFields
Currently 35,000 feet up on his way to NYC to be interviewed by @PM_TV!

@StellaCavill
I wondered how long it would take him to get in touch about that interview.

@TuesdayFields
I preempted it. Thought I owed it to @PM_TV for watching both our backs this year.

@StellaCavill
That's true – and you did get the world exclusive.

@TuesdayFields
It was the least I could do to get @PM_TV first dibs in America.

@StellaCavill
And what about you? Any interest stateside, as I suspected there would be after that interview of yours with the infamous war hero?

@TuesdayFields
One or two phone calls. But I've been in this business long enough to know they'll probably amount to bugger all.

@StellaCavill
Exciting though, no?

@TuesdayFields
Interesting, yes. Anyway, I'm looking forward to seeing how @PM_TV's interview with Jake turns out.

@StellaCavill
@PM_TV's bosses must have been thrilled he got him.

TuesdayFields
Thank God @JakeJacksonLive was up for it. The ABC connection with @PM_TV helped convince him it was a good idea. >> Well that, and me begging.

@StellaCavill
Did you tell @JakeJacksonLive what was at stake, i.e. @PM_TV's ratings and less importantly his Twitter bet with @LordTw1tter?

@TuesdayFields
No. Wanted Jake to make his own mind up about whether it was something he wanted to do and luckily he thought it was.

@StellaCavill
Well let's hope your war hero can save the day for @PM_TV then.

@TuesdayFields
9PM your time. ABC. Primetime.

@StellaCavill
I'll be watching. Let's hope the rest of America is.

@TuesdayFields
Something tells me that they will be.

***

@StellaCavill

OMG.

@TuesdayFields

Told you there was nothing to worry about . . .

@StellaCavill

I got the gist of it from your interview with @JakeJacksonLive but @PM_TV getting a whole hour to grill him . . .

>> . . . what he went through sounds straight out of a Bourne film!

@TuesdayFields

Glad they biffed the other guests and gave it the time it deserved.

@StellaCavill

God how terrifying. @JakeJacksonLive's bloody lucky to be alive, Tuesday.

@TuesdayFields

Yes he is.

@StellaCavill

@PM_TV must be singing from the rooftops after that interview. Best thing I've seen him do in ages.

@TuesdayFields

You mean better than his cake-baking feature with @LindsayLohan? Surely not?

@StellaCavill

Well, maybe not that, although I did laugh when @PM_TV hinted that she'd got the recipe in Amsterdam.

@TuesdayFields

Her 'people' must have thrown a fit.

@StellaCavill

Not when she's so desperate for airtime. So, any feedback from @PM_TV?

@TuesdayFields

He DM'd me to say ratings are through the roof and the network had a new contract waiting for him in his dressing room when he came off air!

@StellaCavill

Bingo. Definitely made the intended impact then?

@TuesdayFields

And then some.

@StellaCavill

I've just looked at my news feed. @PM_TV like the cat that got the cream on Twitter too.

@TuesdayFields

So I see. @PM_TV's fantasy is at long last a reality. He's trending worldwide!

@StellaCavill

And take a look at his follower count – it's finally on the rise.

@TuesdayFields

Wonder if he'll reach a million by New Year's Eve after all?

@StellaCavill

Can't see @LordTw1tter being very impressed at losing out to @PM_TV in the eleventh hour, but a bet is a bet.

@TuesdayFields
And there's more than just pride riding on this one.

@StellaCavill
Boys will be boys. Speaking of which where's @JakeJacksonLive now?

@TuesdayFields
He's supposed to be on a jet plane coming back home, but ABC wanted a word . . .

@StellaCavill
A word?

@TuesdayFields
Probably just a debrief following the stuff he did for them in Afghanistan and his interview with @PM_TV.

@StellaCavill
Probably.

@TuesdayFields
You sound less than convinced, Stella . . .

@StellaCavill
I'm just wondering . . .

@TuesdayFields
Wondering what?

@StellaCavill
Well, after the headlines @JakeJacksonLive's made you don't think they'd offer him a permanent gig stateside?

@TuesdayFields
I don't know. Oh God. I'm not sure I can handle it if they did.
Not after everything it's taken to get us here.

@StellaCavill
You might want to start thinking about packing your bags,
permanently . . .

@TuesdayFields
That's some step.

@StellaCavill
That's been this year though, hasn't it? Steps we never thought
we'd take or make.

@TuesdayFields
All of a sudden I'm craving Gordon again.

***

@StellaCavill
Happy Christmas!!!!

@TuesdayFields
Happy Crimbo, S! Is @Supermodel_1971 laying on a spectacu-
lar spread?

@StellaCavill
Considering she's not seen the inside of an oven for years she's
doing a pretty good job,
> Albeit with @AllThatGlittersIsGold's housekeeper at her side.

@TuesdayFields
And @BugsBunnyMovie?

@StellaCavill

Coping admirably bearing in mind that he's Jewish and he shouldn't have to suffer any of this!

@TuesdayFields

It must be love.

@StellaCavill

He's bought me a present. Or rather an envelope, which @Supermodel_1971 says I'm not allowed to open until after lunch.

@TuesdayFields

Never had her down as the traditional type.

@StellaCavill

Dare I say it, but @AllThatGlittersIsGold is having a positive effect on her.

@TuesdayFields

So how's @BugsBunnyMovie going down in @AllThatGlittersIsGold's Central Park West apartment?

@StellaCavill

He's quite the raconteur, but then we always knew that.

@TuesdayFields

I imagine he is! The stories he can tell . . . The thing's he's seen . . .

@StellaCavill

You're never going to let me forget that, are you?

@TuesdayFields

Of course not!

@StellaCavill
Fortunately that's not the only tale @BugsBunnyMovie has in his repertoire.

@TuesdayFields
@Supermodel_1971 and @AllThatGlittersIsGold suitably impressed?

@StellaCavill
@AllThatGlittersIsGold keeps guffawing and @Supermodel_1971 is more than enjoying the attention, so, yes.

@TuesdayFields
What is it about our boyfriends and our mothers? @Mum all over @JakeJacksonLive. Frankly, it's embarrassing.

@StellaCavill
And there you were thinking she wouldn't approve of a younger man . . .

@TuesdayFields
I'm not saying she wants to shag him, Stella, at least I don't think she does.
>> Oh God, what a thought. Just been a little bit sick in my mouth.

@StellaCavill
That's disgusting, Tuesday! I've still got to get through lunch.

@TuesdayFields
As is the thought of @JakeJacksonLive and @Mum.
>> Not just me who would be mortified at that either, Dad's taken quite a shine to him too.

@StellaCavill
Really?

@TuesdayFields

They're going down the driving range together tomorrow, while @Mum and I no doubt make turkey and cranberry sandwiches.

@StellaCavill

Does @JakeJacksonLive even play golf?

@TuesdayFields

Not until about 20 minutes ago, no, but he recognises the good sense in indulging Dad nonetheless.

@StellaCavill

As every future Son-in-law should!

@TuesdayFields

Whoo there, Miss Cavill. Reign it in. It's still early days . . .

@StellaCavill

But so far, so good.

@TuesdayFields

So far, so good.

* * *

@StellaCavill

I know you're probably watching a double bill of Doctor Who but if you're not, tweet me back.

@TuesdayFields

I'm not.

@StellaCavill

Good. I'm having a crisis.

@TuesdayFields
Oh God, why? It's not @BugsBunnyMovie is it? Everything alright?

@StellaCavill
Better than. The envelope contained an @NetJet's schedule.

@TuesdayFields
I'm saying nothing. Where are you going?

@StellaCavill
LA. But Jerry's banned me from using my Crackberry from Boxing Day through to New Years Eve!

@TuesdayFields
Hats off to @BugsBunnyMovie. He's achieved more in a short spell than @MerchBanker managed in years.

@StellaCavill
This isn't funny, Tuesday. You know how I rely on that bloody thing. How on earth will I get by?

@TuesdayFields
Just like you did before.

@StellaCavill
Before what?

@TuesdayFields
Before Blackberries and Stellar Shoes were what they are now.

@StellaCavill
Which is?

@TuesdayFields
Your everything! Stop being such a control freak. It's like you said.

@StellaCavill
What did I say?

@TuesdayFields
There would come a point where you wouldn't be needed 365/24/7. This is that time. Take your foot off the gas, Stella. Relax, will you?

@StellaCavill
And do what instead?

@TuesdayFields
I can think of one thing . . .

@StellaCavill
What?

@TuesdayFields
@BugsBunnyMovie for starters!

@StellaCavill
Told you your advice wasn't always all bad. Anything left to tweet before I sever ties with civilization and disappear into the wilderness?

@TuesdayFields
See you on New Years Eve, Stella Cavill.

@StellaCavill
See you then, Tuesday Fields.

@StellaCavill
PS. I'll be the one in the sleepsuit.

@TuesdayFields
In which case I'll bring a spare Leger.

#EPILOGUE

STELLA

Tuesday will have a field day with this.

I'm peering out of the window of seat 1K– who'd have thought I'd be sitting up here this time last year, willing the plane to taxi quicker towards Terminal 3? I cannot believe volcanic ash has got in the way of my best laid New Year's Eve plans.

TUESDAY

Stella is going to kill me.

Mum is doing her level best to make me late for Peter Mignon's New Year's Eve party. Dammit. There is no logical reason whatsoever to hang about here in the country and wait for Marjorie to turn up with fresh eggs. Just Mum showing off her most recent fixation and for some reason I'm too chicken to leave.

STELLA

It was all so perfectly planned – reminiscent of the Stella of old, before all the dramas of this year. I was back in control, even if everything was being booked at the last minute.

I would land in NYC from LA, sign off on the necessary Stellar Shoes' paperwork (so I could have an undisturbed jaunt to Thailand after Peter Mignon's NYE bash), then a hop, skip and a jump onto the day flight to London and a much longed for reunion with my cyber pen-pal.

But now there is no way I'll have time to check-in at Blakes, make myself presentable and appear at Mignon's soiree, in The Ferret and The Trouserleg, with a good hour or so to spare before he starts belting out a tuneless rendition of Auld Lang Syne.

Tuesday will enjoy this spanner in the works. She'd cackled with laughter on the phone when I told her my hastily re-arranged travel schedule, but she didn't give me grief for any of it – she knew for the first time in almost a year I was doing something for Stella, not Stellars. It was about time.

TUESDAY

I had tonight mapped out perfectly. That was before Marjorie and her eggs showed up on the front door of Mum and Dad's to throw everything awry.

What was supposed to happen is not what is happening and any minute now I'm going to blow.

It wasn't so long ago Marjorie was making Mum's life a living hell! Well, selling copies of The Daily with Mum on the front cover in the village shop, which translates to being the same thing.

And now, and now . . . here she is sitting in the kitchen with her feet under the table sipping tea from Mum's favourite china and scoffing scones.

I should have left ages ago but I'm trapped in suburban purgatory, when where I need to be is hoofing it up the A1 to The Ferret and Trouserleg for a Gordon, or two.

At least Stella won't curse me when I stumble through the door late, again. It's not like we haven't both been there or here before.

STELLA

I elbow my way through so I'm first off the plane – somewhat easier when you're turning left not right, it has to be said. I could get used to this. Hopefully my cattle class days are far behind me. However, I seem to have found the one and only problem with flying Upper Class. In typical rush-to-wait fashion I arrive at the carousel well before my luggage.

Time ticks on and I start to wonder if my bags are going to turn up at all. I experience an involuntary shudder. As highly amusing as arriving in a red baby gro at The Ferret and Trouserleg might be, I have a feeling this particular joke would wear thin extremely quickly – for me at least. After Tuesday's mishap last New Year's Eve I was tempted to travel hand luggage, but the Thai trip tomorrow put paid to that.

Thailand. I can scarcely believe that I agreed to go, let alone that I'm going to be getting a proper holiday. Have I gone completely mad?

Maybe, but this is the new Stella. Chiva Som promises to balance my mind, body and soul and I couldn't need it more. I have sworn, again, not to touch the Crackberry, but we'll see. Well, it takes time to break an addiction, doesn't it?

With a detox on the cards I fully intend to live it up tonight with Tuesday. She'd be the first to advocate total intoxication before duly reversing the process – if you can't maximize the experience what's the point?

I don't believe it. This is so typical. Everyone else has their luggage apart from me. Even those in the cheap seats. This can't be happening. After everything, I'm now contemplating a panic phone call to Tuesday request-ing a dress after all . . .

And then, could it be? Yes. Just before I throw every toy out of the pram, my bag appears. Relief. Unfortunately, one glance at my watch and the window I reserved for Blake's has well and truly disappeared. There's nothing to be done for it. I sprint towards the airport loos, wheeling my precious cargo behind me.

TUESDAY

Right, that's it. I can take no more nor stay any longer. I have to go. Bye Mum, bye Marjorie. London is calling.

Bloody traffic! I knew I should have bolted before Mum had a chance to scupper my smooth passage back into town. Must be mainly Arsenal fans making their way back after a surprising home victory over Stoke. Mignon will be relieved, maybe even pleased. It's not been the best of seasons so far for his beloved club. No doubt he'll want to pour over every twist, turn and bad penalty decision with me later. Grin and bear, Tuesday, grin and bear. I put on the radio and flick through the channels trying to find a way to ease my frustration and take my focus away from the never-ending snake of cars blocking my route to unadulterated fun and inevitable football analysis.

I settle on Radio 2. Radio 2? How old am I? Apparently old enough to genuinely appreciate the sounds of a 'distinctive mixed music and speech service'. Well, that's how the Beeb bill it and here I am, on the A1, loving every single minute of Dermot O' Leary's early evening nostalgia fest.

I'm daydreaming. I can't help it. It's the sounds of yester-year, they are throwing up all sorts of memories of the one just gone. I get to thinking how very different this Tuesday Fields is, stuck on the motorway in her Audi A3, to the one who boarded a flight to New York this time last year. Gone is the desperate wreck of a girl broken by a bad man in Hugo Prince. She's long since been replaced by a woman ready to conquer the world with a nice boy on her arm to do it with.

Take That breaks my train of thought. Gary Barlow and Dermot O'Leary all in one afternoon. I'm suddenly grateful for the hold up. And here's another thing, while I might be late for Mignon's party, at least on this occasion I'll be dressed in something more suitable than a sleepsuit.

Stella, however, well that rather depends on the reliability of Virgin Atlantic. I remind myself to pop a spare Leger in my handbag just in case and for old time's sake.

STELLA

There are certain shades of limelight that can wreck a girl's complexion.

The woman staring back at me in the mirror looks like – well looks like she's had the year, and especially the past week of multiple time zones, that I've had. My mother's words ring in my ears: 'you always get the face that you deserve – and I deserve the one I paid for'.

Well, Coco Chanel had it right when she said, 'nature gives you the face you have at twenty; it is up to you to merit the face you have at fifty'. My eyes are puffy and now the Botox is beginning to wear off, thank God, I certainly look my age. This year has made me realise how much I do love my mother, but I also love myself enough not to listen to everything she says nor worry about trying to freeze everything– or at least my face – in time, despite her nudging otherwise. I choose to grow old gracefully. She clearly doesn't. I just hope her teenage-like behaviour around my main investor doesn't start to grate and end up in me losing my backer . . .

But then, and with an extremely pleasant jolt, I remember this month's sales figures. Reality is that I don't need All That Glitters Is Gold anymore. Mother and he can do precisely what they like.

Underneath the strip lighting, I see myself stripped bare. I realise the choices I've made – eventually – have been the right ones. I have Tuesday to thank for much of that. I can't imagine life without her now.

With a start it occurs to me that I could well be standing in the loos that Tuesday hid in after the infamous Monaco incident with No1 Sportsman, when The Daily put two and two together and came up with sixty nine.

Monaco. God, that seems so long ago. So does Will. As I slather on the touché éclat, I think about where he might be right now. Shanghai, that's where. I now know for sure that splitting up was the right thing to do, for both of us. We'd grown apart, simple as that. It happens.

So here I am, almost 35, and I feel as though finally I'm on my way, that I've found the right path. And I can't wait to see the girl who shared all the highs and lows of this year with me and pointed me in the right direction.

TUESDAY

I fly through the front door of my Kensal Rise flat and shoot up the stairs straight into the bathroom I now share with a significant other. Has a bomb dropped? Certainly looks like it. What is it about bloody boys and bathrooms?

Admittedly it's taking me longer than I thought it would to get used to sharing my tiny pad with another but is it really too much to ask to put the loo seat down? I hate that he doesn't, ever!

Mind you if that's all I've got to complain about then life must be good, and it is.

I locate my worse for wear make-up bag somewhere under a mountain of discarded towels and tip the contents into the sink.

As I sponge foundation over my face it finds new lines to hide in. Maybe next year I'll give in to peer pressure and have fillers after all.

Well Stella did!

I used to be so competent in the application of war paint but tonight I'm all fingers and thumbs.

It's true that since I secured the sofa slot at Wake Up Britain I've been spoilt rotten. Hair washed, blow-dried and styled and make-up administered with care and acute precision every day. Well, after Susan left at least. It's no wonder I've forgotten how to do it myself.

My God. When I think back to how this year started, to Tuesday Fields the sports reporter, being caught on camera face planting off a Boris bike, baring her bottom to the nation at Ascot and filling, badly, a three minute banter window with Anchor Man . . .

I can't believe I got here.

It all seems so long ago. So does Hugo Prince and No1 Sportsman. I sweep a large dose of bronzer over my cheekbones and wonder where they both are now. Hugo Prince is probably mulling over what might have been. A political future full of potential scuppered by a slapper girlfriend. A daub of lip-gloss and then I'm done. No1 Sportsman? As is the case with most sportsmen, while he's winning he's still a hero. After that, who knows?

I'm ready, for tonight and whatever comes next in life. I grab a dress from my cluttered wardrobe and out of the door and into a black cab to see Stella we go, the girl who's more than a little bit responsible for showing me the way.

STELLA

My phone beeps. Has my luck changed? My Addison Lee is easy to find, parked up just outside arrivals. Within minutes we are in a people carrier bumping along the M4 towards Peter Mignon's infamous pub.

Driving through these familiar streets feels strangely odd. Despite sounding like I belong, I'm an outsider in London now. In NYC I sound as if I'm a stranger, when in fact it's very much become my home.

I wonder for how much longer? I'd finally got LA on this trip. The weather, the lifestyle. And the people, well other than being surgically enhanced, underneath it all, they weren't all bad.

Could I live there? After swearing to Tuesday I never would / could, it's something I'm suddenly pondering. Have I lost my mind? But everyone says the winters are getting worse in NYC and being stuck in snow boots for six months is nothing to write home about. Or to Tuesday.

There they go again! The butterflies in my stomach. I couldn't feel more excited about seeing Tuesday again. I wonder what she'll make of the surprise I've got in store for her tonight . . .

How our lives have turned upside down in one short year. It's strange how much easier it's been on so many levels to confide in someone through writing, living a world away, than someone on your doorstep. An independent observer who I haven't needed to keep up appearances with.

And then, all of a sudden, we arrive at The Ferret and Trouserleg.

I know this place is Mignon's pride and joy but at this precise moment I can't think why. It's a perfectly nice gastropub, in a perfectly nice area of London, whose local newsagents invariably sell out of The Daily, daily, but it's so less flash and brash than its owner.

Peter Mignon is full of contradictions, but then who isn't. And anyway without him where would I be? Bankrupt and sans Tuesday.

In I walk, no sign of Tuesday but I cannot help but break into a smile. Mignon is mincing around in a truly horrific outfit – I really do think he's outdone himself this time. Mauve velveteen with a frilly shirt – he looks like Austin Powers. Of course I tell him I didn't realise it was fancy dress. He swats me. I duck, spin around – and see her.

TUESDAY

I'm here, at the headline-making pub Mignon is so fond of, The Ferret and Trouserleg. It is heaving. How many people has Mignon invited along this time? The usual crew of models and modelisers are here, although they look horribly out of place in this setting. For fuck's sake. I don't know why I'm surprised. Typical Mignon to over extend the hand of generosity. Where is Stella? I can't see her anywhere.

It might be the last day of December but it's hot as hell in here. I need a drink. I need to reacquaint myself with Gordon and then I'll go and hunt down my friend. A bald American is at the bar knocking back the one expensive offering of red that Mignon has on his menu.

America . . . could I? Should I? Should we? Is it too soon?

There is so much to weigh up. I love New York but I don't know if I want to move my life there. What would Stella say? I'll ask her later, when we have a moment away from the masses.

Then there's the question of work. After a shaky start, Anchor Man and I are getting on better than ever and I love the team at Wake Up Britain. Even The Boss has his good points.

But then there's Jake. His time in Afghanistan has made him an overnight sensation in the States. While I've been sounded out about a morning show on HLN and it's given me something to think about, the offer Jake is considering from ABC might just be too good to turn down. At some point we're going to have to talk, properly, about the future.

But that can wait. Tonight is about having fun with friends. With that thought in mind I catch sight of Mignon. What has he come as? Either he's sticking two fingers up to the GQ fashion police or, more worryingly, he genuinely thinks he looks the business. He's bragging to someone or another about a recent opinion poll which has somehow found him to be in the world's top 20 most influential people, and then I see . . . it's Stella!

STELLA

Tuesday is positively glowing. To her side, and holding her hand as if his life depends on it, is a particularly handsome twenty-something, Jake Jackson. Neither could look happier.

Tuesday and I exchange a cheeky glance. Well, if Bugs had biceps like that I'd make him wear a t-shirt like Jake's in late December too.

But Bugs has his own benefits. A brain the size of Britain for starters and charm in spades, which he immediately puts into action on the young lovers that now stand before us.

Naturally, Mignon tries to muscle in on the action. With Jake's interview in the can, predictably Mignon makes a beeline for Bugs. Jerry looks at me, looks at Tuesday, winks at us both and dismisses Mignon rather cruelly before returning his attention back to our happy foursome. Oh, Mignon will get his exclusive, but for tonight Bugs is under strict instruction from me to wind him up mercilessly.

TUESDAY

Stella is beaming. On her arm is a familiar face, the American I saw seated at the bar. Of course, Jerry Reuben. He looks nothing like Bugs Bunny. In fact, I'm pleasantly surprised.

The picture Stella painted wasn't the most flattering, but the self-assured man standing in front of Jake Jackson and I looks quite the part.

So does Jake. My God he's handsome. Sometimes when my alarm sounds at hideous o'clock I find myself just staring at him while he sleeps, this beautiful boy lying to my side.

Jerry and Jake are already chatting like old pals when Mignon tries to get involved. Stella and I know exactly what he's up to. After his exclusive with Jake he's after another with Jerry. Jerry though is playing hard to get. We all stifle laughs while Mignon goes on a shameless charm offensive. He'll get what he wants but not yet, not tonight.

Stella and I catch each other's eye, make our excuses and head for the loos.

STELLA

Tuesday has never struggled to make me laugh in 140 characters or less. Tonight she can barely string a sentence together without us dissolving into fits of giggles.

I ask her about Jake – she doesn't need to say much, it's written all over her face and apparently he's her Mum's newest obsession. As for a move to NYC? Well it appears it's an option.

Oh the irony. My turn: I'm not sure how much longer I'll be there. I can see her concern. I know she's worried Bugs and I are moving too fast but I steady her fears. I tell her in Jerry I've found someone who treats me better than I've ever been treated and loves me like I've never been loved. Someone who understands what Stellar Shoes means to me. Someone who also realises that every now and then I need reminding that work is not the be all and end all. She gets it. Of course she does. Why wouldn't she?

And then she pulls out a surprise for me. Hervé is here. More laughter.

We've spent long enough gossiping. Time to go and find our men, save them both from Mignon. We link arms and take our places back at the table, just in time for his speech.

TUESDAY

Stella and I are convulsing with laughter at Mignon's shameless attempts to secure an interview with Jerry. I'm glad that tonight we aren't restricted by 140 characters. There is just too much to say.

I tell her Bugs seems charming and much more attractive than she'd alluded to. Apparently she agrees because she then says she's thinking about a move to LA!

What? How sodding typical is that, what with Jake and I thinking about upping sticks to NYC she's considering a world of plastic fantastic with Jerry. I can't hide my shock when she first moots it as an option, not least because it all seems very fast but she knows

I know things have never been this good for her and Bugs has played a major role in that.

I get it. Of course I do. Why wouldn't I?

I pull out the Leger I've stuffed in my handbag and offer it to her with a broad grin on my face. She doesn't need it or want it but it triggers a memory and makes us both giggle.

I can hear a tinkling of glasses out in the dining area. It's Mignon. We rush back out to the assembled party as he starts to speak.

STELLA

Mignon has declared we need to announce our New Year's Resolutions.

We have already drunk plenty enough to be frank.

Tuesday's is to stay out of The Daily for an entire year.

Mine is to switch off my Crackberry occasionally as part of an effort to embrace a work/life balance.

Mignon's is to hit another million followers on Twitter by the end of the year.

Tuesday and I roll our eyes. We've heard it all before. We get our phones out and send our final tweets of 2012 . . .

The End.

#ACKNOWLEDGMENTS

For Georgie:

Air kisses to the following . . .

Piers Morgan for fatefully introducing me to Imogen. You will always be my most favourite benevolent uncle.

Caroline Michel and Sam Hiyate for always loving *The Twitter Diaries* first as an idea and later as a book.

To all at Bloomsbury, particularly Stephanie Duncan and Miranda Vaughan Jones who I suspect now think in tweets and no longer in full sentences. Sorry.

To superwoman incarnate and one of my oldest friends Nic Stephenson and her team at Mission for all their efforts both in London and New York with our PR.

Rob Noble, you are a technical genius and I can't thank you and Great Fridays enough for your support online and otherwise.

Mum, for being a little bit like @Mum and an endless source of inspiration, in a good way. Dad and H for providing any necessary filters. For keeping me on the straight and narrow in London: SJ, the best flat mate and girlfriend in the world, my boarding school pals George, Tam, Nat and Zannie and my rock solid assistant Gee. For keeping me on the straight and narrow in life: as above. To whatever happens next . . . XO.

Imogen Lloyd Webber for being the friend who not only knows all my best stories but has lived them with me.

For Imogen:

A big thank you to the following . . .

Piers Morgan for introducing me to my soul sister Georgie at his New Year's Eve party and for not waging Twitter war on us. Yet.

Alex Finlay, who is much younger, prettier and more successful than @StellaCavill but who, with her @finsforhim shoes, was a fabulous inspiration.

Sam Hiyate and Caroline Michel for being amazing agents through thick and thin.

Stephanie Duncan, Miranda Vaughan Jones and everyone at the brilliant Bloomsbury.

Nicola Stephenson and everyone at Mission for all their help with our PR.

Rob Noble, Mark Carrington and the team at Great Fridays for their webbie genius.

My mother for being nothing like @Supermodel_1971. All my family. For keeping me sane in NYC: Soleil Nathwani, Liz Furze, Michael Kaplan, Bill Schulz, Jorge Mora and Godfather Peter Brown. For keeping me sane forever: Ele Wilkinson, Darryl Samaraweera and Daniel Bee.

Georgie Thompson for making me realise that everything will be OK in the end and if it's not OK – it's not the end.